COME TOGETHER

BUTLER, VERMONT SERIES, BOOK 7

MARIE FORCE

D1637041

Come Together
Butler, Vermont Series, Book 7
By: Marie Force

Published by HTJB, Inc.
Copyright 2021. HTJB, Inc.
Cover Design by Kristina Brinton
E-book Layout: E-book Formatting Fairies
ISBN: 978-1952793202

The Green Mountain and
Butler, Vermont Series

The Green Mountain Series

The Butler, Vermont Series

(Continuation of Green Mountain)

More new books are always in the works. For the most up-to-date list of what's available from the Butler, Vermont Series as well as series extras, go to *marieforce.com/vermont*

CHAPTER ONE

"If you love large, you've got to hurt large."
—Sarah McLachlan

The rattle of his alarm clock woke Noah Coleman at five o'clock as it did every weekday morning without fail. Keeping his eyes closed, he reached over to silence it, took a deep breath and let it out slowly. He was on his way back to sleep when his backup alarm went off five minutes later. That one usually did the trick because he had to get up and cross the room to shut it off.

Shivering in the early morning cold, he went directly to the woodstove downstairs, added wood and had it putting out heat five minutes later. Then he went back upstairs to make his bed before heading to the shower, which was part two of his wake-up ritual. He kept the water on the chilly side until he felt fully awake. That's when it was safe to add some hot water. Otherwise, he might fall back to sleep right there in the shower.

Noah was famous for his ability to sleep anywhere, any time, under any conditions. The single greatest challenge he had as a self-employed construction contractor was getting his ass out of bed every morning. Thus, the multiple alarms and the rituals.

Lately, however, that wasn't his greatest challenge. Getting up in the morning had nothing on the pain-in-the-ass architect from Boston overseeing his latest project.

But he didn't need to think about her—or deal with her—for another hour or so. He planned to fully enjoy that hour, because the minute he got to the site, she'd send his day spiraling into multiple forms of hell that would last eight hours.

He followed the same routine every day with few exceptions. This time of year, he often skipped shaving the scruff that helped keep his face warm in the frigid Vermont winter. Dressing involved layers—lots of layers—topped with a red plaid flannel shirt that he tucked into flannel-lined jeans he bought at his family's Green Mountain Country Store.

After grabbing the lunch he'd made the night before and the three bottles of red Gatorade that kept him hydrated from the fridge, he donned his Carhartt work coat and emerged from the house twenty minutes after the second alarm. He did a double-take when he saw his mother standing next to his truck. Wearing boots and a heavy parka over flannel pajamas, she held a travel mug that she handed to him.

"What's this?"

"Coffee."

"Thank you."

"You're welcome."

He took a sip of the coffee fixed just how he liked it, with cream and a dash of sugar. "What's the occasion?"

"No occasion. I just hadn't seen you in almost two weeks, so I figured I'd try to catch you before you left for work."

"Sorry I haven't been around. We've been busting ass at the inn." Mrs. Hendricks had hired his company to rebuild the Admiral Butler Inn after it burned last year.

"I know. It looks good. Everyone is saying so."

"Glad to hear it."

"We missed you at Christmas."

"Sorry. I had some stuff to take care of."

"What kind of stuff?"

"Nothing important." He'd checked into a hotel in Stowe and had spent the holiday skiing. These days, Christmas was just another day to get through, and he found it easier to endure the day by himself than to be with his family, even if he knew that probably hurt his mother's feelings. Eager to change the subject, he said, "So whose truck is that in your driveway?"

She looked over her shoulder to her house a few doors down. "Ray's."

"What's it doing in your driveway at five thirty in the morning?"

"Wouldn't you like to know?"

"I would. That's why I'm asking. Seen it there a lot lately."

"We're, you know, spending time together."

"Overnight time?"

She gave him a withering look. "No, he leaves his truck at my house and takes a cab home."

Her reaction amused him. He knew whose truck it was and how many nights it had spent in his mother's driveway, not that he was keeping tabs or anything. Ray was a good guy, and if his mother had found happiness with him, who was Noah to begrudge her that? His dad had left her with eight kids to finish raising when Noah was fourteen. If anyone deserved a second chance at love, it was her.

As long as it wasn't him. Noah was good with second chances for other people. He'd learned the hard way to steer clear of shit like what his mother was doing with Ray.

"I'd ask you not to out me to your siblings, but since you never talk to any of them, I suppose there's no need to be worried about that."

"I talk to them."

"When do you talk to them?"

"Gray came by the site last week. I gave him a tour that involved talking. Izzy has been photographing the construction for a book Mrs. Hendricks wants to do about the inn's history before and after the fire. I talked to her while I showed her around. Vanessa called me last week when her toilet wouldn't flush, and I talked her through a repair to the ball cock. I talk to them."

"I'm glad you do. They look up to you."

"No, they don't. They look up to Gray." His brother Grayson was the eldest of the Colemans.

"They look up to both of you and Izzy. They remember how the three of you stepped up for our family when we needed you."

She meant after their father left, but she didn't have to spell that out. He got it.

"We did what anyone would've done."

"You did way more than you should've had to, and I'll never forget it."

"Thank you, but is there a reason we're taking this trip down unpleasant-memory lane at five thirty in the morning when it's dark and freezing?"

"I just wanted to see you."

"Now you've seen me." He gave her a spontaneous kiss on the forehead, which took her by surprise. That made him feel guilty for neglecting her. He'd try to do better. "Thanks for the coffee."

"You remind me of myself, you know."

He didn't know that. "How so?"

"When shit goes sideways, you retreat into yourself."

Noah had no idea what to say about that.

"I don't know what happened with Melinda, but whatever it was, you haven't been the same since, and I miss you. I miss the Noah you were with her."

He wanted to snap at her and tell her not to mention *her* name to him ever again, but because she was his mom and he loved her, he didn't snap. But he wanted to. The Noah he'd been with her had been a blind fool. He'd never again be that guy. "As much as I've enjoyed our visit, Mom, I gotta go to work."

"Have a good day, son, and don't be a stranger."

"You have a good day, too."

Noah got into his truck and turned on the engine to get the heat going. He'd forgotten to use the remote starter the way he did most days while in the early-morning brain fog. He waited until his mom was safely inside her house before backing out of the driveway and heading for the diner to pick up the breakfast Megan had waiting for him every morning.

He took comfort in the routine he'd established for himself since the disastrous end of his marriage. It allowed him to bury himself in work and kept the residual pain and anger locked away where it couldn't fuck with him every minute of every day, the way it had at first. On the weekends, he headed for the hills, either hiking or skiing until he was so exhausted, he fell into bed and slept like a dead man. Whatever it took to get through the day without the ghosts.

One mention of her name was all it took to erase all that hard work and effort to run from the past.

Fucking Melinda.

She'd ruined him in every way it was possible to ruin a man. Breaking his heart would've been more than enough, but she'd also destroyed his ability to trust just about anyone.

Well, that wasn't entirely true. Noah trusted his siblings and the ten Abbott cousins who'd grown up with them. Any of them would take a bullet for him, and vice versa. He didn't see them every day, but he knew they were always there for him, as was his mother, his grandfather, his aunt Molly and uncle Linc.

Anyone else? Forget it. He couldn't imagine any scenario under which he'd trust another living being who wasn't a blood relative. That was Melinda's legacy.

He gripped the wheel tighter than usual, his entire body vibrating with the tension that filled him any time he let his mind wander in her direction. Which was why he never let that happen. Why'd his mom have to mention her and stir up shit that was better left locked away in a dark corner of his mind that he rarely visited?

5

She might never have existed for the time or attention he gave her these days, which was zero.

Until someone mentioned her name and brought it all back like it'd happened yesterday rather than three years ago.

Noah slammed his hand against the wheel in frustration, which only made his hand hurt. It didn't do a damned thing to address the ache in his chest that resurfaced any time *she* slithered out from under the massive rock he kept over her and the memories of her. He'd give everything he had never to have to think about her again.

But alas, the brain didn't allow you to disassociate from memories you'd rather not keep. Nope, you got to hang on to the good, the bad and the hideous. How lucky were humans to carry around a gelatinous mess in their heads that could serve up a lacerating memory any time you were feeling good about the progress you'd made in moving on from something painful?

So lucky.

At some point, he needed to do something about the fact that he was still legally married to her. He'd resisted anything that would put him back in contact with her, even via lawyers. Eventually, he'd get around to taking care of that but not today.

Noah pulled up to the diner and left his truck running while he ran in to pick up the coffee and breakfast sandwich that Megan had ready for him five mornings a week. His cousin Hunter's wife was a sweet, welcoming woman who always greeted him with a cheerful smile and a friendly word. She was a bright spot in the gloom that was his life, and he looked forward to seeing her every day. Add her to the small list of people he trusted, not that he ever shared anything more with her than *good morning* and *how're you today.*

When he stepped into the diner, he was surprised to see his uncle Linc and grandfather Elmer sitting at the counter. "You boys are out early today," Noah said as he accepted the to-go bag and coffee from Megan. "Thank you." She had his credit card on file, and he insisted she add a twenty percent tip to each order.

Elmer Stillman whirled around on his stool to greet Noah with a big smile. Elmer was the best man Noah had ever known, with Linc coming in a very close second. The two men had been there in every way they possibly could be for Noah and his siblings after their father left, and he loved them both.

"How's it going, son?" Elmer asked.

"Not too bad. You?"

"We were talking about Linc's father. He passed away the other night." Linc had just seen the man for the first time in forty years, after a rift none of them had known about until recently when Linc's father asked to see him.

"I'm sorry to hear that," Noah said to Linc. "Are you okay?"

"I am, but thanks for asking. We knew this was coming."

"Still…" Noah said.

"Yeah," Linc said, grimacing. "Still…"

"The blessing in this is that Linc is back in touch with his three siblings," Elmer said.

"That's true," Noah said, aching for his uncle. Family shit could be so very painful, especially the stuff you had no control over, like a father turning his back on his children. Until Linc recently heard from his estranged father, Noah hadn't known the Coleman siblings had so much in common with their uncle.

Mike Coleman had resurfaced a year or so ago, after more than twenty years of silence, looking for bone marrow from one of the children he'd abandoned.

Audacious, to say the least.

Gray had donated to him, albeit reluctantly, but Mike's return on the scene was hardly welcome by any of his children. His deadbeat father was another thing Noah would prefer to never think about again. "I've got to get to work. I'm sorry again for your loss, Linc."

"Thank you, son."

Noah loved when his uncle called him that.

"I'd like to come to see the progress at the inn one of these days," Elmer said.

7

"Stop by any time, Gramps."

"Will do."

"Have a good day, you guys," Noah said as he headed for the door with a smile and a wave for Megan.

And with that, he'd exchanged more words with others by six a.m. than he usually said in a full day. He got back in his truck and drove the ten seconds it took to get to the parking lot at the inn, sat in his warm truck to eat the bacon and egg sandwich on a grilled English muffin and drink the coffee fixed just the way he liked it.

There were pluses to living in a small town where everyone knew you. There were also minuses to being so well known.

Noah had thought about moving somewhere that no one knew him, so there'd be no chance of anyone mentioning *her* name out of the blue like his mother had done this morning. His mom didn't know the details of what'd gone down with her. If she had, she'd never mention Melinda's name to him. Noah didn't blame his mother for having questions. Of course she did. One minute, he was happily married, and the next, he wasn't.

The last thing on God's green earth he wanted to do was relive that nightmare, even if it meant his mother would never again say her name in his presence. Since he didn't want to talk about what'd happened, he supposed he had to put up with the occasional question even after all this time.

But he didn't have to like it or the way he felt after he had to confront memories that put him in a foul mood.

As prepared as he could be to face another frigid day on the job, he got out of his truck and headed toward the framed outline of the inn, which was barely visible in the mist of early morning.

He stopped short at the sight of the architect, Brianna Esposito, her white project manager hard hat covering dark curly hair. She stood outside the back door, hands on her hips, glaring at him with fire in her dark eyes.

What now?

She drove him mad in more ways than one. For one thing, she micromanaged every aspect of the job—or at least she tried to. For another, any time she looked at him with daggers in her brown eyes, the way she was now, he went hard as stone. He told himself it was just because he hadn't gotten laid in a while, but he'd started to think it was something much worse than that.

Because there was absolutely *no way* he could be attracted to the feisty, bossy, pain-in-his-ass, know-it-all architect from Boston.

No way at all.

CHAPTER TWO

"Truth is everybody is going to hurt you:
You just gotta find the ones worth suffering for."
—(Author unknown, sometimes credited to Bob Marley)

*B*rianna wanted to take a hammer to his head ninety percent of the time. Unfortunately, the rest of the time, she wanted to kiss the nasty scowl off his too-handsome-to-be-true face. The wanting-to-kiss-him thing was super annoying since he was such a cranky jackass. Of course, after seven years in a male-dominated business, she knew how men could be toward a woman who had a working brain and wasn't afraid to use it.

"Good morning, Brianna. How are you on this fine Vermont morning?"

Fully aware that he couldn't care less how she was, she didn't fall for his nonsense. "Don't try to charm me, Coleman. What did I tell you about signing for materials?"

"I believe you told me not to sign for anything."

"And yet you signed for the lumber delivery yesterday afternoon after I had to leave early for a work meeting." She'd told him she had to take the meeting at home where there was a landline. Cell service was nonexistent in Butler.

"Yes, I did sign for the lumber delivery."

"Why did you do that when I *specifically asked you not to?*"

"Because I assumed you'd want us to be able to finish the framing today as planned. Without that lumber, my team would've been twiddling their thumbs. We would've lost today and possibly tomorrow, too, waiting for the redelivery of lumber that was sitting right in front of me. I signed for it, and I'd do it again."

She wanted to punch him in his smug, sanctimonious face, but sensing he'd probably enjoy that a little too much, she refrained. "I'm sure you checked the quantities against what was ordered to ensure the amount delivered was correct."

"Nope. That's your job. I'm just the dumb contractor who does all the work."

"So, you signed for a delivery with no idea whatsoever of what you were signing for?"

"Not true. I signed for what we need to keep things moving. Isn't the goal to get it buttoned up as soon as possible so we can bring in heaters for the indoor work?"

"Yes, that's the goal, but—"

"No buts. If we didn't get that delivery yesterday, we'd fall further behind. So again, I have zero regrets."

Brianna let out an exasperated growl and spun around, intending to storm off before she did something stupid like hit him with a hammer, but she slipped on an icy puddle and nearly went flying.

Noah grabbed her arm and saved her from a nasty fall. "Careful," he said, his voice full of amusement that made her furious.

She pulled her arm free of his hold. "Shut up."

He cracked up laughing.

Just another day in paradise.

Brianna hated this job with every fiber of her being. She

hated that one of her bickering-brother bosses had sent her to middle-of-nowhere Vermont to oversee the rebuilding of his third wife's cousin's inn, which had partially burned—although she had her own reasons for being glad to get out of Boston for a few months. She hated being so cold all the time that her teeth had gotten sore from chattering nonstop. But more than anything, she hated the contractor she had to work with every day. And on top of that, she hated that she hated him.

She'd been raised not to hate anyone.

Noah Coleman was an exception to every rule. He was rude, arrogant, noncommunicative, challenging, exasperating and every other adjective she could think of to cover the full range of jerk descriptors. It wasn't bad enough that Noah was a grumpy ass. No, he also had to be incredibly handsome and sexy as all hell, too. If she didn't stab him or knock him over the head with a shovel before they finished this job, it would be a miracle.

He made her crazy just by the way he looked at her with barely concealed disdain for her very existence.

Noah either didn't like working with architects, or he didn't like working with women. Either option made him even more unbearable than he already was.

After the first week she'd spent locking horns with him on the job, she'd done some light recon in town to get the lowdown on him—the second of eight kids, his father left the family when he was a teen. He was a first cousin to the Abbotts, who owned the magical country store next door to the inn. And, most interesting of all, three years ago, he'd split with his wife of two years under mysterious circumstances. No one knew why they'd broken up.

Although why she gave a flying you-know-what about Noah was a further source of aggravation when she had more than enough on her plate as it was. Why in the world had she even bothered to ask Mrs. Hendricks about him? God, what if the nosy, buttinsky woman who owned the inn ever got the big idea to tell Noah that Brianna had been asking about him? The very thought of that made Brianna cringe. The last thing in the world she'd want was him thinking she cared one iota about his story.

All that said, Mrs. Hendricks's info had given her some insight into why he was the way he was. Maybe he was still bitter over his father's desertion, and God only knew what level of hell his wife had put him through. She certainly knew what it was like to have a marriage blow up in her face. Her husband had put her through the nuclear level of hell, and she felt for anyone who'd endured the breakup of a marriage.

But having a marriage go bad didn't give him permission to act like a jackass ninety-nine-point-nine-nine percent of the time.

In addition to him signing for materials, which she'd expressly asked him not to do, she had to tell him the fireplace his workers had roughed out yesterday was in the wrong place. She dreaded that. She dreaded every second she had to spend on this godforsaken job in which she froze her ass off for eight hours a day and had to deal with *him*.

Six weeks into the project from hell, she was ready to quit her job and find a new profession. Nothing about being an architect was anywhere near as much fun as she'd thought it would be back when she was eighteen years old and under tremendous pressure to pick a college major.

If only she didn't have so much riding on the timely completion of this project, she would quit, but that would leave her without the references she would need to find a new job. The nonstop personal drama of the previous year had her skating on thin ice with her employers even before she came to Vermont. Quitting this job before she finished it was not an option. Neither was committing contractor murder, but a girl could dream.

The Butler Inn was the only place in town for visitors to stay. Butler needed the inn, and Mrs. Hendricks needed to get her business reopened. Brianna would get that taken care of and get the hell out of Butler the second the last nail was driven.

In the meantime, she had to deal with Noah Coleman. Steeling herself for yet another confrontation—there'd been so many, she'd lost track of how many—with the contractor from hell, she went to find him. They'd been able to salvage the front half of the building and were rebuilding the back portion while bringing the front portion up to code with a sprinkler system and other required upgrades.

A sprinkler system would've quickly extinguished the fire, but older buildings weren't required to have them. The new inn would be much safer than its predecessor had been, which had been one of Mrs. Hendricks's primary goals for the project.

Brianna was always so cold, she could barely think when she was on the job. The only thing that got her blood running hot was the predictable arguments with Noah. That was the one benefit to their frequent disagreements. They warmed her up for a few blessed minutes when her heart rate soared, and the blood pumped faster through her veins.

Inside the construction warzone, the sound of hammers on the roof competed with the roar of a table saw. The noise was enough to jar her teeth loose.

She found Noah in the kitchen, which had been framed the week before. He had squatted to measure something.

"Can we please talk about the fireplace in the reception lounge?" she asked in the calmest tone she owned.

"Sure."

"It needs to be redone."

He looked up at her over his shoulder, eyebrow crooked. "Why?"

"It's off by six inches."

"No, it isn't."

"Yes, it is."

"No. It isn't."

Brianna summoned the massive amount of fortitude it took to stand her ground and not blink in the glare of the sexiest gray eyes she'd ever seen. "Are we going to do this all day, or will you listen to me?"

"I'm not going to listen to you telling me that fireplace is six inches off, because it isn't."

"Then you'll have to come with me so I can show you."

He took his own sweet time standing to his full six-foot-something height. Since his back was turned, Brianna got a good look at how he filled out his Levi's. And he filled them out well. Very, very well. Not that she was looking.

Much.

He spun around suddenly and caught her staring at his ass.

Awesome.

When she looked up at him, a smug smile stretched across his face. "See something you like, darlin'?"

"Yeah, the most attractive part of you." Brianna was rather pleased with that comeback if she did say so herself. Usually, she thought of good responses hours after she'd gone ten rounds with him.

"I've always been told I have an exceptional ass. I'm glad you agree."

She pretended like she hadn't heard him. "What's that you said? People say you're an exceptional ass? I couldn't agree more."

His laughter followed her from the room as she headed for the reception area. Hopefully, he would get there eventually so they could fight about the fireplace that was six inches too far to the left. They were completely rebuilding the chimney, so that wasn't the issue. If they left the fireplace where it was, it would interfere with the fire escape on that side of the building. It had to be moved.

They'd ventured straight into the realm of unprofessional and inappropriate, which gave her pause. Dear God, did she have to discuss *that* with him, too?

Ugh, probably.

She found it interesting that he never raised his voice with the men who worked for him. They took their orders from him and seemed to respect him as a boss and friend. No, he argued only with her, or so it seemed.

By the time he made his way to the reception lobby, Brianna had plans rolled out on a makeshift table constructed of sawhorses and plywood and was ready to do battle.

Noah stopped in what would eventually be the doorway from the first-floor hall and eyed the work his men had done the day before.

"If you'll come look at the plans, I'll show you how the chimney will interfere with the fire escape. I need those six inches."

"So much I could say to that."

Was he flirting with her? No way. He couldn't stand her. And she couldn't stand him. He was *not* flirting. She ignored his suggestive comment and focused on the plans. A now-predictable wave of warmth overtook her when he came closer so he could see what she was pointing to. The bastard had to smell good, too. Life wasn't fair.

"You're right," he said. "It's off. We'll redo it."

Brianna was so shocked that she found herself momentarily speechless. And anyone who knew her well would say that was a rare, rare thing. "Would you mind repeating that? I'm afraid I didn't hear you properly the first time."

"I said you're right. It's off. And we will redo it."

"Wow, I need a minute to enjoy this victory."

Again, he flashed the grin that did such incredible things to his usually austere face. "Knock yourself out."

"You ought to do that more often."

"What's that? Tell you you're right?"

"Definitely—and smile. It looks good on you."

"I didn't smile."

"Yes, you did. Twice so far today, actually."

"That's not true. Don't be making shit up."

It was no wonder she wanted to smack him ninety percent of

the time. "Oh my God, are we really going to fight about whether or not you smiled?"

"Yes, we are, because I don't smile as a rule."

"That's the dumbest thing I've ever heard. Who makes a rule about not smiling?"

"I do."

"No wonder you're so cranky. Anyone who has a rule against smiling is a good time had by all."

"Are you having a good time? Because you seem wound sort of tight."

"I'm wound tight because I have to deal with you!"

"Oh *Lord*," a third voice said from the doorway.

Brianna and Noah spun around to find Mrs. Hendricks standing in the future doorway, watching them with dismay. On top of the hood to her full-length parka, she'd placed the red hard hat Noah had given her so she could visit the site and see the progress.

"I can't bear to hear the two of you fighting," she said, looking almost tearful and resembling a giant mushroom with the hard hat teetering precariously on top of her hood.

"We're not fighting," Noah said. "We're *communicating*."

"Now, don't you sass me, Noah Coleman. I know fighting when I hear it, and that was fighting."

"We occasionally disagree about things, but we're working it out," he said. "Isn't that right, Brianna?"

She knew she ought to agree with him so they could send their customer away happy, but Brianna couldn't bring herself to lie to the woman's sweet face. "We fight nonstop, actually."

Noah sent her a look of complete disbelief.

"That just won't do," Mrs. Hendricks said. "I want the two of you to go to dinner tonight and work this out."

Brianna was shaking her head before the woman finished her sentence. No way was she going to dinner with him.

"In fact," Mrs. Hendricks said, rifling through her massive

purse, "I just got this coupon for the Pig's Belly Tavern in the mail." She pressed it into Noah's hand.

"Thank you," he said, "but—"

As if he hadn't spoken, she said, "Go have a nice dinner and talk it out. You young people need to learn how to communicate properly. You're all so tied to those silly phones that you've forgotten how to *talk* to each other."

Brianna wanted to remind her that no one was tied to a silly phone in the cellular nowhere land known as Butler, Vermont. Their motto ought to be "The place where cell phones go to die."

"Tomorrow, I'll be back to see how it went. I hope you two can work out all this nonsense and find some harmony. Life is too short to spend it fighting."

"Is that why you came by?" Noah asked, his jaw tight and his teeth clenched. No doubt the idea of spending time with her outside of work was every bit as revolting to him as it was to her.

"I heard there'd been some squabbling, and I wanted to nip that in the butt."

Brianna tried to contain the snort of laughter that erupted from inside her at the way the woman mangled the expression "nip that in the *bud*."

Noah cleared his throat as if he were also trying not to laugh.

"I'll see you two in the morning. You have a nice dinner now and put all this bickering to rest." She turned and walked away before either of them could think of anything else to say to her.

For a full minute after she left, neither of them said a word.

Finally, Noah broke the silence. "Way to go."

CHAPTER THREE

"It is when we hurt that we learn."
—Steve Maraboli

*W*hy couldn't she have just gone along with him when he said they were communicating, not fighting? If she'd done that, he wouldn't be showering and shaving the scruff off his face to go back out. No, he'd be throwing logs on the woodstove and settling in for a long winter's night of reading. Instead, he had to go another ten rounds with the architectural equivalent of Muhammad Ali. She exhausted him.

And she turned him on.

God, he hated that. He hated to be feeling anything resembling desire for the first time in three long years—long enough that he'd worried the plumbing had broken—only to have it return for someone who drove him *mad*.

She wasn't even his type, for Christ's sake. He usually went for the frosty blondes, but Brianna had curly dark hair, curves on top of her curves and sharp brown eyes that didn't miss a trick. One of his guys had referred to her as a "smoke show."

Noah had asked him what that meant.

"You know, smokin' hot," the young man had said, looking at Noah as if he were ancient.

It wasn't possible to be more "out of it" than he was. No cell phone, no social media, a TV he rarely turned on, a computer he used only for billing and work-related activities and little to no contact with people other than the men at work. And he kept his distance from them. He'd learned the hard way not to get too buddy-buddy with his employees.

After Mrs. Hendricks had dropped her bomb—and her coupon—on them, Noah had spent the rest of the day supervising the redo of the fireplace. His foreman, Carlo, had been full of apologies for misreading the plans.

Noah had told him not to worry about it, but he couldn't help yearning for Miguel, who'd been with him for years before everything between them went to shit in the most spectacular way possible. Before that horrible day, Miguel had been the other half of Noah's brain. He didn't ever have to be supervised or told what to do. He just knew.

In the end, Noah had paid a hefty price for trusting his foreman so implicitly, but he didn't wish to think about that nightmare when he needed every ounce of fortitude he could muster to deal with the current one.

A night out with Brianna Esposito was his idea of hell. What would they talk about? *Ugh.* Mrs. Hendricks was a lovely lady. She'd once been his Cub Scout leader when he and her son Jud had been kids. After Noah's father left their family, Mrs. H had started driving Noah to all the activities he and Jud did together —football, baseball, basketball and Scouts. Often, she'd drop off a meal, claiming she'd made way too much of whatever her family was having for dinner, and somehow ended up with more than enough to feed nine extra people.

Noah had been old enough to know how dire their situation had been, and the kindness of people like Mrs. H, as he'd called her then, had gone a long way. He'd never forget it. That was why, when she asked him to take Brianna to dinner at the Pig's

Belly Tavern, he would take Brianna to dinner at the Pig's Belly Tavern.

Even if he didn't want to.

He *soooo* didn't want to.

He was dying to get back to the spy thriller that'd kept him up way too late the night before. He'd been thinking about the story all day and wanted to know what happened next. But nope, that wasn't happening. Not until later, anyway.

He found a navy sweater his sister Izzy had given him for Christmas and pulled it on over his usual thermal Henley and the well-worn jeans that counted as "dress up" jeans because he'd never worn them to work. And they were clean. With that, he'd put more effort into his appearance than he had in years.

What did it matter what he wore or how he looked? Who cared? Not him, that was for sure. He didn't care about much these days, except his family and his job. That was about the extent of the things that got any time, mental energy or emotion from him. They were all things that were, for the most part, incapable of hurting him in any significant way.

Noah had learned to avoid people and situations that could cause him grief. He'd had enough of that for one lifetime.

Ten minutes before leaving, he used the remote to start his truck and get the heat going. He bundled up and headed out into the frozen wilderness that was Northeastern Vermont in the winter and got into the still-freezing truck cab.

After work, he'd spent ten minutes collecting the discarded coffee cups and other trash that had accumulated on the floor of the passenger side. No one ever rode in his truck but him and occasionally one or both of his aunt and uncle's dogs when he was taking care of them.

His life was dull and boring, and he liked it that way. He'd taken a walk on the wild side of the road and found out what can happen when the wild side goes bad, and he never wanted to experience that again. He was better off staying in his lane and not risking things he couldn't afford to lose, such as his heart, his sanity and his ability to trust anyone other than family members.

And yes, he was self-aware enough to know that bitterness was the reason for his disconnectedness. But that was now so much a part of who he was that he wouldn't recognize himself without it. His first experience with the emotion had come from what his father had done so many years ago, and then life had dealt him new cards that added to his stores of bitterness.

As he drove to the house Brianna was renting near his cousin Will's place, Noah tried to think of things he might talk to her about over dinner. It would serve his digestion—and hers—if they stayed away from anything to do with the project that had put them in this predicament in the first place.

People were always interested in what it had been like to grow up as one of eight siblings and ten close first cousins who'd been like extra brothers and sisters to him. That was probably a safe topic. He could tell her about the years he lived in California when he'd attended USC on a full scholarship for mechanical engineering. While there, he'd survived an earthquake that registered a 6.9 on the Richter scale and killed people two blocks from where he'd lived at the time. That made for a good story.

Hopefully, that would be enough to get them through the appetizer part of the meal.

Noah couldn't overstate his level of dread for this outing.

He pulled into her driveway and thought of his school friend Kent Barclay who'd lived in the house when they were kids. His dad had split the year after Noah's dad left. They'd had that in common. Kent had once joked that Noah's dad had given his father the idea to cut and run. Noah wondered where Kent was now and whether his family still owned the house.

A light was on over the front door. Did that mean Noah was supposed to go to the door to get her?

No, that would make this too much like a date, which it was *not*.

Noah didn't date anymore. He hooked up once in a while with a friend from high school who'd been through a nasty divorce—weren't they all bad?—and was now a struggling single mother to three kids. Glenda was a nice person, and they had fun in bed together every couple of months, but that was all it would ever be, because neither of them wanted anything more than the physical release.

Wanting more led to ruin, which they'd both learned the hard way.

He was about to beep the horn to let Brianna know he was there when the door opened, and she appeared in the doorway, framed by the glow of the outside light.

She flashed him the one-minute sign and turned away from the door.

Her sidewalk was framed by three feet of snow on each side from four different snowstorms. This time of year, the snow tended to pile up, one storm on top of the other. Noah wondered if she shoveled her walk or paid someone else to do it.

People who hadn't grown up in Vermont tended to be overwhelmed by the amount of snow they got. His brother's fiancée, Emma, and her sister Lucy, married to Noah's cousin Colton, had grown up in New York City. He'd heard Emma say once that she'd had no idea it was possible to get as much snow as they got in Vermont and not be buried under it. She said she had dreams about being stuck under a ton of snow and trying to find her way out.

"I'd come looking for you," Grayson had said with the goofy, lighthearted smile he wore all the time now that Emma and her daughter, Simone, were in his life.

Noah was glad Gray was happy. He'd shouldered far more than his share of the load after their dad left, and he deserved to find someone who made him smile all the time.

However, Noah was never going down that road again. He was happier alone, and he was okay with that.

Brianna came out of the house and turned to use her key to lock the dead bolt.

Back before their pristine state had become a hub for heroin, oxy and other drugs, no one had ever locked their door. Now, he never left home without locking up and was glad that Brianna did, too, although that had probably become a habit after living in Boston.

He didn't like her very much, but he certainly didn't want anything to happen to her.

She walked slowly and carefully down the sidewalk to the driveway.

Get out and get her door for her.

His grandfather's voice was so deeply ingrained in him that Noah couldn't help but want to heed the directive from Elmer.

I'm not getting the door for her because that's date bullshit. This is not a date.

Because his grandfather had raised him to be somewhat of a gentleman, Noah leaned across the bench seat to open the door for her. When he realized she was almost too short to use the step to get in, he offered her a hand that she gratefully accepted.

The second his hand connected with hers, a jolt of energy traveled up his arm, and he immediately understood he'd made a significant error by touching her. He let go the second her ass connected with the seat.

It took about three seconds for the captivating scent of woman to overtake the small space.

Great.

If only it weren't so butt-ass cold, he'd put down the window to flush out the extremely appealing scent. But since that wasn't feasible, he had to live with it and the fucking boner that Brianna's nearness had caused.

"Thanks for picking me up. I'm not a big fan of driving around here in the dark, with the moose that stands in the road and the various life-ending drop-offs."

"You heard about the moose, huh?"

"Uh, yeah, like on day one. Wasn't it your cousin's wife who hit him?"

"Yep. Cameron met Fred about one mile into the town of Butler. Will found her knee-deep in mud with her face and car smashed up, and the rest, as they say, is history."

"I can't believe she stayed here after that."

"I think she stayed for my cousin, but you'd have to ask her that."

"Nothing could keep me here after this job is finished."

"Is it safe to assume you don't like our little corner of the world?"

"Very safe to assume. The snow is ridiculous, there are moose in the road, every mile you drive is like a video game—and not the fun kind where you can crash into stuff and walk away unscathed—there's nothing to do, and the people are grumpy."

"All people or one in particular?"

"One in particular. Unfortunately, the one I'm forced to spend the most time with."

Noah winced even as he tried not to laugh. He had to give her points for putting it right out there. "Well, other than the grumps, Butler is a great little town, especially this time of year. People come from all over to ski on Butler Mountain."

Out of the corner of his eye, he caught her wrinkling her nose. "I've never understood the attraction of spending hours in the cold to sled down a mountain standing up."

"Have you ever done it?"

"*No*, because I *hate* being cold."

"If you dressed properly, you wouldn't be cold."

"Yes, I would. I'm always cold, which is another reason why Butler and I don't get along."

"What're you wearing for underwear?"

"Excuse me?"

Noah laughed at her indignant tone, and yes, he was aware that he'd laughed twice since she got in the car. He hadn't expected to find anything about this evening funny. "I meant *long* underwear. What kind is yours?"

"The usual thermal stuff, not that it's any of your business."

"Granted, but they sell this silk stuff at the store that's a thousand times better than the thermal stuff. I'll get you some." The words were out of his mouth before he could weigh the impact of offering to buy her underwear.

You don't like her, remember?

Trust me, I remember, but that doesn't mean I want her to suffer in the cold if she doesn't have to.

Shut up.

You shut up.

No, you.

There, she had him arguing with himself. He couldn't help but think she'd enjoy knowing that. Not that he planned to tell her. He'd already said more than enough in the first ten minutes.

"I don't need you to get it for me. I'll get it."

"Sure, whatever works, but you'll be much warmer with that."

"Thanks for the tip."

"You might want to invest in a long coat and better boots, too."

"What's wrong with my coat and boots?"

"Your coat is too short, and your boots are for style, not function. Winter is serious business up here. They can fix you up with everything you need at the store. Not that I'm plugging the family business or anything. Full disclosure, I have no stake in it."

"Didn't your grandparents start it?"

"They did."

"How come you don't have a stake in it?"

"When my uncle Lincoln became the CEO, he and my aunt Molly, who is my mother's sister, made an offer to buy out my mom and their other siblings. Since the others didn't have any interest in the business, they took the offer. Linc, Molly, their ten kids and my grandfather own the business in equal shares. When my grandfather dies, his portion goes to the twelve of them."

Why was he talking so much? To her of all people? He never talked to anyone if he could avoid it.

"That's very interesting. I love the dynamics of how family businesses work. Three brothers own my company. Two of them don't speak to each other, which makes for a nightmare for the third one."

"Why don't they speak to each other?" *And why do you care? Shut up. I don't care. I'm just making conversation.*

"I guess one of them slept with the other's wife."

"That'll do it."

She laughed—hard—and Noah couldn't help but smile at the sound of her laughter. It filled the small space every bit as powerfully as her scent had.

"The husband caught her in bed with his brother, and all hell broke loose. Because they have such a successful business, they're forced to work together still even if everyone knows why they don't speak."

"Awkward." Noah's heart ached for the brother who'd been wronged. He knew all too well what that was like. He could only thank God he hadn't caught his wife with one of his brothers.

"Seriously."

"Did the wife and the wrong brother end up together?"

"Nope, which makes it worse, in my opinion. If you're going to do something like that to your brother, shouldn't it be for true love and not just to scratch an itch?"

"First of all, I wouldn't do that to my brother—or anyone else, for that matter." Once it'd happened to you, you're cured of any desire to dally with a married woman. Not that he'd ever done that. After what'd happened with his parents, it was a wonder that Noah had ever worked up the courage to get married in the first place.

Melinda had known what he'd been through with his family,

and she'd still ended up in bed with the wrong man, which was why Noah trusted no one, except his own family. Hearing what'd happened with Brianna's bosses made him wonder if even that was safe.

He stopped that thought before it could develop. His family was solid. He didn't doubt that any of his siblings or cousins would take a bullet for him—and vice versa. There's no way they'd ever cross lines with each other's significant others. That was one thing in his life he was sure of.

"Where're we going, anyway?" Brianna asked as Noah navigated the twisting, winding roads that took them into "downtown" Butler.

That's what people called the collection of buildings that made up Elm Street, home of the Green Mountain Country Store, the diner, the inn, a bank, the post office, the requisite white-steepled church that was a staple of most New England towns, an art gallery, a pizza restaurant and a few other smaller stores. It wasn't much, but it was home.

"A few towns over."

"What's this place Mrs. Hendricks is sending us to? The Pig's Belly? Is it really called that?"

"It is, and despite the name, the food is fantastic. Some of the best barbecue I've ever had."

"I assume you've been outside of Vermont?"

He didn't want to be amused by her, but he was, nonetheless. "In fact, I have. I lived in Southern California for six years and traveled a lot for my job."

"Which was what?"

"I worked for a commercial engineering firm for a couple of years after college before I came home eight years ago to start my business."

"You're an engineer?"

"That's right. A licensed PE." He assumed she knew that PE stood for professional engineer.

"Hmm."

"What?"

"That's just surprising."

He didn't want to ask. Honestly, he didn't. He was much better off when he found her annoying. "How so?"

"I just didn't take you for a PE."

"What did you take me for?"

"You really want me to answer that?" she asked, her tone infused with delight.

"Yeah, probably better to leave that to my imagination." After a long pause, he said, "I'm sorry that I've been unwelcoming toward you. That wasn't my intention."

After a very long pause, she said, "And I'm sorry that I've come on too strong. My boss is on me constantly about getting this job done on time and under budget, and as I mentioned, I hate being cold. Butler is cold, and that hasn't helped my disposition."

"Maybe if we warm you up, you'll feel better about being here."

Noah hoped she knew he was talking about the clothing he'd recommended and nothing else. He wasn't available for that kind of warming. Not with her, anyway. They rode the rest of the way in silence, but it wasn't uncomfortable silence, which was a vast improvement over what he'd expected of this evening.

He hated to admit it, but maybe Mrs. Hendricks had been right. Perhaps if they spent some time together away from the inn, they could begin to understand each other and get along better on the job.

But he refused to go so far as to start *liking* her.

CHAPTER FOUR

*"Hearts will never be made practical until
they are made unbreakable."*
—The Tin Man, The Wizard of Oz

ho was this man, and what had he done with Noah Coleman? Brianna could deal with grumpy, annoying, exasperating Noah. This almost-charming, self-deprecating version of him left her feeling off her game and out of sorts. Was it possible that she almost liked him? No. No way.

"Can I ask you something?" she asked.

"I guess so."

He sounded wary, and considering their past interactions, she couldn't blame him. "Is it me or women or architects in general you don't like?"

His deep sigh conveyed a world of angst. "None of the above. I have four sisters, three close female first cousins and was raised mostly by a single mom with a lot of help from her sister. I have nothing against women. I promise you that."

"Is it me, then? You just took an immediate dislike to me?"

"No, not at all."

"That leaves architects, then."

"I'm not a huge fan of architects. I'll admit that."

"Ah-ha! We have a winner. What is it about my colleagues and me that you don't like?"

"It's not that I don't like architects. It's that your people always think you know better than the person doing the actual work."

"Often, we do know better."

He grunted out a laugh at her sassy reply. "I shoulda seen that coming."

"Well, it's true. We're the ones who drew the plans. Doesn't it stand to reason that we might know the project a tiny bit better than the contractor?"

"Not necessarily. What do you think I do first when I land a new job?"

"I have no idea."

"I learn those plans inside and out. I don't just show up and start banging nails."

She laughed, which she hadn't expected to do with him. "You don't?"

"Nope. You heard the part about me being a professional engineer, right? I do know how to read a set of plans, and yours were exceptional."

"Really?"

Nodding, he said, "You did a great job of melding the new portion of the inn with the historical elements of the remaining portion and bringing the building up to current code."

"That was my goal. I'm glad you liked what I did."

"My biggest concern when Mrs. Hendricks told me she was bringing in an architect from Boston was that the new inn wouldn't fit the aesthetic of the town."

"Before I did anything, I spent days researching the town, the inn, its history. I even read about Admiral Butler and your family's store. I came and took photos and explored every corner of the town and the area. I did my research."

"I'm impressed."

"I can't believe you thought the Boston architect would just phone in a job like this."

"I didn't think that. Exactly."

"Right…" The cab was dark, so he couldn't see her roll her eyes to high heaven. "Well, now you know that's not what I did. And PS, that fireplace was off by six inches."

"Yes, it was. I already conceded that one to you."

"And the order from the lumberyard was off by ten percent."

He looked over at her. "Was it?"

"Yep. Fortunately, we hadn't touched it yet, so I was able to prove to the yard that they shorted us."

"Huh. Well, sorry about that."

"I didn't ask you not to sign for stuff because I don't trust you. I did it because the budget is on my shoulders, and I need to be aware of what's coming in and making sure it matches up with the order."

"I've been duly chastised."

"If it weren't for the fact that Butler is a cell phone never-never land, this wouldn't have happened. You could've called me, I could've told you what I ordered, and you could've confirmed it was correct before you signed. But it doesn't work that way around here."

"You get used to it."

"I will *never* get used to being without my phone during the day."

"Soon enough, we'll have Wi-Fi working at the inn again, and you'll be back in business."

"Somewhat. Being here is still like stepping out of the twenty-first century into the stone ages."

"Now, that's not true. We don't have cell service. That doesn't mean we're stone-aged."

"Yes, it does! You don't even know how the rest of the world works."

"I do know. Believe it or not, I get off this mountain once in a while and venture into the real world. I even *own* a cell phone."

"Gasp," she said. "You do not!"

"I do, too. I bought it last year when I was working in Rutland and driving back and forth, figuring I ought to have a way to call for help if my truck broke down."

"What do you do with it?"

"Stuff."

She snorted with laughter. "You can't do a damned thing with it in this town."

"I know it might surprise you to hear that I don't spend my entire life in this town. The Butler Inn is the first project I've had inside Butler itself in two years. I do stuff all over the Northeast Kingdom as well as other parts of Vermont."

"Wow, you're a regular man of the world."

"Yes, I am. You did hear me say I lived in SoCal for six years, right? I became a regular cell phone professional during those years."

"I'm suitably impressed."

"Gee, thanks. Impressing you was my only goal tonight."

She turned in her seat so she could better see him. "You set goals for tonight? What're the others?"

The low rumble of laughter coming from him felt like a victory. Brianna had discovered he didn't laugh or smile very often. "I walked right into that trap, didn't I?"

"You did. So are there other goals?"

"Mostly, I hoped to survive dinner and get home as quickly as possible." He turned on the windshield wipers to contend with the sudden onset of snow. "But so far, I've discovered you're not completely awful away from work."

"Oh gosh, that's like the best compliment I've ever received. Did you get that from a book on how to charm a difficult woman?"

"I wasn't aware that I was trying to charm you."

"Yeah, charm isn't one of your talents."

"You've noticed my other talents? What are they?"

"Hmm, let me think. You operate a mean nail gun. You appear to be quite talented in the area of grumpiness and surliness. Let's see." She tapped her chin. "What else?"

"That's more than enough, thank you very much."

"Why are you so cranky? Were you always that way?"

His grip on the steering wheel tightened ever so slightly, but she noticed. "Not always."

"What happened?"

"Life happened."

"Ah, yes. Good old life. She can be a bitch when she wants to be, huh?"

"Yeah."

"You want to talk about it?"

"God, no."

"With me or anyone?" she asked.

"Anyone. What's the point of talking about shit that happened years ago?"

"There's no point unless the past is affecting your present. I learned that in therapy."

He took his eyes off the winding road for a second to glance at her. "What else did you learn in therapy?"

"That until you deal with the past, the present is always going to be a bit of a mess."

"Is your present a mess?"

"Kinda. I'm working on fixing that, but these things take time. That's the one good thing about being here. It gets me away from the crap I left at home."

"I don't want to be curious about you, but alas…"

"Ah-ha," she said with a laugh. "You just can't help yourself, can you?"

"Easy, slugger. I said I was curious. That's a long way from intrigued or enthralled."

"FYI, intrigued and enthralled mean the same thing. Just like curious and interested mean the same thing."

"I'm *not* interested."

"But you *are* curious. Intriguing."

"You're starting to irritate me again."

"I wasn't aware that I'd ever stopped irritating you."

"You didn't, but you started irritating me *less*."

She laughed again, surprised to be having way more fun than she'd expected to, and they weren't even to their destination yet. "Where is this place we're going, anyway?"

"Coming up in a mile or so."

The snow was much heavier than it'd been even ten minutes ago.

"Do we need to be worried about the snow?" she asked warily. She'd never seen snow come down the way it did here.

"Nah. No biggie."

"To you, maybe."

"When you grow up with it, you get used to it."

"I'd never get used to this kind of snow. It's as high as my boobs on my sidewalk!"

Noah sputtered with laughter. "Is that an official measurement?"

"In this case, yes."

"Well, you're not exactly… How should I put this?"

"Shut up. I know I'm short. I don't need you to tell me that."

"I never said you were short. I was going to say you aren't exactly tall."

She hoped the withering look told him what she thought of that. But he didn't see her withering look because he was so intent on keeping the truck on the increasingly snowy road. "Maybe we should turn back."

"And have to tell Mrs. H that we wimped out? Not happening."

"It's not wimping out if we're concerned for our safety."

"No self-respecting Vermonter would be afraid to drive in this."

"You people are certifiable."

"We hear that a lot."

They inched along until a neon sign with the outline of a pig appeared in the gloom. The official name of the place was Pig's Belly Tavern and Publick House. Delightful.

Brianna expelled a deep breath full of relief. "If the snow is this bad now, what'll it be like after dinner?"

"Don't worry. I won't drive you off the side of the mountain or anything."

"Thank you. That sets my mind at ease."

Noah parked the truck and turned off the engine. "Wait for me to come get you so you don't fall."

Brianna wanted to tell him she didn't need his help but wasn't sure if that was true, so she waited for him to walk around the truck and open the passenger door. When he offered her a hand, she reluctantly took it so she wouldn't fall face-first into a snowdrift. "Are you sure we shouldn't just go home now before it gets worse?"

"I'm sure. Hold on to me so you don't slip."

She didn't want to be holding on to him for dear life, but she also didn't want to fall. They trudged through shin-high snow to the front door, which Noah held for her.

The man had manners. She had to give him that much. After pounding the snow off their boots, they proceeded inside, where a gold statue of a huge pig greeted them. The restaurant was crowded and noisy, the atmosphere nonexistent. Music that might've been live was coming from the back, and the smell of barbecue had her mouth watering and her stomach growling.

"Two, please," Noah told the hostess.

Judging by the crowd, Brianna was the only one concerned about the snowstorm happening outside. If they weren't worried, maybe she shouldn't be either. Noah grew up in these hills and knew how to get around in the snow. She needed to chill and try to relax.

The hostess handed them menus and a list of specials.

"What can I get you to drink?"

Noah asked what they had on tap and settled on a Sam Adams Winter.

Brianna ordered Grey Goose and soda with a lime. Vodka was the only alcohol she ever drank because it had no taste. She hated the taste of everything else and barely drank anything except for at times like this when it paid to be sociable. And when her nerves were shot by having to dine with the cranky contractor during a snowstorm.

The menu consisted of every form of rib, pork, pig's feet and even pig's knuckles. No part of the pig went to waste in this place. "What do you usually get here?"

"I'm particular to the pork jambalaya myself, but it's all good. My cousin Hunter had his rehearsal dinner here, and I had the ribs that night. They were *so* good."

"He had his rehearsal dinner *here?*"

Noah laughed at the face she made. "The scene of his first date with his now-wife, Megan."

"Is she the same Megan who runs the diner?"

"One and the same."

"She's very nice—and very pregnant."

"She's both those things. She's made my cousin very happy."

"When is she due?"

"Soon. I'm not sure of the exact date."

"Is it me, or are you related in some way to just about everyone in Butler?"

"Not everyone, but when you're one of eighteen cousins, many of whom still live in town, there're very few degrees of separation."

"You guys must've been something when you were kids."

"We had a lot of fun, got into a lot of trouble—the good kind —and had all the laughs together."

"That must've been nice."

"Do you have siblings?"

"A much older brother who left for college when I was seven

and never lived at home again. I think I was an 'oops,' not that my parents ever admitted to that."

"No cousins?"

"One that I'm very close to. Dominique is my third cousin. We went all through school together and have always been the best of friends. Her mom and my mom are first cousins."

"Wouldn't that make her your second cousin?"

"Nope, her mom is my second cousin."

"I'm gonna need a minute to wrap my head around that."

Brianna laughed. "It's simple. Her mom is my second cousin, and Dom is my third cousin."

"If you say so."

"You were lucky to grow up in a pack."

"I've always known that even if it could be crowded and loud. I feel like I should add that it wasn't always great. My dad left when we were kids."

"I might've heard something about that in town."

His mouth set in an expression that conveyed his displeasure. "People still can't believe a man could leave his wife and eight children."

"That must've been rough."

"It was."

"How old were you?"

"Fourteen. I was the second oldest, so a lot fell to me and my older brother, Grayson."

"I'm sorry that happened to you."

He shrugged. "It was more than twenty years ago now."

"Some things don't get better with time." She knew that all too well.

The waitress came to the table. "Sorry to keep you waiting. What can I get you?"

Noah gestured for Brianna to go first.

"I'm going to do some sides—the baked beans, coleslaw and cornbread."

"That's it for you?" the waitress asked.

"That'll do it."

"And for you, sir?"

"I'll do the full rack of ribs with fries and slaw."

"I'll put that right in for you."

After she walked away, Noah said, "No pig for you?"

Brianna gave him a sheepish grin. "I'm a vegetarian."

He stared at her, stunned. "Why didn't you say something?"

"Mrs. H's orders were clear. I didn't want to get us in more trouble."

"We could've gone somewhere else, Brianna."

"And miss all this?" She gestured to the chaotic energy of the place. "Not on your life."

He looked at her with what might've been new respect, but Brianna didn't want to jump to any conclusions.

"You know all about me, and I know very little about you other than you're an architect from Boston and have an older brother."

"That's about the extent of it."

"No way." He dove into the basket of cornbread like he hadn't seen food in a year. "There's got to be more to it than that. Ever been married?"

"Unfortunately, yes."

"See? I knew there was more to the story. What happened?"

"It'd be easier to tell you what *didn't* happen."

"I'm intrigued."

Brianna didn't want to talk about this, but he was right. She knew a lot about him and his family, but he didn't know anything about her. "Do you know what a sociopath is?"

"I picture serial killers when I hear that word."

"That's what I thought, too, until I encountered one in person. They lie, cheat and steal with no regard for consequences or the feelings of others. I was lucky enough to be married to that. I still am because he's refusing to divorce me after he all but ruined me in every possible way. So, there. That's my life."

"I'm sorry."

Kindness from someone she'd been so at odds with felt better than she would have expected. "It is what it is. Cost me more than twenty thousand dollars in therapy to get to the point where I could look at it as something that was outside my control. He has antisocial personality disorder, and there was nothing I could've said or done differently to change what he is. I just wish I'd listened to my gut before I married someone who seemed too good to be true."

She'd said more to him than just about anyone other than her therapist since the shit hit the fan last Christmas. It felt good to speak about her nightmare with someone who didn't know Rem or them as a couple. For some reason, she wanted to tell him the rest.

"A lot of people in my life didn't believe he was capable of the things he did, because they all liked him so much. That's the ultimate dichotomy. Sociopaths are often extremely likable people who charm others into their web of deceit. By the time you realize what you're dealing with, you're in so deep, it feels like you'll never break free of the nightmare."

Noah didn't offer platitudes the way many other people did. He just listened and let her talk, which she appreciated.

"How did you find out he wasn't what he seemed?"

"One of my friends saw him having lunch with another woman. He didn't notice her, but she watched him until she was sure it wasn't platonic. Imagine the hubris it takes to be married and take someone else out to lunch like it was no big deal. She called me, told me what she'd seen, and at first, I didn't believe her. I thought maybe she was jealous of our marriage or something, but then I started to dig. It wasn't hard to uncover his trail because he hadn't done anything to try to hide it. There were credit card charges at hotels and restaurants all over Boston, dating back to before we were married."

"Shit, Brianna. That must've been so awful."

"It was horrific. I went from being happily married to realizing it was all a big lie in the span of a few hours. I couldn't eat or sleep or work for more than a month. And despite all the proof I had, Rem claimed he was being set up and refused to leave our home. I had to move back in with my parents just to get away from him. All these months later, he won't sign divorce papers. He says the marriage isn't over as far as he's concerned."

"I wish there was something more I could say than I'm sorry. That doesn't feel adequate."

"Thank you."

Noah took a long drink from his beer. "I caught my wife in bed with my foreman."

"*What?*" The word left her on a long exhale. "God, Noah."

"Yeah, it sucked pretty bad. Miguel had worked for me for more than five years, and I relied on him for everything. He was also one of my closest friends. And my wife... We'd been married two years, and I thought we were mostly happy. Like you, I suddenly found out otherwise."

She shook her head in dismay. "Why do people have to hurt the ones who love them the most?"

"I'll never understand that part of it. I was good to them both. I treated Miguel like a member of my family. Trusted him with everything, and she knew she was the most important part of my life. I thought the three of us were the best of friends. I had no idea what they were doing behind my back."

"Like you said, saying I'm sorry seems so inadequate."

"You want to know something else?"

"Only if you want to tell me."

"Not even my mother knows why my marriage ended."

CHAPTER FIVE

"You don't get to choose if you get hurt in this world.
But you do have some say in who hurts you."
—John Green

hy was he confiding in her this way? If you'd asked Noah before he left the house if he'd tell Brianna what happened with Melinda, he would've said you were crazy. He never talked about that topic with anyone, so why would he tell her, of all people?

But after hearing what had happened to her, he'd felt compelled to let her know he got it. Strangely enough, it made him feel a little better to know that shit like that happened to other people, too, even if he'd never wish that kind of heartache on anyone.

Brianna had been a revelation in more ways than one. There was nothing not to like about her away from work. In addition to being funny, she was also very, very pretty, which, of course, he'd noticed before tonight. If he were honest with himself—and really, what's the point of lying to yourself?—he'd have to admit to being instantly attracted to her on day one. Perhaps that was why he'd allowed himself to be so easily annoyed by her.

"Why do you feel the need to keep what happened to yourself?" she asked as she sipped her cocktail.

"It's embarrassing."

"To whom?"

"To me. My wife was screwing my employee."

"Isn't it a bigger deal to you that he was your friend?"

Noah shrugged. He hated to think about that time in his life, let alone talk about it. "The whole thing sucked."

"I'm sure it was awful, but to keep it completely to yourself is to give it power over you long after it should be a distant, unpleasant memory."

He eyed her with newfound respect. "Did your therapist tell you that?"

"Among many other things. She made me see that Rem's actions weren't a reflection of me. They reflected *him*. I was a victim of his cruelty. You were a victim of theirs."

"I hate that word. *Victim*."

"I hate it, too, because people think victims are weak. But we're the strong ones because we survived something that could've ruined us. What I told you about my ex-husband is like one one-thousandth of the full story. I'm sure there's more to your story, too, things that others will never know, but you'll never forget. There's nothing weak about being a victim of someone else's cruelty."

It was the best articulation of what he'd been through that Noah had heard since his life blew up in his face, and it was a huge relief to know that someone else got it. "You're very wise."

"No, I'm not wise at all, or I would've seen him for what he was long before I did. My dad saw it. He told me if someone seemed too good to be true, he probably was. I didn't want to hear that. I was in love and determined to have it all with him. If only I'd listened to my dad, who's the wisest person I know, I could've avoided a lot of hell and heartache, not to mention financial ruin."

"He ruined you financially, too?"

She nodded. "I was a fool to allow him to oversee our finances. My credit was all tied up in his, and by the time I realized the full extent of what he'd been doing, we were nearly bankrupt. He'd wiped out our accounts, maxed out the credit cards and had stopped paying my student loans. I couldn't even afford to hire a divorce attorney or get an apartment of my own after I left him. I had to borrow money from my parents that I'm still paying back, and my cousin's husband is handling my divorce pro bono."

"God, what an asshole."

"He played me every which way and weaponized my love for him. He was shocked when I left him. He never expected that to happen because he thought I loved him so much, I'd never dare to leave him."

"I'm so glad you got free of him."

"I'm not completely free yet, but I'm working on it. He's refusing to sign the divorce papers, but I have a court date in a couple of weeks that might force the issue without his consent. I've got proof of all the shit he did, which my lawyer says will matter to the judge. We got lucky with a female judge who has no patience for men who prey on women."

"I hope she sticks it to him."

"I hope so, too. I'm looking forward to being completely free of him, but it's going to take me years to dig out of the financial hole he left me in."

"You ought to sue him."

"That's what my lawyer says, too, but that would cost more money and just extend the nightmare."

"And I get why that's not something you want to do, but why should you be stuck paying his tab?"

"The thought of dragging it on is so nauseating to me."

"I'd think the idea of paying off his debts would be even more sickening."

"You sound like my dad. He'd like you."

Before Noah could respond to that, the waitress returned with her sides and his ribs.

She took a bite of the beans and made a sound of pleasure that traveled like an arrow straight to his groin, making him thankful for the cover the table provided. For God's sake, now he was getting turned on by her in a restaurant? Before he met her at the start of this job, he'd had reason to wonder whether he'd ever again be interested in another woman for anything more than the random physical release. She'd answered that question rather definitively on more than one occasion since she came to town.

With this massive job at the center of both their lives—and a lot riding on it for everyone involved—he needed to keep this relationship professional, no matter what. The last thing he needed with the biggest job of his career only half finished was any kind of romantic entanglement with the architect running the show.

Tell that to your dick, jackass.

My dick needs to stand the fuck down and stop paying attention to her.

And now he was having conversations with himself about his dick.

He devoured the delicious ribs and tried to ignore that everything she did was sexy.

The waitress returned to refill their water glasses from a pitcher. "How is it?"

"Delicious as always," Noah said.

"Fantastic," Brianna replied.

"You folks from Butler?"

"We are," Noah said.

"We hear there was a big accident about four miles south of here. A car off the road. They expect the road to be closed most of the night. Since the snow is coming down hard, and you'd have to drive around the mountain to get home, we're offering free rooms upstairs for the night to anyone who can't get home.

One per party. Let me know if you want me to grab one for you."

Noah's mind went completely blank as he stared across the table at Brianna.

She looked up at the waitress. "We'll take one. Thank you so much."

"No problem. I'll get you a key. Be right back."

Noah wanted to say no way in hell to spending a night upstairs with her. That was the worst thing they could do with his little brain running roughshod over his better judgment where she was concerned. But driving more than an hour around the mountain in a raging snowstorm wasn't something he was eager to do either.

Fuck.

"I know it's not ideal, but I was already afraid of driving back in the snow before I heard a car was off the road. And by 'off the road,' does that mean 'off a cliff'?"

"Probably an embankment."

"Which isn't quite as terrifying as a cliff, but enough to make me want to stay put."

"My cousins are firefighters. They're probably on the scene."

"I hope everyone involved is all right."

"Me, too. I'm sorry about this."

"Don't be," she said. "It'll make for a funny story to tell Mrs. H."

"She'll be thrilled we had to spend the night. This whole thing was a fix-up anyway."

"You think so?"

"Oh, hell yes. My grandfather and uncle probably gave her the idea to send us off on an outing together. This entire evening is right out of their playbook. I wouldn't have put it past them to arrange the accident to keep us here, too."

"For real?"

"Well, not that part about the accident, but it wouldn't surprise me to learn they were behind the idea for us to come here in the first place. They've made it their mission in life to get all my cousins and siblings happily settled down, and their track record has been shockingly good so far."

"How so?"

"I could give a ton of examples, but my favorite one so far has to be what they did with my cousin Hannah. Her first husband was killed years ago in Iraq."

"That's so sad."

"It was awful. We grew up with Caleb, and his loss hit us all hard. He was a great guy, and they'd been together since they were kids."

"I'm so sorry for her."

"It was rough for a long time. In the last few years, we started to realize that another of our childhood friends, Nolan Roberts, had a thing for Hannah. He was a close friend of Caleb's, so it was messy, you know?"

"I can imagine. What did your uncle and grandfather do?"

"Nolan is the mechanic in town. That's his shop down the street from the diner."

"I know him. I took my car there for oil a couple of weeks ago. He and his coworker, Skeeter, took excellent care of me."

"Skeeter is a whole *other* story. Anyway, Hannah had a standing date with some friends once a week that she looked forward to. My grandfather and uncle waited for a week when everyone else was unavailable and then messed with Hannah's car so it wouldn't start when she was ready to leave. She had no choice but to call Nolan, and while he was there, he finally worked up the nerve to ask her out. They're married now with an adorable little girl named Caleb, but they call her Callie, and another baby on the way."

"That's seriously the sweetest thing I've ever heard."

"They're both great people who deserve to be happy."

"We're both great people who deserve to be happy, too," Brianna said.

Noah was slightly terrified of where she might be going with that. "Is that right?"

"It is. We deserve it after what we went through with *them*."

"My definition of happy changed after that. Happy to me is a drama-free life."

"I understand that. The kind of drama that happened to us is the worst, but neither of us went looking for it. We didn't cause it, and we can't let it completely ruin our faith in other people."

"How can you have faith in anyone after what he did?"

"It's not easy, but I choose not to let the actions of one person color my outlook on everyone."

"You're a bigger person than I am if you can still trust people. I don't think I'll ever trust anyone the way I did her and Miguel." Noah finished the last of his ribs and took a drink of his beer. "That mistake with the fireplace never would've happened on his watch. His attention to detail was meticulous. Carlo is great, but he misses shit all the time and makes mistakes that Miguel never would've made."

"It's tough to replace someone like that."

"He's irreplaceable at work, which makes me hate what he did even more. I gave him the keys to my kingdom, and he ran off with my queen."

"Are they still together?"

"I don't know, and I tell myself I don't care."

"You could find out easily enough."

"What difference would that make to me?"

"Maybe if it was a love match, you'd feel better about it."

"No, I wouldn't. They had to betray me to get their 'love match.' So why would I want to know that?"

"If I were you, I'd prefer to know that what they did was about more than scratching an itch at your expense."

"Eh, I don't care either way. It happened. It sucked. It's over. I've moved on."

"Have you, though?"

~

BRIANNA COULDN'T BELIEVE SHE WAS TALKING TO HIM THIS WAY, about the worst time in both their lives. But it was comforting to meet someone who understood what that kind of betrayal did to a person. It ripped apart the fabric of your entire life and left you shredded. She was still putting the pieces back together more than a year after uncovering the full extent of her ex-husband's deceit.

If there was one good thing about being in Vermont, it was being far away from all the misguided sympathy from friends and family at home who'd wanted to do something to help—at first. But what could they do? What could anyone do? She'd given her heart to a monster, and he'd trampled all over it. After a while, her friends and family had grown weary of hearing the latest episode in her ongoing drama, leaving her more alone with her heartbreak than she'd been at first. Her cousin, Dom, was the one exception. She'd been there through it all and had never wavered in her devotion. For that, Brianna would be eternally grateful.

"I think I have," Noah said in response to her question. "Moved on, that is. It's been three years."

"Do you date?"

"Not really. I have a friends-with-benefits thing with a woman I've known since high school. Neither of us is interested in anything more than that, so it works out well."

"So that's it? A friend with benefits for the rest of your life?"

"I don't know about that, but it works for me right now."

"I get it. What's the point of risking anything if there're people out there like your ex and mine, right?"

"Right. I did that once. Risked everything, and it didn't work out, so why bother with the hassle of that again?"

"Can I ask you something—and you don't have to answer if you don't want to."

"Sure. I mean, I've already told you more than anyone else knows."

"Thank you for trusting me with that. I promise it won't go any further."

"What did you want to ask me?"

"If you were happy with your wife before it went bad."

"I was, which made it so much worse when I caught her with Miguel. I'd had no idea that anything was that wrong. I mean we had our issues, but who doesn't? It reminded me of what my mom said after my dad left, that she'd had no clue he was unhappy enough to do something like that. Sure, things had been 'off' between them for a while, but she didn't see *that* coming." He took a drink of his beer. "What about you? Were you happy before you found out who he was?"

"Blissfully. No one in the history of love had ever been more in love with anyone than I was with him. I'm sure I was completely annoying to everyone who knew us with the way I'd go on and on about how wonderful he was. Only to find out it was all a con. Everything that happened between us was part of his master plan to ruin my life."

"Why would anyone spend the limited amount of time they have in their lives ruining someone else?"

"I've done a lot of reading about the mindset of the sociopath, and I've come to understand that it's not intentional on his part. It's just how his mind operates. His goal is to maneuver a situation to his optimal benefit at the expense of anyone and everyone who gets in the way. I wasn't a person to him. My feelings had no bearing on him, so it was nothing for him to hurt me the way he did. It took me a long time to under-stand the psychology of it. My therapist is the one who first used the word sociopath to describe him."

"Do you ever wonder..." He fiddled with a paper-wrapped straw that the waitress had left on the table.

"What?"

"How it's possible you lived through something like that and continue to function somewhat normally?"

"All the time. When I look back on those first few months, all I see is the darkness. My life imploded in one twenty-four-hour period. Everything went from fine to not fine in the literal blink of an eye. For a long time, *weeks*, I didn't think I would survive it."

"How did you?"

"When the full extent of what he'd done became clear to me, I started to get angry. Strangely enough, that helped."

"I know about that kind of anger. I never thought I could kill someone, but when I saw them together..."

"Which one would you have killed first?" she asked with a grin.

"Him."

"Why not her? She was the one you were married to."

"Because he was screwing me twice over by screwing her."

"I can't believe you had to see them together that way." She shuddered. "That had to be the worst."

"Took a long time to scrub those images from my mind."

The waitress returned to take their plates, handed a key for a room upstairs to Brianna and asked if they were interested in more drinks or dessert.

"Since I don't have to drive, I'll have another," Noah said. "Anything for you, Brianna?"

"I'll have one more, too. And I wouldn't mind seeing the dessert menu."

"Coming right up," the waitress said. "The band is here until midnight." She moved on to tend to other tables.

Brianna looked at him through thick lashes. "I just want to say... I didn't expect to talk to you like this, and it's been nice. Thanks for listening to my tale of woe."

"Likewise and thank you for listening to mine. It's strangely cathartic to meet someone who's been through something similar, although yours was much worse. At least my ex didn't also ruin me financially."

"You're lucky."

The waitress brought their drinks and the dessert menu. When Brianna didn't see anything that tempted her, the waitress placed the check on the table.

Noah handed her the coupon Mrs. H had given him and his credit card.

"Let's split it," Brianna said.

"No worries. I've got it. And I was going to say that I already owned my house and my business when she came along, so my brother, the attorney, strongly suggested a prenup. I was so pissed with him for thinking I'd need that." Noah smiled at the irony. "He said, 'You just never know what's going to happen, and you have assets to protect.' Thank God I listened to him."

"You dodged a second bullet with that."

"No kidding. I probably ought to thank Grayson for that one of these days."

"You really should. He saved you an even bigger headache than you already had."

"It's funny… I hated having to tell her that my brother was recommending a prenup. I thought that was a shitty way for her to start with my family. But she said she understood he was protecting me and signed it without another word about it. In the end, it was no big deal between her and me, but it sure saved my ass when shit went sideways."

"Jeez, no kidding, huh? Imagine having her as your partner in the business after what she did."

Noah cringed as he laughed. "Thanks for putting that thought in my head."

"Sorry."

"I feel like I've had three years' worth of therapy over one dinner," Noah said. "Thanks for that."

"I'd say it was my pleasure, but I sure hate to hear that anyone else has had a similar thing happen. I've found it helps to talk about it, though. Keeping it all bottled up inside isn't healthy. I don't want to hold on to all that shit."

"Yeah, I suppose you're right. My MO has been to keep it all to myself, if for no other reason than it was so freaking embarrassing. My wife and my best friend-slash-top employee? *Seriously?* Like was there no one else for her to screw? It had to be *him?*"

"That makes it so much worse than it would've been if it had just screwed up your marriage."

"So much worse."

"If you want to move on from it, you should tell people what happened. You're not the villain in that story, Noah. Someone did this *to* you. No need to suffer in silence over it. The longer you do that, the longer the two of them get a pass with the people in your life."

"That's true. If my sisters ran into her somewhere, they'd probably be glad to see her. They liked her."

"Yeah, you need to tell them what she did. She doesn't deserve to be treated well by anyone in your life."

"How much do you charge for this advice?"

"Free of charge in exchange for some baked beans and coleslaw."

"Don't forget the cornbread and vodka."

"Ah, yes, that, too."

"Not to mention deluxe accommodations at the Pig's Belly Tavern."

"And for this, I went to medical school."

"Did you?" he asked, stunned.

She cracked up. "No, I was just rolling with the shrink thing."

As Noah laughed—again—he realized he'd done that more in the last couple of hours than he had in years. He'd lost his sense of humor along with his best friend, his wife and the life he'd thought he was going to have with them both by his side. "Enough of this depressing shit. Let's go dance."

CHAPTER SIX

*"Being hurt by someone you truly care about leaves
a hole in your heart that only love can fill."*
—George Bernard Shaw

They danced until the band quit at midnight. Brianna hadn't had that much fun in more than a year. She was sweaty and disheveled and possibly drunk after that devil Noah kept the drinks coming while they danced. This evening had turned out much differently than she'd expected when she set out to dine with the man who'd been such a thorn in her side for weeks now.

It turned out he wasn't mean, just wounded. Brianna certainly understood how the kind of heartache they'd both endured could turn someone into a moody asshole. She could only hope they'd had a breakthrough tonight, and things would be better on the job.

The dancing had served a secondary purpose of postponing their stay upstairs until the last possible minute. As the band packed up, Brianna sat with Noah at the table that had been their home base and finished the last of her latest drink. She'd lost track of how many she'd had and would pay for that in the morning.

Whatever.

It'd been worth it to have fun again.

In a year full of abject misery and heartbreak, the word *fun* had been a long way from her vocabulary. Something about sharing their experiences had given them the liberty to cut loose and enjoy themselves.

Brianna had polished off the last of her drink when a loud burp came from somewhere deep inside and had everyone still in the room looking at her.

She covered her mouth as her face heated with embarrassment. "'Scuse me."

Noah laughed harder than he had all night.

"Stop! It's not funny." She hiccupped on the word *funny*, which made him laugh some more.

"We should get you upstairs before you fall over."

The hiccups intensified until they were coming one right after the other.

Smiling, Noah stood to offer her a hand up.

She took hold of his hand and let him haul her to her feet. The second she was upright, the whole world seemed to tilt, which had her reaching for him to keep from falling.

He put his arm around her. "Easy. I've got you."

"I'm not much of a drinker."

"You don't say?"

"Stop making fun of me."

"I'm not!"

"You are, too!"

His low chuckle was confirmation that he was, in fact, making fun of her. He half walked, half carried her up the stairs to room four. Using the key the waitress had given them, Noah somehow managed to keep her upright while unlocking the door. After they staggered into the room, Noah got her to the bed and waited for her to sit before releasing her.

Brianna promptly slid right off the bed onto the floor, where she lost it laughing and hiccupping. She laughed so hard, she feared she might wet her pants. Wouldn't that be the kicker?

Noah offered her both his hands. "Let's try this again."

Brianna wasn't sure why she pulled on them, but he fell almost on top of her, setting off another round of hilarious laughter.

He just barely missed landing right on top of her.

Pity.

"Are you trying to kill us both?"

Hiccup. "Nope."

He rose to his knees and looked at her with amusement in his lovely eyes. Had she ever noticed how gorgeous his eyes were? Probably not, because she'd been too busy being furious with him most of the time.

"You have lovely eyes."

He rolled them. "Thank you. Now, do you want to sleep on the floor, or would you prefer the big comfy bed?"

"Bed." Hiccup. Giggle. "Please."

Standing, he offered only one hand this time and helped her to her feet, grabbing her with the other hand when she swayed.

"I gotta pee."

"Awesome. Let's go." He perp-walked her to the bathroom. "If I let you go in there by yourself, you're not going to fall and crack your head open on the sink or anything, are you?"

Hiccup. "Try not to."

"Do that, since there's no way to get to a hospital in this snow." He released her at the door and waited until she'd crossed the bigger-than-expected bathroom to get to the toilet. "Closing the door now. Do not fall."

She smiled and waved her fingers at him. "K."

Fortunately, she had enough sense to heed his concern about not being able to get to the hospital if she hurt herself and managed to take care of business without falling. Out of curiosity, she looked inside the closet and was shocked to find a wide variety of sex toys, lube and condoms along with combs, tooth-paste and toothbrushes. The Pig's Belly was full of surprises.

When she opened the bathroom door, he stood with his arms propped above his head on the doorframe. He'd removed his sweater, leaving him only in a thermal Henley that displayed his considerable muscles.

Yum.

"All set?"

The sight of him waiting there for her did something to her insides, making her feel even more light-headed than she already was.

He offered his arm and escorted her to the king-size bed. When she sat on the edge, he stood by to grab her if she slid off again. "Sit back. I'll help you get your boots off."

Brianna leaned back on her elbows so she could watch him as he untied and removed first one boot and then the other. A wave of heat came over her as she watched him concentrate on the task, the muscles in his arms and shoulders flexing under the Henley. Had she ever noticed before how seriously ripped he was? No, not really. He wore tons of clothes to stay warm at work, so how would she know?

"I'll crash on the sofa."

"The bed is huge. You can sleep on the other side." Hiccup. "I'll try to resist mauling you in your sleep."

"You're funny when you're drunk." He sat in a chair to remove his boots. "I never would've suspected that."

"Why, because I'm such a professional on the job?"

After a long pause, he said, "Something like that."

"I think it's safe to say a lot of things about this evening have been surprising."

Noah put the safety lock on the door before he stretched out on the far side of the big bed. "Lots of surprises all around. Like this room, for example. It's way nicer than I would've expected from the Pig's Belly."

"There's stuff in the closet," Brianna said in a scandalized whisper.

"What kind of stuff?"

"Toys."

"Like Legos?"

She snorted with laughter that only intensified her hiccups. "*No!*"

"Oh, *those* kinds of toys. This I need to see." He got up and went into the bathroom, closing the door to use the facilities before opening it again so she could hear his comments about the items in the closet. "Holy cow. They aren't messing around."

"Don't you mean holy pig?"

"I guess I do," he said on a low chuckle.

"I had no idea I was missing out by being a vegetarian. They don't have this stuff at the vegetarian restaurants."

Noah came back to the bed and lay down again. "I'm trying to picture my buttoned-down cousin Hunter finding that stuff in the closet. That must've been funny."

Brianna was suddenly so sleepy, she could barely keep her eyes open, but she didn't want this night to end. Once they returned to Butler, would the magical bubble surrounding them burst? Would they go back to normal, fighting all the time? She was tired of fighting with him over stupid shit that didn't matter. "I don't want to fight with you anymore."

"I don't want that either." He looked over at her. "I really am sorry if I made you feel unwelcome in Butler. I wasn't raised like that."

Smiling, she said, "How were you raised?"

"To be nice to the flatlanders who come up to our mountains to visit."

"Is that what I am? A flatlander?"

"If you're not a native Vermonter, then yes, that's what you are."

Brianna yawned and then hiccupped again.

"Try holding your breath."

She took a deep breath and held it.

"Push out from your diaphragm." He gestured to his abdomen to show her what he meant. "Don't let it go until you can't hold it any longer."

Brianna held her breath until she had stars in her eyes and then released it slowly. "I think you cured me."

"Hope so."

An extended period of silence ended with another loud hiccup that made them laugh.

"Try holding your breath again."

Brianna repeated the ritual several more times before it seemed that she'd beaten the hiccups. "I'm not cut out for this drinking stuff."

"Did you have a good time?"

"I had the best time that I've had in ages."

"Then it was worth the hiccups."

Brianna looked over at him. "Did you have fun, too?"

"I did," he said, "and I never have fun."

She turned on her side to face him, hands under her face. "That's sad. You're too young to have given up on fun."

"It seemed easier that way."

"To me, it sounds lonely."

"Maybe a little, but nothing I can't handle. I've got a huge family all around me. I can be with people any time I want to be."

"How often do you hang out with them?"

"Not very."

"Noah... Why would you let two people who aren't worth it do that to you?"

"Do what?"

"Turn you into a recluse?"

He shrugged. "I didn't want to answer questions about what happened to my marriage, so I fell into the habit of avoiding everyone."

"Did you ever consider just telling everyone so you could move past it?"

"Nope, because that'd require me to *talk* about it, and that's the last thing I want to do."

"You talked about it with me."

"That's different."

"How so?"

"I don't know you that well. You didn't know my ex or us together, and you've been through something similar. All of that made it easier for me to talk to you about it."

"I'm glad you talked to me. My therapist has helped me to see that none of what happened was my fault. That's true for you, too."

"I figure it must've been partly my fault if she wanted to sleep with someone else."

"That's on her, not you. If something wasn't right for her with you, all she had to do was tell you, and you could've tried to work it out. What she did was evil on several levels." She closed her eyes, just for a second, and immediately regretted it when the room started spinning. "Ugh, room spins."

Noah moved closer to her. "Hang on to me. That'll stop the spinning."

She glanced up at him. "Are you sure that's a good idea?"

"It's better than puking in the bed."

"That's very true. Okay, here goes." She placed her hand on his shoulder and tried closing her eyes again. The room tilt was less severe than it had been before.

"Breathe through the spins."

"You seem to have some rather significant experience with room spins."

"A little. The bottle was my friend after my life imploded."

"You're lucky you could find that oblivion. I couldn't keep anything down for months. I survived on water and soup. Lost twenty pounds, so that was the good news."

"You don't have twenty pounds to lose."

Since the spinning had stopped because she held on to him, she kept her eyes closed. "I did then. I still have trouble eating sometimes. I get this lump in my throat that won't let anything by." She took a deep breath and released it, hoping she wasn't killing him with booze fumes. "Do you ever miss her? The person she was before she did what she did to you?"

"Sometimes, and I hate that."

"Me, too. I find myself yearning for the life I had before I found out the truth, even though now I know it was all lies. He never loved me. He's not capable of loving anyone but himself. I think that was the hardest thing to accept."

"He didn't deserve you."

"No, he didn't."

That was the last thing she said before she fell asleep, still clinging to him.

SHE HAD AN ADORABLE LITTLE SNORE THAT MADE HIM SMILE AS HE listened to the rhythmic sound of her breathing.

He wanted to laugh at how this evening had unfolded. He'd gone from dreading the outing to sleeping next to Brianna, with her holding on to him for dear life. In addition to her adorable snore, she was also a cute drunk.

Noah also couldn't help but notice he felt strangely lighter after confiding in her about the most painful event in his life. The breakup of his marriage had made his father leaving the family look simple by comparison, when it was anything but.

He was awake for a long time, picking over the things they'd talked about and wondering if maybe she was right. He'd allowed what his wife and former friend had done to make him into a cranky recluse who avoided interactions with other people as much as he possibly could—even the people closest to him.

Take the way his mother had cornered him first thing in the

morning, wanting to lay eyes on him for the first time in weeks when they lived on the same street. He took care of shoveling her snow, but he rarely stopped in to say hello to her. That needed to change. None of the shit that'd happened to him was her fault, and after everything she'd done for him and his siblings, he owed her better than what she'd gotten from him the last few years.

Noah eventually dozed off, but a sound had him jolting awake sometime later to realize it was Brianna, whimpering in her sleep. He wasn't sure what to do, so he moved a little closer and rested a hand on her back, which seemed to settle her.

"Please," she whispered. "Don't do this."

Was she talking to him?

He raised his hand from her back, and she whimpered again. So, he put it back.

"Rem... Don't go. *Please.*" A sound that might've been a sob came from her, and Noah's heart broke for her.

"Brianna," he whispered. "Wake up."

He'd left the bedside light on in case she woke during the night and forgot where she was, which was how he saw her eyes flutter open.

She blinked several times, her brows furrowing in surprise, maybe, to see him there.

"I think you were dreaming."

"Oh." She licked her lips. "Did I say anything?"

"You were talking about your husband."

Her eyes filled and then closed, tears leaking out the sides. "That hasn't happened in a while."

"What hasn't?"

"Dreams. About Rem. Used to happen a lot. I'd wake up and realize I'd dreamed about everything being normal, and I'd have to remember what happened all over again. That was torture."

"I've had a few of those dreams, too. It's the worst. Fucks me up for days afterward."

"Yeah."

"You want some water or something?"

"That might be good. My head is pounding."

"Coming right up." He got off the bed and went to the bathroom to fill a glass with tap water. In the closet, he rifled through the various offerings until he found a packet of painkillers. The good old Pig's Belly thought of everything. He brought the items to her and sat on the edge of the mattress. "Found some pills."

"Oh good. That'll save tomorrow from being a total loss." She took the glass and downed the pills, chasing them with a drink of water. "It's not like me to party on a school night."

"You're a good girl, then, huh?"

"I always tried to be. For all the good that did me."

"Remember what you said to me? None of this was your fault."

"And I believe that. I honestly do. But I can't help but wonder why he chose to target me. What was wrong with me that made him think I'd make such an easy mark?"

Noah couldn't help himself. He reached out and tucked a stray curl behind her ear, even though he knew as he was doing it that touching her was a mistake. "There is nothing wrong with you."

"There must be *something*. He played me so easily."

"You cared about the guy. Any time you care about someone else, you're taking a gamble. Some gambles pay off. Some don't. But it takes guts to risk yourself that way."

"Do you think you'll ever be able to gamble again?"

"I don't know. How about you?"

"No idea. I've kind of lost my nerve."

"You'll get it back when the time is right."

"You think so?" she asked in a wistful tone.

"I do."

"Will you?"

"I hope so."

They stared at each other for a long, breathless moment.

Noah could hear his better judgment screaming at him to move away from her, to go back to his side of the bed and stay there. But he didn't do that. It was almost as if he couldn't move, even if he'd wanted to, which he didn't, not with her soft hair curling around his fingers.

He wasn't sure who moved first, but later, he would decide it was her. It made him feel better to think he hadn't kissed her. No, *she* kissed *him*, and he let her. That was how it went because it would be highly inappropriate for him to kiss the architect overseeing the biggest job of his career.

It'd be super inappropriate for him to like kissing her or to wrap his arms around her and slide his tongue into her open mouth. Not to mention going with her when she fell back onto the bed without breaking the kiss. This was complete insanity. They worked together. They fought like cats and dogs all day, every day. What in the name of hell was he doing kissing her like he'd just found a boat after a year on a deserted island?

He'd stop this. He would. In a minute. Or two.

CHAPTER SEVEN

"Suffering is the price of being alive."
—Judy Collins

*B*rianna should *not* have been kissing Noah Coleman as if her life depended on it. This might count as the single stupidest thing she'd ever done, and considering her track record with men, that was saying something. Surely somewhere in architecture school, they'd told her not to make out with her general contractor, hadn't they? If not, that should've been on the day-one agenda. Twisting tongues with the contractor when the job was only half finished wasn't a good career move.

But damn if she could be bothered to care about her career when Noah's lips were so soft and his kisses so hot and dirty. And was that his hand sliding under her sweater and branding her back with its heat? God, no one had touched her this way in so long, she'd almost forgotten what it was like to feel desired. If the hard length of him pressing against her core was any indication, Noah wanted her.

While she knew she ought to put a stop to this, she couldn't seem to find the wherewithal to do it, not when her sweater slid up and over her head or when he released the front clasp on her bra and pushed aside the cups so he could get to her nipples. She didn't stop him when he kissed and sucked on the hard tips or when he moved down to unbutton and unzip her jeans.

That really should've been the end. Brianna was about to say no more when his hand slid inside her pants, and one finger ended up deep inside her.

Stop. The word was on the tip of her tongue, but unfortunately, her tongue was super busy at the moment, wrapped as it was around his. With his hand inside her pants, she didn't think it would matter much—in the grand scheme of things—if she unbuttoned his jeans and returned the favor.

One of them would come to their senses before this went too far, before something happened that they couldn't undo.

Any minute now.

He'd call this off. Or she would. She definitely would. But not quite yet, not when he was stroking her *there* and making fireworks explode within her entire body. Not when he was pulling off her jeans and panties or moving down to replace his fingers with his tongue. That'd be a terrible time to stop him.

Oh *God.*

And was he ever *good* at that. He had her holding back a scream in a matter of seconds. Usually, it took her months to feel comfortable enough with someone to let them do *that,* but Noah didn't ask if she was comfortable. He just did it, and as she launched into an explosive orgasm, she was damned glad he had.

She was still panting as he kissed his way up the front of her.

"Tell me to stop," he said in a gruff, sexy voice.

"No, I don't think I will."

"Brianna, seriously."

She pushed at his jeans and stroked the long, thick cock that had breached the top of his boxer briefs. Who'd a thunk he had *that* going on inside the faded jeans he wore to work? It really would be tragic to let that go to waste.

"Brianna." His breath was hot against her nipple, which tingled from the brush of his whiskers against it.

"Hmm?"

"Tell me to stop."

"No."

"Yes."

"*No.*"

Now, this was more like their usual bickering routine, only usually they were fighting over construction priorities or supplies or invoices or something that simply didn't matter. As the wind howled outside and the icy snow pinged against the glass, Brianna wondered how long they'd be stranded at the Pig's Belly. They might as well enjoy themselves before they had to return to reality.

"Do you have a condom?"

He stared at her, his face flat with shock. "No, I don't have a condom."

"There're some in the cabinet. You want to get them, or should I?"

"Are you still drunk?"

"I don't think so."

"You must be drunk if you're not telling me to stop."

"I'm not drunk, and I'm not telling you to stop." She stroked him with a firm grip, from root to tip. "Unless you're telling me to stop."

"Not saying that," he said through a clenched jaw.

"Why don't you go see what kind of condoms the Pig's Belly left for us."

He gave her a long, intense look as if he was waiting for her to say "April Fools" or "psych" or something that meant *game off.*

She said nothing.

Noah lifted himself on his arms and pushed off the bed to go into the bathroom and root around in the cabinet. When he returned, he stood by the side of the bed, the hem of his Henley hiding his erection. "Last chance to say no."

"Not saying no. Are you?"

"I should."

"But you're not?"

"I don't seem to be."

"Take your shirt off."

He did as directed, revealing a well-defined chest and abdomen covered by dark blond hair that got darker at his waist.

"Now, your pants."

Brianna propped herself up on her elbow so she could watch him strip for her. If she was going to cross every line, she might as well enjoy the show. She held out her arms, inviting him to come back to where he'd been before he'd gotten up.

He hesitated. "Tell me this isn't going to make everything between us weirder than it was before tonight."

"I won't let it if you won't."

"I won't. And it's just this once, right?"

She smiled at him. "Maybe twice if the first time goes well."

A grin stretched across his face, which softened his hard edges. It was shocking to discover how genuinely handsome and sexy her adversary had turned out to be.

Brianna drew him into another one of those fantastic kisses that had led to all this nakedness. The brush of his chest hair against her nipples made her gasp from the pleasure that touched every part of her.

Fourteen months ago, the thought of being naked in a bed with anyone other than her beloved husband would've been ludicrous. Since then, every aspect of her life had changed. Not one thing was the same, except for her family.

Never in her wildest dreams had she pictured herself in a bed above the Pig's Belly Tavern in Somewhere, Vermont, with a sexy contractor named Noah Coleman, who had been, as recently as this afternoon, the most irritating human being she'd ever met. When it came to unlikely lovers, she and Noah had to take the prize.

They might be unlikely, but they moved together like they knew what they were doing, the desire drowning out everything other than the urgent need to see this through to the logical conclusion.

"Condom," she said. "Now."

He pulled back from her, grabbed a condom from the strip of five he'd brought from the bathroom and rolled it on.

Brianna's mouth watered at the delicious sight of aroused man and the knowledge that he wanted her badly enough to say to hell with all the reasons why this might turn out to be the worst idea either of them had ever had.

As he pushed into her, moaning from the connection, it didn't seem like such a bad idea. No, it didn't seem so bad at all. If anything, it was really, really good.

He was big, and the fit tight, which made for intense pleasure as he pushed into her slowly, giving her time to accommodate him before he went farther.

Brianna sank her fingers into the muscles on his back and held on for the wild ride they took each other on. Her better judgment screamed at her with outrage that she was *screwing* the cranky contractor.

But it had turned out, shockingly, that he wasn't cranky so much as wounded, and that was something she certainly understood.

God, it felt good to be held and touched and caressed by a man again. For a time, she'd wondered if she'd ever be able to do this with someone else. Noah had answered that question rather definitively. As she climbed toward another incendiary release, she was overwhelmed with relief at knowing it was possible to not only do this with someone other than Rem, but to truly enjoy it.

Noah thrust into her, triggering the release that'd been brewing.

She held on to him as she rode the waves of pleasure that knocked every other thought out of her head. There was only right here and right now. Nothing had been able to wipe her mind clear like sex with Noah had, which was another thing to be thankful for.

Afterward, he came down on top of her, breathing as hard as she was.

"That went well," he said after a long silence.

Brianna laughed. "Sure did. Maybe we should do it again to make sure it wasn't a one-off."

"I'd be down for that. Just give me a minute to recover."

He withdrew from her and moved to his side, facing her with an arm around her.

"That was the first time I've done that since everything happened," she said softly.

"Yeah?"

"Uh-huh."

"How do you feel?"

"Other than conflicted about being naked in bed with a work colleague?"

Smiling, he said, "Other than that."

"Pretty good." She rested her hand on his arm. "For a long time after, I wondered if I'd ever do that again. I mean, if I couldn't be with him, would I want to be with anyone else?"

"Took me six months to go looking for it with someone else," Noah said. "I was numb with shock for so long."

"Did it help? To get back on the horse, so to speak?"

"A little." He sighed. "I mean, it doesn't change what happened, you know?"

"Yeah, I do. And while this doesn't change anything, it made me feel good, so thanks for that."

"I aim to please, ma'am."

Brianna giggled at the exaggerated drawl he affected with the statement. "Maybe it's a good thing Mrs. H meddled in our business, and then it snowed."

"Doubt this ever would've happened without her involvement."

"Definitely not. I wanted to stab you, not, you know..."

"Fuck me?"

"Stop! Oh my God. You had to say it like that?"

"What would you call it?"

"Not that."

"Such a good girl. I need to dirty you up a bit."

"Didn't you already do that?"

"Nah, that was just the appetizer. We'll get dirty on the next round."

"Um, not sure how I feel about that."

"Trust me. You'll like it."

Brianna was so tired and so sated that she didn't ask for more info. If he said she'd like it, she probably would. She dozed for a long time before the brush of his lips over her nipple awakened her. At some point, he'd turned off the light, and she had no idea what time it was or if it was still snowing. What did trivial stuff like that matter when Noah was teasing her nipples with his tongue and fingers?

Brianna closed her eyes and floated on a wave of contentment. Right here in this gorgeous room in the most unlikely of places, she felt wonderful for the first time after a very long and harrowing ordeal. Maybe she and Noah would go back to locking horns when they returned to the jobsite. Maybe whatever this was between them would never be more than a snowy interlude at the Pig's Belly.

If that's how it worked out, that'd be fine. No matter what happened next, this evening with Noah had given her hope for a future that wasn't all gloom, doom and crushing disappointment.

He turned her onto her belly and rained kisses down her back. Then he tugged her up to her knees and caressed her bottom with a light touch that made her skin tingle and her clit ache with desire.

She was about to beg him for relief when he pushed into her from behind and nearly made her come with one deep thrust.

"Not yet," he whispered gruffly in her ear.

Brianna bit her lip as she tried to hold back the need to let go.

He withdrew from her, making her whimper from the loss. "Easy," he said. "You'll get what you want if you're patient."

"I have no patience."

"That's good to know." He slid his fingers through the liquid heat between her legs, but studiously avoided the one place that burned for his touch. "You need to get some."

"I've never had any."

He set out to torture her until she was nearly wailing from the effort it took to hold back the release that was bursting to break free.

"Noah," she said on a sound that resembled a sob. "*Please.*"

"Is this what you want?" he asked as he drove into her and triggered an orgasm for the ages.

It was so intense, she nearly blacked out from the overload of pleasure that coursed through her body.

Afterward, she felt utterly wrecked. She couldn't have moved if the place was on fire.

Noah withdrew from her and went to dispose of the condom and retrieve a towel to clean her up.

Brianna didn't do a thing to help him.

"You all right down there?" he asked, placing a kiss in the middle of her back.

"Mmmm."

"I need words."

"Yes, I'm all right."

"You're sure?"

"Uh-huh. How are you?"

"Pretty damned good."

She was glad to hear him say he felt good. That was her last thought before a ringing phone woke her from a dead sleep. She opened her eyes to daylight.

Noah shifted next to her as he reached for the phone. "Hello." Pause. "Yes, sure, that sounds good. Hang on a minute." To

Brianna, he said, "The road to Butler is still closed, and the snow hasn't let up. They're offering breakfast delivery."

"That's nice of them. What's on the menu?"

"Eggs, pancakes, French toast."

"Oh, pancakes, please. And coffee. Lots of coffee."

Noah placed the order, requesting an omelet for himself, and put down the phone. He curled up to her and moved her wild hair out of the way so he could kiss the side of her neck. "Did you sleep okay?"

"Like a dead woman."

"Me, too. Haven't slept that well in a long time."

"Me either."

"We're stuck here, then, huh?"

"Looks that way. I should call Carlo and tell the guys to stay in bed." He sat up again and made the call to his foreman.

Brianna dozed to the sound of his voice. She marveled at how his voice had gone from a source of irritation to one of comfort during an unforgettable night. She'd expected to feel conflicted this morning, but she didn't. Sure, she still didn't think sleeping with a colleague was the wisest thing she'd ever done, but mostly she just felt… good.

When was the last time she'd woken up feeling good? Before the implosion. Every single day since then had been shitty. Not every second, of course, but most of the time. Feeling like shit sucked the life out of a person and made everything difficult, even the most mundane tasks.

The next thing she knew, Noah was pulling the bedcovers up over her shoulders. "Stay put. They're here with the food."

Brianna snuggled deeper into the comfortable bed, delighted that they were stranded and didn't have to spend the day in the frigid tundra.

Noah carried in their tray and set it on the coffee table. He went into the bathroom and came out with a robe that he held up for her. "Madam, your breakfast is served." His most excellent chest was still on display since he was wearing only his jeans with the top button undone. Adding to his morning sexiness was the golden-blond stubble on his face and jaw. He was rather lovely to look at.

She tore her eyes off him and got up, eager to put the robe on. "Thank you." The wave of shyness made her feel silly considering what they'd done during the night. She quickly stuck her arms in the sleeves and tied the robe around her waist.

He held her chair at the table and sat across from her to take the catering covers off their plates.

"Holy cow, that's a feast," she said.

"It's holy *pig*, remember?"

"Oh, right. You want my sausage?"

"Since you had mine, I'll take yours."

She sputtered with laughter. "I can't believe you said that."

"Sure, you can."

They ate the delicious breakfast that also included Vermont maple syrup for her pancakes and a fruit bowl to share.

"The Pig's Belly is my new favorite place," Brianna said after her third bite of pancake. "In fact, I think I'd like to live here."

"That's quite a statement for a vegetarian."

"I know! Meat is so not my thing."

Noah gave her a dirty look that had her face heating with embarrassment.

"Stop it."

"You're cute when you're mortified."

"I am not."

"You are, too."

"Glad to get back to normal with you." She eyed him over the rim of her coffee mug. "Back to arguing."

"Feels like old times from just yesterday."

"You mean when you were trying to tell me it was no big deal that you signed for supplies after I explicitly asked you not to?"

"That seems like such a long time ago."

"Does it?"

"Uh-huh. We've traveled light-years from there."

"Maybe so, but you're still not signing for supplies when we get back to work."

"Yes, ma'am."

She glowered at him. "Don't call me that."

"What should I call you?"

"Brianna works."

"Brianna it is."

"Do you have any idea how difficult it is to be a female project manager when your entire team is men who think they know much better than you ever could?"

"No, I guess I don't, seeing as how I've never been a woman."

"I worked construction for four summers when I was in college because I wanted to learn the business from the ground up."

"Is that right?" Noah asked, surprised.

"I did it all, from roofing to drywalling to finish work to apprenticing with the plumbers and electricians, so I'd understand their roles."

"That's impressive."

"From the first time I ever stepped foot on a jobsite, I was treated as someone who didn't belong there. They acted like I was going to get hurt and cause them problems when all I wanted to do was learn their trade."

"How'd you get hired in the first place?"

"A family friend owned a construction business, and when I decided to major in architecture, he told me I should learn the business from the construction side first. He offered to give me a summer job if I wanted it. My parents weren't thrilled about me spending summers with a bunch of grown men, but our friend ran a tight ship and put the word out that they were to leave me alone and teach me. I give him so much credit for starting me off the right way."

"That's cool you did it that way. I really am impressed."

"For all the good it did me. I still have to fight for respect on every job. It gets tiresome after a while."

"I'm sorry I made you feel disrespected."

She shrugged. "It's fine. I'm used to it by now."

"It's not fine. My shitty attitude has nothing to do with you, as you know by now. I've been guilty of letting my personal crap spill over into work, and I am sorry if I mistreated you. You have a job to do just like I do. What happened to me three years ago certainly isn't your fault."

"It's not yours either."

"I have trouble believing that. I must've done something to create the opening for my ex to do what she did."

Brianna looked him directly in the eyes. "You did *nothing* to deserve what she did. I don't care what failings you might have had as a husband. If she wanted out, all she had to do was say so. To sleep with someone else is disgusting. To sleep with her husband's best friend and highly valued employee is despicable."

His lips quivered with the start of a smile.

"I'm serious!"

"I know you are."

"So then why are you trying not to laugh?"

"Because you're cute when you're fierce."

She scowled at him. "Quit calling me cute. No grown-ass woman wants to be told she's *cute*."

"Sexy, then. Is that better?"

"I can live with that."

When he smiled, it transformed his face, taking him from hard and unreachable to sweet and eminently accessible.

"You ought to smile more often. It does good things for you."

"Makes me feel good, too. My face sorta hurts from all the smiling I've done since I picked you up last night."

"Didn't expect that, did you?"

"Not so much. But neither did you."

"Nope. I was kinda dreading having to go to the Pig's Belly with you, of all people."

"The thorn in your side."

"More like a gigantic pain in my ass than a thorn in my side."

He tossed his head back and laughed hard, which made her laugh right along with him.

"What should we do with this unexpected day off?" Noah asked.

"I'd love a shower, and then I might go back to bed for a while."

"I could be convinced to participate in both those activities if I'm invited."

"You're definitely invited."

CHAPTER EIGHT

"Disappointment hurts more than pain."
—American proverb

Noah couldn't recall a day he enjoyed more than the one they spent stranded at the Pig's Belly. They napped, used two more of the condoms, watched a *Mission: Impossible* movie and played pool downstairs, which was where they were when they got the word that the road to Butler had reopened.

He was almost sad to see their time at the tavern come to an end. The unexpected interlude had been fantastic. They returned to their room to retrieve their coats and other belongings before bundling up to head out into the frigid late afternoon. The sky was dark and gloomy, the snow hip-deep and the roads treated but still slippery.

Noah took his time on the winding highway that led back to Butler. About four miles from the Pig's Belly, they came upon the scene of the accident. A new wooden guardrail marked the spot where the car had left the road the night before. "Don't look down," he said.

"Too late. I can't imagine driving off that embankment."

Noah noticed several trees had been knocked over, probably by the car or rescue teams. "I hope everyone is okay."

"I may never drive in Vermont again after seeing that."

"You just have to go slow."

"Those drop-offs are terrifying."

"Accidents happen, but we're used to that up here. Our EMS is amazing. Two of my cousins are firefighter-paramedics, and they can tell you some stories. My cousin Lucas got hurt in the inn fire. His identical twin, Landon, rescued him and Amanda, the woman Landon is now engaged to."

"Wow."

"That was a crazy night, by all accounts."

"Thank goodness Landon was able to rescue them both."

"I know. I can't imagine Landon or Lucas without the other one."

"How identical are they?"

"I have to take a close look before I call either of them by name, except in the winter when Lucas grows a beard. There're two sets of twins in that family. Hunter and Hannah are twins, too."

"It wasn't enough that she had ten kids. Your aunt had to have two sets of twins, too."

"My aunt Molly is an overachiever."

"I'd say so."

They were back in Butler far too quickly for his liking. Would he drop her off, return home and only see her at work going forward? That thought immediately depressed him and ruined the first good mood he'd had in three years. Five minutes later, when he pulled his truck into her driveway, he was no closer to figuring out how to hold on to the upbeat feeling he'd found with her.

"Someone plowed your driveway."

"My landlord sends someone to do it, but he buried my car, as usual."

"I'll help you dig it out."

"You don't have to do that."

"I don't mind. It'll take you hours to do it alone."

"Believe me, I know. I've had to do it before."

"Next time snow is forecast, park it at the end of the driveway facing out. That way he can push the snow to the back, and it won't trap you."

"Well, duh. Why didn't I think of that?"

"You're not a native Vermonter. We're born knowing that stuff." He got out of the truck and went around to give her a hand down. "Do you have an extra shovel?"

"Yeah, there are two of them in the garage. I'll grab them. Thanks for the help."

"No problem. I can't leave you stranded."

They worked together for more than an hour to dig her car out of the massive drift.

"Do you want to make sure it starts before I go?"

"Sure. Let me run inside to get my keys."

While she was in the house, he used the scraper to clear the ice off her windshield.

She came out and unlocked the car, but the driver's door wouldn't open.

"It's frozen." Noah began chipping away at the ice around the doorframe.

"I never knew that could happen until I came up here."

"Your door never froze in Boston?"

"I keep the car in a garage there."

"Ah, okay." He continued to work on the ice until he was able to open the door. "There you are."

"Thank you so much, Noah. I appreciate the help."

"No problem."

Brianna got in the car and tried to start it. At first, it made a chugging noise, but then it started. "Phew. I'm not sure what that sound was."

"It's just cold. You should be good to go."

She turned off the car and got out. "Thanks again."

"Sure thing." He wasn't sure if he should kiss her or say, *see you tomorrow*, or how to leave things with her. Though they'd only left the tavern a little over an hour ago, it seemed like much longer now that they were back in Butler. "I, um, well… I guess I'll see you in the morning."

"Do you want to come back for dinner?"

He replied before she finished asking. "Yeah, that sounds good. What time?"

"Around seven?"

"I'll see you then." Elated to know he'd see her again soon, he started to walk away but then turned back. "What can I bring?"

"Whatever you want to drink?"

"Sure. What can I get for you? Oh, wait. Vodka. I can do that."

She smiled, which made her whole face light up. God, she was pretty, and yes, he'd known that from the first second he met her. But now, after spending the night wrapped up in her, he'd decided *pretty* wasn't a good enough word to describe her. *Stunning* was a much better word.

He took a few steps back, so he was standing within kissing range, and leaned in, hoping she'd meet him halfway.

She didn't disappoint him.

As her lips connected with his, all the agitation he'd been feeling only a minute ago disappeared in a matter of seconds.

Noah had to force himself to pull back from her, lest the goodbye kiss turn into something more, out in the open where anyone might see them. "I'll, ah, just be going now. I'll see you at seven."

"Sounds good."

"Go on inside before I leave."

"Why? What're you afraid of?"

"Nothing. Just want to make sure you're safe."

She surprised him when she gripped his coat and kissed him again. "Be careful, Noah Coleman. I might start to think you're a nice guy."

"Don't you dare spread that rumor."

"Your secret is safe with me."

"Thanks," he said, strangely moved by the words *safe with me*. They had all-new meaning to him these days. "Good to know. Now go on inside before I forget I was supposed to be going."

Flashing a saucy grin, she turned and walked away from him.

He watched her go, noting the attractive sway of her backside encased in tight denim.

She went up the back stairs and into the house, flashing the light over the back door to let him know she was all set.

As Noah walked to the truck he'd parked in the street, he checked his watch to see how many hours it would be before he could come back. Two and a half. That seemed like a long time. "Jeez, get ahold of yourself, man. You're acting like a fool after one night."

It was a great night, the kind of night that makes a guy act like a fool if it means he can have more of her.

"Is that what you want?" Noah asked himself as he drove home. "You want more?" He thought about that for a second. "I don't know what I want. All I know is I liked being with her, talking to her. I like everything with her, which is funny when I thought I couldn't stand her before last night."

He turned the heat up as high as it would go. "You didn't know her before last night. Not really." It pained him to realize he'd jumped to several unfair conclusions about her without taking the time to get to know her. Did he like being bossed around on a jobsite by an architect from Boston? No, but she was just doing her job, the same way he was, and he needed to be less of a dick in general.

Maybe Brianna was right, that it was time to tell his family what went down with Melinda so he could stop feeling like he needed to avoid them and their questions. What had seemed so complicated made perfect sense after Brianna had spelled it out for him. It had helped to talk to someone who understood how he felt, not that he'd wish that kind of pain on anyone. But it made him feel better to know that he wasn't the only one who'd been taken for a ride by someone he loved.

After last night with Brianna, he had reason to wonder if it might be possible for him to feel again the way he once had for the woman he'd married. Not that he expected anything to come of whatever this was with Brianna, but she'd shown him a different path forward, one that wasn't full of doom and gloom and lonely brooding about things he couldn't change. That got old after a while.

He pulled onto his street and was surprised to see a line of cars in front of his mother's house. His siblings' cars. What the hell? What had he missed? And why were the lights on in his house? Noah parked behind Grayson's SUV and got out of the truck. He'd no sooner walked into the mudroom at his mother's house when he was descended upon by siblings.

"Thank God, Noah." His youngest sister, Sarah, hugged him as tightly as she had in years. "You're all right."

"I'm fine. What's going on? What're you doing here anyway? And where's Mom?"

Sarah, Henry, Jackson, Vanessa and Ally all lived in Boston and came home to Vermont only for holidays. They'd all just been there for Christmas, which only added to Noah's concern.

"There was a huge accident last night," Vanessa said.

"I heard about that."

"It was Izzy, Noah," Grayson said. "Her Jeep went off the road and crashed in a ravine. They had to use the jaws of life to get her out. She's in the hospital."

The news hit Noah like a punch to the gut. "Can we see her?"

"We're waiting for Mom to call," Henry said. "She was going to let us know as soon as she was stable."

"Wait, so she's *not* stable?" Noah asked, swallowing hard.

Izzy was one of his favorite people in the world, and before he'd shared his nightmare with Brianna, his sister had been the only other person who knew what went down with Melinda—and Miguel.

"They were working on her the last time Mom called," Vanessa said. "They said she needs surgery, but not until she's stable."

"We were worried when we couldn't find you," Sarah said.

"Where were you?" Henry asked, sipping from a mug of coffee. At some point, Noah's youngest brother had grown a full beard that made him look older than his twenty-four years.

"I went to dinner at the Pig's Belly and got stuck there when they closed the road because of the accident," Noah said. "I came home as soon as the road opened. I'm sorry you guys were worried about me."

"We didn't think you'd mind if a few of us crashed at your place," Vanessa said, leaning into him.

He put his arm around his sister. "Of course I don't mind. When did you guys get here?"

"Around five o'clock this morning," Ally said. "After Gray called last night, the four of us jumped in Ally's car and came up together."

"Where's Jack?" Noah asked.

"Skiing in Wyoming," Sarah said. "We left a message for him."

Emma came in the mudroom door with her daughter, Simone. They went straight to Grayson, who embraced them both. "Is there any news?" Emma asked her fiancé.

"Nothing since I last talked to you."

"Can we go there?" Noah asked.

"Mom thought it might be better for us to wait here," Henry said.

"Better for who?" Noah asked.

"Us, I guess?" Sarah said.

"Let's go," Noah said, glancing at Gray, who nodded in agreement.

"I can't bear to sit around here any longer," Gray said.

"Some of you guys come with me," Noah said. "I'll drive."

They trooped out of their mother's home and got into two vehicles to drive to the hospital.

Ally, Sarah and Vanessa came with him. Henry went with Gray, Emma and Simone.

"Did someone tell Cabot?" Noah asked.

"Oh, um, is that like a thing now?" Sarah asked.

"I think so." It had primarily been a flirtation, but from what Izzy had told him about it, Noah had a feeling she'd want Cabot to know about the accident. "Do one of you have a number for Wade?" Izzy had met Cabot at their cousin Wade's wedding to Cabot's daughter, Mia, in Boston last June.

"I do," Vanessa said.

"I'll call him in the morning." Noah pressed the accelerator to get them to the hospital. In the back of his mind was something he was supposed to do, but damned if he could think of anything other than getting to his sister as fast as he possibly could.

AT EIGHT, BRIANNA WENT AROUND BLOWING OUT THE CANDLES she'd foolishly lit, thinking they'd started something special the night before that would continue now that they were back in Butler. After he'd left earlier, she'd ventured out to the grocery store to get what she needed for chicken Marsala, one of several dishes she could make reliably without much difficulty.

The Marsala was now a thick, gelatinous mess, the pasta had gone rubbery, and the too-familiar ache in her chest was back with a vengeance.

It was one thing to be a fool once. But when it happened repeatedly, that was on her and her piss-poor judgment when it came to men. She should've kept Noah in the pain-in-the-ass category, where he'd been before they left for the Pig's Belly.

Standing in the living room window, she looked out at the snowy landscape and wondered why he'd said he'd come and then didn't show.

You'd think she'd be used to being disappointed by men after what she'd been through, but alas, you'd be wrong. She hadn't expected this from Noah. Despite how they'd begun as adversaries on the job, they'd connected on a deep, intense level last night, and to think he might've been playing her to get her into bed made her feel sick.

Moving away from the window, she went to the kitchen, flushed the ruined dinner down the garbage disposal and put the pots and pans in the dishwasher. After starting the dishwasher, she locked the doors and shut off the outside light she'd put on for a man who wasn't coming.

She changed into her warmest pajamas and went to bed, pulling the covers over her head to form a cocoon.

Maybe he'd been in an accident, or his truck wouldn't start. He didn't have the number at the rental, so he couldn't call her. She preferred the possibility of him being injured to him having stood her up out of callous disregard for her feelings.

After last night, Brianna wanted him to be different. She wanted him to be what he seemed and not some illusion that disappeared like a wisp of smoke up a chimney, never to be seen or heard from again.

It wasn't as if he could avoid her when they still had at least two more months to go on the inn.

Her loud groan echoed through the bedroom. "This is why you don't sleep with colleagues, Bri, because when they stand you up, you have to see them every day at work."

God, this sucked so bad. She hated the awful feeling that came with this kind of disappointment. After the horrors that'd ended her marriage, she'd become accustomed to keeping crap like this to herself, but she needed to talk to someone. She came out from her blanket cave and reached for the portable phone on the bedside table.

Before she arrived in Butler, she hadn't used a landline in years.

Her cousin, Dominique, answered on the third ring. "Hey, is this my cousin calling from Antarctica?"

"Not quite, but I think it's colder here than it is there. Are your kids in bed?" Her cousin had gotten married two years before Brianna and had two kids, a four-year-old daughter and a son who was two.

"Out cold, and I just poured myself a glass of wine. I'm glad you called. I was thinking about you today and wondering how it's going up there."

"I was going to text you this week, but my Wi-Fi has been acting up."

"I don't know how you can stand not having cell service."

"It's been an adjustment."

"I'd die," Dom said with typical bluntness. "How's the job going?"

"It's okay. It'll be better when we can move completely inside and get some heaters."

"I also couldn't do that. I hate being cold, and so do you."

"It's horrible. I have so many clothes on that I can barely move."

"Better you than me, girl. I loved the latest pictures you sent, though. It's going to be beautiful when it's finished."

"Yeah."

"What's wrong, Bri, and don't say nothing, because I can hear it."

"I did a bad, bad thing."

"Do tell."

"I slept with the contractor."

"The bitchy guy you hate?"

"Yep."

"Um, you're gonna have to tell me how *that* happened."

Brianna relayed the story of Mrs. Hendricks playing match-maker and the evening she and Noah spent at the Pig's Belly.

"It sounds like you had a blast."

"We did."

"And you finally got back on the horse. How was it?"

"Excellent. Not at all awkward, and I didn't cry like I thought I would if I ever did it with someone other than Rem."

Dom made a spitting noise. "Don't even say his name to me. And PS, fuck him and the rail he rode in on. Tell me more about the cranky contractor."

"His name is Noah Coleman." She'd referred to him simply as The Jerk to Dom in prior conversations.

"Is he hot?"

"I had no idea how hot he is because he's always wearing forty layers at work."

"So, you had a great time and got stuck at a place called the Pig's Belly overnight. Why do you sound like shit?"

"Because he was supposed to come for dinner tonight and pulled a no-show."

Dom groaned. "Damn it. And here I was starting to like him."

"Me, too."

"And you have no idea where he is or what happened?"

"Nope."

"Can you call him?"

"I'm not calling him. To hell with that."

"If something came up, could he have called you?"

"I don't think so. The landline in this house is in the name of the owner, who lives in New York, so Noah probably doesn't know who owns the house."

"Well, there you have it. Something happened, and he had no way to get in touch with you. Don't think the worst until you know."

"I'm kinda preprogrammed to think the worst."

Dom made the spitting noise again. "You're not saying his name, but you're talking about *him*, and he is *nothing* to us. He's less than nothing. He's dogshit on the bottom of our oldest pair of shoes."

Brianna giggled. "Tell me how you really feel."

"I have, many times since *he* turned out to be an epic douchebag."

She certainly had, but she'd also been by Brianna's side during the worst of it, and there was no doubt she'd saved

Brianna's life with her unwavering support. At one point, Dominique had gone four days without seeing her own family while she stayed with Brianna through the darkest days of her life.

"I know it's almost impossible for you not to, but don't go to the worst-case scenario until you know what happened tonight, okay?"

"I'll try not to."

"He sounds like a nice guy."

"He can be. He can also be an epic PITA. But I saw a whole new side of him last night, and I liked that side. I want to believe it's real."

"Until he shows you otherwise, you can believe it. I'm sure he'll have a good explanation."

"I love how you're so sure, and you don't even know him."

"I know *you*, and there's no way in hell you would've slept with him if you hadn't felt a connection. Especially since it's the first time you've been with anyone since the asshole."

"I did feel a connection. Noah kind of endured a similar thing with his wife, who slept with his foreman and best friend."

"Ugh, *why* do people do shit like that?"

"I don't know, but we bonded over our shared experience with suck."

"Give him a chance to explain himself, Bri. He might have a perfectly reasonable explanation for not showing up tonight. You're living in a cell phone wasteland where misunderstandings go to fester."

Brianna laughed at how she said that. "True. It's just so hard to have faith in anyone anymore."

"I get that, but you can't blame him and every other man for what one fucking psycho did."

"I'm working on that. Thanks for talking me off the cliff."

"That's what I'm here for. No matter what happens next with Noah, we need to celebrate that you blew the cobwebs out of the tunnel and got your groove on with someone new."

Brianna nearly choked on a laugh. "There were no cobwebs in my tunnel."

"If you say so."

"Let's talk about something other than my cobwebs. Tell me about my niece and nephew. What's the latest?"

They talked for another half hour about the kids, Dom's job as an insurance agent, her husband's legal practice and the progress on the inn.

Brianna was yawning by the time they agreed to talk again soon so she could tell Dom why Noah hadn't shown up for dinner.

"Give him the benefit of the doubt," Dom said as they were ending the call.

"Yes, ma'am."

"And let me know what happens."

"You'll be the first to know."

"Love you, girl," Dom said. "I'm so happy you're back in the saddle."

"And I have the saddle sores to prove it."

They were both laughing when they said their goodbyes.

Brianna felt a thousand times better after talking to the cousin who'd been her best friend her entire life. Dominique had helped put her back together after the shock had begun to recede and her new reality set in. Dom's husband, Joe, had represented Brianna in the ugly and ongoing divorce proceedings. She credited Joe with saving not just her sanity, but also trying to rescue her from financial ruin. If Joe had his way, Rem would be the one ruined by his deceit, not Brianna.

She went to the kitchen to refill her water glass and noticed it was snowing—again. How did people who lived here all the time stand the endless snow for months on end? It would drive her crazy to deal with that kind of snow for so long.

Wherever Noah was tonight, she hoped he was okay and hadn't ended up down the side of the mountain or something equally awful.

CHAPTER NINE

"What if the worst thing that happened to you turns out to be the best thing that has ever happened to you?"
—Joe Dispenza

oah finally got to see Izzy at almost seven o'clock in the morning and almost wished he hadn't been allowed in. She was so bruised and swollen, she barely resembled herself and was attached to beeping machines that freaked him out.

His mom was leaning over the bed rail, stroking Izzy's long hair and speaking softly to her daughter.

"Mom." Noah whispered so he wouldn't startle her. "How is she?"

"She was awake a minute ago," Hannah said. "She doesn't remember the accident."

"I suppose that's a good thing."

"I'm glad to see you. We were worried you'd crashed, too, when we couldn't find you."

"Sorry you were worried. I went to the Pig's Belly, and when the accident shut down the road, I just stayed put there rather than try to drive around the mountain in the snow."

"What took you over there?"

"Long story." He glanced at his sister again and then looked away, not able to bear the sight of her so banged up. "Should I call Wade and ask him to get in touch with Cabot? The others weren't sure if it was a good idea."

"They've spent some time together. Cabot would probably want to know she's hurt."

"I'll take care of it."

"Will you ask Emma to call Ray, too? He must be wondering how we are. Tell him he can come here if he wants to."

"I'm sure he'll want to be with you, Mom."

Hannah shrugged. "If he wants to."

"Don't be so used to doing everything on your own that you can't lean on him when you need the support."

"I'm almost afraid to rely on him."

"I get that, but he seems like a solid kind of guy."

"Your father did, too, until he wasn't."

"Are we under any obligation to call him about Izzy?"

"I suppose we probably should."

"I'll take care of that."

"Thanks, Noah." She glanced up at him, and he noted how exhausted she looked after the sleepless night. "Were you at the Pig's Belly by yourself?"

Usually, he'd hold out on her, but he wanted to tell her something that would make her happy. "Nope."

"Anyone I know?"

"Nope." Right in that second, he remembered he'd made plans to have dinner at Brianna's house and had completely forgotten after he arrived home to the news about Izzy. "Ah, shit."

"What?"

"I had plans last night and forgot after I heard about Izzy."

"I'm sure you'll be forgiven when your friend finds out where you were."

"I hope so." He hated that he'd disappointed her after how

her ex-husband had treated her. Unfortunately, he didn't have the phone number at the house she rented, so he couldn't call her.

Fuck.

Noah was sure the whole town probably knew by now who'd driven off the road. He hoped she'd forgive him when she heard it was his sister. "I'd better go make those calls. Do you need anything?"

"No, I'm good. Thanks."

"I'll be back to check on you in a bit."

"I'll be here."

Noah went to the waiting room and asked to borrow a cell phone from one of his siblings who had Wade's number.

"Emma, Mom was wondering if you could call your dad and tell him he's welcome here if he'd like to come."

"I'll do that. I'm sure he's waiting to hear something."

Ally gave Noah her phone after putting through the call to their cousin.

Noah walked out of the ICU so he wouldn't bother anyone.

Wade answered on the third ring. "Hey, Al," Wade said. "How's Izzy?"

"It's Noah, and she's hanging in there."

"Glad to hear it."

"We thought Cabot might want to know."

"Mia called him last night after we heard the news about Izzy. Somehow, he already knew about it. He's coming up today from a meeting he was at in New Jersey."

"Okay, thanks for letting him know. We weren't sure whether we should call him or what's up with them besides being friends. You know how Izzy plays it all close to the vest."

"I do, and we weren't sure we should call him either, but Mia said we should tell him and let him decide what to do, so that's what we did."

"Good call. Thanks, Wade."

"We're all praying for Izzy."

"Thank you." Noah had a lump in his throat when he ended the call with Wade and put through another to Carlo, dialing his employee's number from memory.

When Carlo answered, he sounded hesitant, probably because he didn't recognize the number.

"It's Noah. I'm calling on my sister's cell."

"Hey, what's up?"

"I won't be at the site today. One of my sisters was in a bad accident the night before last, and I'm with my family at the hospital."

"Oh, damn, was she the one who went off the mountain road?"

"Yeah."

"Sorry to hear it, Noah. Is she going to be okay?"

"Eventually. Do me a favor, will you? Ask Brianna to call me on this number?" He had a phone he kept in his truck for emergencies outside of Butler, but since he was working in town now, it wasn't charged.

"Yep, will do. I'm on the way into Butler, and I'll pass along the message. Anything else?"

"Keep everything moving at the inn. I'm not sure when I'll be back to work."

"Take care of your family, man. I got you covered."

"Thank you. I'll be in touch. Call me on this number or at home if you need me."

"Copy."

Noah ended the call, hating himself for missing Miguel. Carlo was a good dude, but Noah didn't have the same confidence in him that he'd had in Miguel. That two-faced son of a wife-fucking bitch. All this time later, Noah still didn't know when the two of them had become more than friends or how long they'd been going at it before Noah caught them.

He'd shut down any conversation with them after the dreadful day when he'd returned home from an overnight search and rescue with his cousins to find his foreman sleeping naked in his bed with Noah's wife. What did it matter to him how it started or how long it had gone on?

His two-year marriage had ended in the split second that Noah realized his wife had another man in their bed. And not just any other man, but Noah's closest friend and most trusted employee.

Why was he even thinking about this shit? Talking about Melinda with his mother and then Brianna had stirred it all up again. He wished he could stuff it into a trash bag and toss it into an incinerator, so he'd never have to think about either of them again.

He was about to rejoin his siblings in the ICU waiting room when Ally's phone rang with a call from a local number. Hoping it was Brianna, he took the call.

"Hey, it's Brianna. I heard about your sister, and I'm so sorry. How is she?"

"She's in rough shape, but they say she's going to be okay eventually."

"That's a relief. How are you?"

"I'm very, very sorry I didn't show up last night. I had no way to call you, and to be completely honest, the minute I heard about Izzy, I forgot everything else. I feel terrible about it."

"Please don't. I understand."

"Were you upset about me not showing?"

"Of course not."

"Are you lying?"

She chuckled softly. "Maybe a little. I hate that something so awful happened to your sister, but I'm glad you didn't just blow me off for no good reason."

"I didn't. I wouldn't do that to you. I swear."

"I believe you. What can I do for you?"

"Keep things moving at the site. I'll be back to work in a day or two."

"Don't worry about a thing. We'll take care of everything."

"Thank you."

"Can I check on you later to see how your sister is?"

"Sure. That'd be nice."

"Give me your number, and I'll call you tonight."

Noah recited the digits to his home number. "I'll try to be home by nine."

"If you are, you are. If not, I'll call you tomorrow."

"Sounds good."

"I'll let you get back to your family, and I'll pray for your sister."

"Thanks. Hey, Brianna?"

"Yes?"

"I had a great time with you the other night. I never would've blown you off."

"I had a great time, too, and that's good to know."

"I'll talk to you tonight."

"Okay."

He didn't want to end the call and got the feeling she didn't either. "Go to work, Brianna."

"Go to your family, Noah."

Laughing, he pushed the button to end the call and looked up to find his brother Grayson watching him with a strange expression on his face.

"What?"

"You were laughing. I haven't seen that in so long I wondered if you still could."

"Now you know."

"It was nice to see."

Noah honestly hadn't given much thought to how his reclusive behavior had affected the rest of his family. He'd been trying to move past the nightmare with Melinda and Miguel and had no time to be worried about anyone else.

"So, what were you laughing at?"

"Nothing, just something from work."

"How's the inn coming?"

"Right on schedule."

"Heard you're locking horns with the architect."

"Is everyone talking about that, or does it just seem that way?"

"It's winter in Butler, Noah. What else is there to talk about?"

Noah rolled his eyes at his brother. "You think you're so funny."

Grayson grinned. "I know I am, but I also know it's great to see you smile. It's been too long."

"I'm sorry about that."

"Don't be. You went through some rough shit. Or, well, I assume it was rough."

"It was."

"I hope whatever it was is in the past for you now."

"I think it might be." And he had Brianna to thank for that, in part. The evening he'd spent with her had been a realization of sorts that while his last relationship had blown up spectacularly, that didn't mean he wasn't capable of maybe trying again with someone else.

Even having that thought was a huge deal for Noah, because when the shit first went down, he'd been sure that part of his life, the part in which he willingly gave someone else the power to hurt him, was over for good. That wasn't to say he was ready to jump all-in to something new, but the door to that possibility had cracked open ever so slightly.

"I was going to call you today to ask if you could stop by when you get a minute," Gray said.

"What for?"

"I wanted to ask you something."

"Okay…"

"Emma and I are getting married in June."

"Oh, cool. I hadn't heard you'd set a date."

"That's a recent development. I was wondering if you might be my best man."

Noah stared at Grayson, wondering if he'd heard him right. "I, uh…"

"I know you're probably not a big fan of marriage, but I'm so happy with Emma, and I can't wait to take this next step with her and Simone." The rush of words was unusual for his brother, but anyone could see the happiness in him since Emma had come into his life. "Did you hear I'm adopting her?"

"No, I hadn't. That's awesome, Gray. I'm happy for you on all counts, and of course I'll be your best man. I'm honored you asked me—and surprised."

"Why're you surprised? Didn't we grow up together and go through all the shit together?"

"We did."

"Then who else would I ask but you?"

"Thanks for asking." Noah was strangely emotional to know his older brother wouldn't have asked anyone but him to be his best man. He and Melinda had eloped, so he hadn't had a best man, but Gray would've been his first choice, too.

"We've both been around the block a few times, had some highs and lows."

"Ain't that the truth?"

"The one thing that never changes is this." Gray gestured between the two of them and then toward the waiting room where most of their siblings had gathered. "I don't know about you, but I take comfort in that."

"Yeah, for sure." His siblings were always right there if he needed them, not that Noah needed them often. They'd been through a lot together and shared a bond none of them would ever have with anyone else. Gray was right. There was comfort in that.

"Mom wants us to call Dad about Izzy."

"I'll do it," Gray said.

"Are you sure? I don't mind."

"It's fine."

Their aunt Molly and uncle Linc came through the doors to the ICU, stopping short when they saw Gray and Noah in the hallway.

"How is she?" Molly asked warily.

"Still holding her own." Gray hugged them both. "She had a pretty good night."

"That's a relief," Molly said. "And how's your mother?"

"Hanging in there."

The door swung open again with a loud bang as Ray came in. "Could I please see your mother?" he asked Gray.

"Sure, I'll take you to her."

Ray nodded to Molly and Linc as he followed Grayson into the unit.

"I'm thrilled to see you, too, young man," Molly said to Noah. "We had a long day yesterday wondering if you were all right."

Touched by her concern, Noah hugged his aunt. "I'm just fine."

"Thank God for that," Molly said.

HANNAH HEARD HIM BEFORE SHE SAW HIM. SHE SMILED WHEN SHE heard him tell Grayson to take him to her right away. Since Izzy was sleeping after a restless hour, Hannah left her post by Izzy's bed to meet Ray in the hallway.

He came right to her and wrapped his arms around her, holding her so tightly that Hannah almost couldn't breathe. Not that she was complaining.

"I would've stayed with you here last night."

"No sense in both of us going without sleep."

"No sense in you going through this alone."

He'd been with her when she got the call about Izzy's accident, but Hannah had sent him home to get some rest late last night.

"I'm glad you're back."

"I didn't want to leave in the first place."

Hannah leaned into his solid chest, taking comfort from a man for the first time since her husband left so many years ago.

It'd become her habit to go it alone, but Ray had shown her she didn't need to do it that way anymore.

"Your sister and brother-in-law are here."

"I'll see them in a minute." She tightened her hold on Ray. "Could I have a little more of this first?"

"You can have as much of this as you want for as long as you want."

"Might be a while."

"I've got all the time in the world for you, sweet Hannah."

She pressed her face against his flannel shirt and breathed in the scents of soap and fabric softener that she associated with him. They'd become the scents of comfort in recent months. She'd thought that part of her life was over and done until he came along to show her otherwise, and now she felt like a giddy teenager in the throes of first love when he was around.

"Whatever you and your daughter need," he said gruffly, "I'm here for you, Hannah. I hope you know that."

"I do. Thank you."

He kissed her right there in the busy ICU. "Sorry," he said when he seemed to realize what he'd done. "I didn't mean to do that."

She smiled up at him. "I'm glad you did."

CHAPTER TEN

"Never to suffer would never to have been blessed."
—Edgar Allan Poe

*W*ith his aunt and uncle settled in the waiting room, Grayson took the cell phone he rarely used anymore with him when he went down to the lobby to call his father. He hadn't talked to him in almost a year, since he'd donated the bone marrow that had saved his father's life. He'd heard from others that Mike was doing better and in remission, but other than a note he'd received in the mail a month after the transplant thanking him for the life-saving gift, Grayson hadn't had any further contact.

And that was fine with him.

Yes, he'd donated to save his father's life, but that was the end of it as far as Gray was concerned. He'd never forgive Mike for abandoning their family when Gray was sixteen or the changes that action had brought about for all of them, but mainly their mother, him, Noah and Izzy. As the three eldest, they'd had to take on way more responsibility than any of them should've had at sixteen, fourteen and thirteen.

Before he could talk himself out of making the call, he pressed the single word on his contact list: Dad.

"Grayson?"

"Yes, it's me."

"Is everything all right?"

He had to give Mike credit for knowing there was no way he'd hear from any of his eight children unless something was wrong.

"Izzy was in a bad accident the night before last. She's in the ICU."

"Is she... Will she be all right?"

"Eventually."

"Which hospital?"

"Northeastern. There was some talk yesterday of transferring her to UVM in Burlington, but they were able to treat her here."

"Is she stable?"

"She is after surgery to remove her spleen and repair some other internal damage. She also broke her arm and two ribs. Her face is banged up, too."

"Poor Izzy. How upset you all must be."

"We are."

"Could I... I mean, would it be okay if I came by to see her?"

"I suppose so but let me know when you're coming."

"I'll try to get there today or tomorrow, and I'll give you a heads-up. Thank you for calling, Gray."

"Yeah, no problem."

He ended the call and sat in the busy lobby for a long time, trying to contend with the emotions that always came from hearing his father's voice. People talked about "triggers." Mike Coleman's voice triggered Grayson and took him right back to an awful time in his life that he'd much sooner forget than relive.

"I wondered where you'd run off to."

Grayson perked up at the sound of his favorite voice in the world, smiling at his fiancée as she took the seat next to him and reached for his hand. How had he ever lived before he had Emma and Simone to love him and be loved by him? He could barely remember what life was like without them, and that was just fine with him.

"I had to make a call for my mom."

She looked at him the way only she ever had. "Why do you seem wrong in the eyes?"

"The call was to my father."

"Oh."

Emma knew better than just about anyone how difficult his recent interaction with his father had been for him. When they'd discovered he was a perfect match, he'd donated the bone marrow and acted like it was no big deal. But Emma knew how gut-wrenching the entire thing had been for him, how Gray had briefly considered declining the donation request. In the end, Gray hadn't been able to deny his father a second chance at life, even though he had every reason to.

"How was it?"

"No biggie. I just told him about Izzy."

"What did he say?"

"He asked if he could come to see her."

"Are you going to let him?"

"My mom said it was okay with her if he wanted to. Not sure Izzy would want to see him, but we're not going to bar the door. We'll see if he even shows up. He's the king of good intentions that never pan out."

She reached for his hand and curled her fingers around his. "I hate the way he steals your joy every time you have to deal with him."

"Aw, baby, he can't steal my joy when I get to look at your beautiful face every day and kiss your sweet lips and sleep with you in my arms."

Her small, satisfied smile lit her up eyes. "You do have a way with words, Counselor."

"I have the best muse to inspire me. Thanks for coming to be with us."

"Of course we came to be with you. We love Izzy and you and your family."

"They love you and Simone, too." He kissed the back of her hand. "I finally got a chance to ask Noah to be my best man."

"What did he say?"

"He seemed shocked that I'd asked him, but he said yes."

"That's great. And you're still good with just having Noah and Lucy?"

"It's either two or twenty, and twenty is too many. I wouldn't know where to stop asking siblings and cousins."

"I know, and I agree it's just simpler this way."

"I wish we didn't have to wait five more months to tie the knot. That seems like forever."

"It'll go by so fast you won't believe it."

"You promise?"

"I do, and you know I'm always right."

Grayson laughed at the sassy look she gave him. "Yes, dear, you're always right."

"See that? You're so ready to be a husband."

"Only because I get to marry you."

If he had to see his father, he'd be okay because he could go home to her afterward, and she'd give him everything he needed and then some. He was thankful for her every day, but never more so than at times like this when his painful past reared its ugly head. Knowing he had her—and Simone—made everything better.

NOAH DROVE HOME JUST AFTER EIGHT, BRINGING HIS SISTERS Sarah, Ally and Vanessa to spend the night at his house. Henry was going to stay at their mom's but had promised to come over to hang out with the rest of them at Noah's. For once, Noah was glad to be surrounded by his younger siblings to help keep his mind off the stressful day at the hospital.

Izzy was doing okay, but she looked rough. Her face was bruised and swollen, her bottom lip split open, and her left arm broken. And those were just the injuries they could see on the outside. The internal damage had been of far more concern initially. The nurse had told them that Izzy would probably leave the ICU in the next couple of days if she continued to improve.

That was the good news.

The bad news was that she faced months of recovery that might include inpatient rehab.

"I feel so bad for Iz." Vanessa's soft words broke a long silence. "She won't be able to work for months."

"I know," Sarah said. "It's terrible, and I hate that I can't stay to help her when she gets home. I have to get back to Boston soon. I can't miss any more classes, or I'll never catch up."

She was a nursing student at Northeastern, in the fourth year of a five-year program.

"You can take my car," Ally said. "I'm going to stay for a bit. I can work from anywhere." As an account executive with a marketing firm, she had a lot of leeway.

"I'm going to stay, too," Vanessa said. "I'm job hunting, and I can do that from here."

"What happened to your job?" Noah asked.

"Her boss got handsy with her, and when she reported him to HR, he tried to have her fired, so she quit," Sarah said.

"*What?*" Noah asked. "Did you tell Gray about this?"

"No," Vanessa said with a sigh. "I've barely told anyone. It's all so embarrassing. I was just trying to do my job, and he wouldn't leave me alone. But he's a VP, a rainmaker, they call him, and I'm just a lowly admin, so they weren't about to take my side."

"Vanessa, that's a lawsuit looking for a place to happen," Noah said. "You need to tell Gray and ask him what he can do for you."

"Maybe. I don't know. I'll think about it."

"You have to," Noah said, feeling more agitated by the second. The thought of a man hassling any of his sisters was enough to make him see red. "You can't let them get away with that shit. It's harassment."

"We've been telling her that for weeks," Ally said.

"I'll talk to Gray," Vanessa said. "Now drop it. I don't want to think about that right now."

Noah reached across the center console to put his hand on top of hers.

Vanessa turned her hand up to squeeze his. "Thanks for caring, big brother."

"Of course I care. I'd like to go beat the shit out of the asshole who harassed you."

She laughed, which made him feel better. "Don't do that, but thanks for wanting to."

"Hell yes, I want to."

"We all do, Nessa," Sarah said. "It's total bullshit what he did —and how they covered for him. How much you want to bet it's not the first complaint they've gotten against him? But as long as he keeps the money coming in, they look the other way."

"Total crap," Ally said emphatically.

Noah pulled onto his street, wondering whose car was in front of his house with the lights on.

"Who's that?" Sarah asked.

"Not sure." As he got closer, he noticed the Massachusetts license plate and realized it was Brianna.

And why did that realization make him feel so happy? When was the last time he'd felt anything close to that? And what the hell was wrong with him?

"Who is it, Noah?" Nessa asked.

"One of my work colleagues."

"What's he doing here?"

"I don't know what she's doing here, but let's find out." He pulled into the driveway and got out of the truck as Brianna got out of her car. She looked cute with a knit hat holding her wildly curly hair down. "Hi there."

"Hi. I hope you don't mind that I asked Mrs. H where you live. I thought you guys might be hungry. I brought you some food."

Touched by the sweet gesture, he couldn't stop the smile that stretched across his face. He'd been doing a lot of that lately. "That's so nice of you. We were going to send my brother to Kingdom Pizza."

"Now you don't have to."

"Now we don't have to." He couldn't stop staring at her, drinking in every detail of her pretty face as his heart fluttered erratically. She'd come to his house with food. What did that mean?

She pressed a button on her key fob to open her trunk.

The smell hit him first, making his mouth water. Garlic and basil. "Wow, that smells good. What'd you make?"

"My grandmother's lasagna. Will you help me carry it in?"

"I suppose that's the least I can do."

She put two big pans in his outstretched arms and grabbed another cloth bag from the trunk before shutting the lid and following him into the house. Shockingly, his sisters had already gone in, but only because they were freezing. They were probably watching him through the window and trying to figure out who this woman was to him.

He'd like to know that himself. Inside, he wiped his feet on the mat and went right to the kitchen to put down the heavy load. "You made a ton," he said when Brianna joined him.

"There are a lot of you. I wanted to make sure there was enough."

"This is really nice of you. Thank you so much."

She shrugged off his thanks. "I wanted to help."

He wanted to kiss her but didn't dare with his sisters nearby. "You did."

Brianna unpacked the bag, which contained a large salad, two big loaves of garlic bread and a pan of brownies.

"I can't believe you did all this," he said, amazed by what she'd brought.

"Is it too much?" she asked, seeming adorably uncertain.

"No, it's very sweet. Thank you again. I'm starving."

"I thought you might be. How's your sister?"

"She's okay, but it's going to be a long road to recovery."

"I'm so sorry she's hurt and that you are because she is."

Before he could respond to that, his sisters came into the room, probably driven by mouthwatering smells as much as a potential scoop. *Noah has a woman in his house.* That would be big news in the Coleman family.

"Brianna, these are my sisters, Ally, Vanessa and Sarah. Ladies, this is Brianna Esposito, the architect in charge of the inn project."

Ally's mouth formed an O as if she'd just put two plus two together to equal God knew what conclusion.

"Brianna brought us dinner. Say thank you, and don't ask any questions that are none of your business."

"Thank you, Brianna," the three of them said.

"Now tell us everything about you," Vanessa said as she made herself at home in Noah's kitchen, getting out plates and silverware.

"You don't have to do that," Noah said, glaring at his sister.

"I don't mind," Brianna said, laughing. "It's kind of a boring story of school, school, more school, followed by a job in Boston that brought me to Vermont to rebuild the inn with your brother."

"Where do you live in the city?"

"Back Bay," Brianna said. "How about you guys?"

"We're in the North End," Ally said. "We all live within a few blocks of each other. Our brother Jackson is there, too. He's skiing in Wyoming with some friends right now."

"He texted that he's trying to get home," Sarah said. "I told him that Izzy is okay and wouldn't want him to interrupt his vacation, but he's coming anyway."

"We'd all do the same thing if we were him," Nessa said. "This lasagna is fantastic, Brianna. I need the recipe."

"Sure, I can get it to you. It's my grandmother's."

"Was she Italian?" Ally asked.

"Full-blooded. I loved to cook with her, and she loved to teach me."

"And Colemans love to eat, so it's a win-win," Noah said.

"I'm glad you like it," Brianna said, seeming embarrassed by their praise.

"You're not having some?" Nessa asked her.

"I ate earlier."

Noah suddenly remembered what she'd told him the other night. "Wait, you're a vegetarian, so you made something for us that you wouldn't eat yourself?"

"I have no issue cooking with meat. I just don't like the way it tastes or the consistency of it. I've never eaten meat. Even as a little kid, I just hated it."

"Well, thank you for taking one for the team for us," Ally said. "It's excellent."

The mudroom door opened, and Henry came in, bringing a gust of cold air with him. "What's this I hear about food?"

"Henry can sniff down food like a bloodhound," Sarah said.

"Everyone has their talents," Henry said.

"I'll get you a plate," Nessa said. "Meet Noah's friend Brianna, who makes the best lasagna you've ever had."

"I'm telling Mom you said that," Sarah said.

"Mom would agree," Noah said. "This is the best lasagna ever."

"You guys are good for a girl's ego," Brianna said with a smile.

"Brianna, this is my youngest brother, Henry. He's a bit feral, but we love him anyway."

"Aw, thanks, Noah. If I'm feral, what the hell are you?"

"Don't anyone answer that question," Noah said with a glare for his siblings that made Brianna laugh.

"What's the age difference between you guys?" Brianna asked.

"Grayson is the oldest," Sarah said. "He's thirty-seven. Soon to be thirty-eight. He's the oldest of all the grandkids. He beat Hannah and Hunter by a month."

"I'm next," Noah said.

"He'll be thirty-six in March," Ally said. "Izzy is thirty-five, Nessa is thirty-two, and I just turned thirty."

"They're all senior citizens compared to us," Henry said, receiving scowls from his older siblings. "Jackson is twenty-eight, I'm twenty-four, and Sarah is the ultimate baby diva of the family at twenty-two."

Sarah stuck her tongue out at her brother. "Shut up."

"You shut up," Henry retorted.

"The two of them have been fighting since the second Sarah was born," Ally said.

"Our family was perfect at seven," Henry said, frowning dramatically. "They should've quit when they realized they'd finally found perfection with me."

"Oh my God," Nessa said. "Are you listening to yourself right now?"

"His voice is his favorite one to listen to," Sarah said.

Brianna lost it laughing. "You guys are hilarious."

"They're ridiculous," Noah said, amused by his siblings. He'd forgotten how fun it was to be with them this way, and even though he felt terrible about Izzy's accident, he was glad to have them home.

The others did the dishes while Noah sat with Brianna, trying to keep things casual, to not give away too much to his perceptive siblings, who'd zoom right in on the attraction he felt for her if he let it show. He kept it together until they'd all left the kitchen to take showers, check in with work or watch TV.

"So that's my family, or most of it, anyway. There're three

more."

"That's a lot of siblings."

"Sure is. You should've seen what it was like when we all lived at home. Utter mayhem."

"It sounds like fun to someone who only had one much older sibling."

"It was, most of the time." At least until his dad left, and then nothing was fun for a long time. But they'd survived. Somehow.

"You're lucky to have each other."

"I know. Gray asked me to be the best man in his wedding. That was surprising."

She took a sip of the red wine he'd poured for everyone. He didn't own wineglasses, so Brianna was drinking hers from an old Scooby-Doo jelly jar. "How so?"

"I figured he'd ask Hunter or someone he was closer to than me."

"What do you suppose it means that he asked you?"

"That he feels closer to me than anyone, which is amazing since we don't see very much of each other these days."

"Doesn't he live here?"

"Yeah, about a mile from here."

"And you hardly see him?"

Noah squirmed under the intense way she looked at him. He shrugged. "We're both busy."

"You ought to see him more often now that you know what you mean to him."

"Is that right?"

"Yes, that's right."

He smiled at the emphatic way she said that. "I'll take that under advisement."

"Is it okay that I came here tonight?" she asked, seeming a bit shy and uncertain, which was adorable considering the way she ran roughshod over him at work.

"It was great that you came. We appreciate the meal. It's been a very long day."

"I was hoping you wouldn't mind if I came without asking you first. In the world I live in, I could've hit you up and said, 'Hey, Noah, how about I drop off dinner for you guys?'"

"I like it better this way. It was a nice surprise to come home to—the food and you." After glancing over his shoulder to make sure no one was lurking, he reached for her hand. "I'm *really* sorry about last night."

"Don't be. You had an emergency."

"And no way to call you, which we need to rectify." He released her hand to grab a pen and a napkin. "Give me the number at your house."

She recited the number.

"And your cell."

She gave him that number, too.

"Thanks. Feel free to use the number I gave you earlier any time."

"You do the same."

"Don't mind if I do." He reached for her hand again, this time linking their fingers. "Were you upset last night? Tell me the truth."

"A little."

"I'm sorry I did that to you. After everything we talked about the other night, I hope you know I'd never do something like that to you on purpose."

"I hoped I hadn't been wrong about you."

"You weren't. I swear. Even if I suddenly decided I didn't want to get together again—and that's not what happened—I never would've just blown you off. I promise you that."

"That's a big promise to make."

"It's an easy promise to make after what we've dealt with in the past."

"True, and I'll promise you the same."

Noah really, *really* wanted to kiss her, but there was no way he could do that with a houseful of younger siblings who could interrupt them at any minute. But oh, how he wanted to.

CHAPTER ELEVEN

"No matter how bad your heart is broken,
the world doesn't stop for your grief."
—Faraaz Kazi

The mudroom door opened, and his mother came in with Ray, making Noah doubly glad he hadn't kissed Brianna.

"Heard there's pizza here," Hannah said.

Noah withdrew his hand from Brianna's and stood to greet his mom and Ray after they'd hung their coats and kicked off their boots. "That was the plan until Brianna came with her amazing lasagna. Brianna, this is my mom, Hannah Coleman, and her, um, friend, Ray Mulvaney."

"I'm her boyfriend." Ray grinned at Noah as he shook hands with Brianna. "So nice to meet you."

"You, too. I should, um, get out of your hair so you can visit with your family."

"Please don't leave on our account, Brianna," Hannah said over her shoulder as she fixed plates for herself and Ray. "This looks delicious. Thank you so much."

"It was no problem."

Hannah turned to face Brianna. "Yes, it was, and it was nice of you."

"I wanted to do something to help out."

"You did. We appreciate it."

"How's Izzy, Mom?" Noah asked, noting the sweet flush in Brianna's cheeks. He wanted more than anything to have a few minutes alone with her.

"She's doing a little better. She insisted I come home and get some sleep so I wouldn't end up in a hospital bed myself."

"That's good," Noah said. "I'm glad she's better and that she talked you into coming home."

"If she didn't, I was gonna," Ray said with a meaningful look for Hannah. "Your mom is running on fumes."

"His mother is in the room and can speak for herself, thank you very much," Hannah retorted with a good-natured grin for Ray.

"Oh, damn, Ray," Noah said. "Watch out for Hannah when she's overtired. It's not pretty."

"She's always pretty," Ray said as he joined them at the table.

"And *she* is in the room." Hannah took a bite of lasagna. "Wow, that's delicious, Brianna."

"Thanks. All the credit goes to my grandmother."

"I need the recipe."

"I'll get it for you."

This was not at all how Noah had predicted this evening unfolding, with Brianna sitting at a table with his mom and Ray, as if that was no big deal. It wasn't a big deal. Of course it wasn't. They weren't dating or anything. They'd gone out once, had a great time and ended up in bed together. That didn't equal a relationship.

But it'd been nice of her to cook up a storm for his whole family. She must've gone right from work to the store and then home to cook for hours. And she'd gone to the trouble of asking Mrs. H where he lived.

Noah held back a groan as he wondered what Mrs. H would

do with that information. She was friends with Mrs. Andersen, the biggest gossip in town. Those two would have him engaged to Brianna in no time. Shit.

Brianna tipped her head, giving him a curious look. "Are you okay?"

When was the last time anyone had asked him that? Well, other than his mother, but she had to ask. It'd been a long time since anyone outside his family had cared whether he was okay. "I'm good."

"Tell me if I'm outstaying my welcome."

"You're not."

"How do you guys know each other?" Hannah asked.

The question seemed innocent, but Noah knew his mother well enough to surmise that she was picking up on a story, or she never would've asked. She'd always been good about not prying into their personal lives. She would say Elmer and Linc did enough of that for everyone.

Brianna looked to him, and he gestured for her to fill in the blanks for his mother. "We're working together on the inn."

"Oh." Hannah took another bite of lasagna, and then her eyes went wide. "Wait, are you the architect from Boston?"

"I am."

"*Oh.*" Hannah glanced at Noah and then back at her plate. "Have you ever been to the Pig's Belly, Brianna?"

Noah held back a laugh at his mother's shameless question.

"I have! We had the best time there the other night, well, until we found out the accident that stranded us there was Noah's sister."

"I love the food there," Ray said, innocent to the major scoop his mother had just scored.

Maybe she wasn't above prying after all.

"It's a very interesting place," Brianna said, her face flushing again.

Damn, he loved when that happened. That slight blush took her from pretty to stunning, and he couldn't say why. It just did

115

it for him. And so did she if he was honest with himself. He'd give anything to be able to clear his family out of the house so he could invite her to stay awhile.

But that wasn't going to happen tonight.

He hoped it happened again soon.

Noah was acting strange, but that was nothing new for him. He was always a little odd, but that made him attractive to Brianna. When she got the big idea to make dinner for him and his huge family, she hadn't expected to sit at a table with his mother and her boyfriend. Meeting the parents usually signified a significant step forward in a relationship.

That wasn't what this was. They'd had one fun night that'd led to stranded-in-the-snow sex. That never would've happened if they hadn't gotten stuck at the Pig's Belly.

Or would it?

No, definitely not. Noah would've driven her home after dinner, and that would've been that. They would've returned to work the next day and probably gone right back to the nonstop bickering that had led Mrs. H to intervene in the first place.

She'd missed him at work today. It'd been weirdly dull without him around to spar with.

Speaking of work… "I, um, I ought to get going home."

Noah seemed reluctant to let her leave, or was she imagining that?

Quit being a simpering girl, hoping the boy you suddenly have a massive crush on wants you to stay. Haven't you learned anything about where being silly over a man can lead you? But Noah is different. He's not like Rem. Look at what he said about being so sorry about last night. Just stop, Brianna. Stop it right now.

"Brianna?"

She realized Noah had been speaking to her while she was off arguing with herself. "I'm sorry. What?"

"My mom was asking if you'd like to come to dinner some night soon," Noah said.

Brianna wasn't sure if he'd want her to accept, but she couldn't be rude. "I'd love to. Thank you, Mrs. Coleman."

"Call me Hannah. Everyone does."

"Thank you, Hannah."

Ally came into the kitchen and stopped short at the sight of her mom and Ray sitting at the table. "I didn't think you were coming home tonight."

"Izzy kicked her out," Noah said.

"That sounds about right," Ally said, smiling. She got herself a glass of water. "You need anything, Mom?"

"I'm good after this delicious meal that Brianna made for us." Hannah cleared her plate and Ray's, rinsed them and put them in the dishwasher, which was almost full for the first time in longer than Noah could remember. "Now, I'm going home to crash until sometime tomorrow."

"Take some brownies with you." Brianna jumped up to cut some for them. She wrapped them in paper towels that she handed to Hannah.

"Thank you again for feeding us."

"My pleasure."

"See you all tomorrow," Hannah said, heading for the mudroom with Ray.

"Dinner was great, Brianna," Ray said. "Thank you."

"You're welcome."

While Noah walked them out, Brianna started doing the dishes that hadn't made it into the dishwasher. She was wiping down the countertop when he came back in, bringing a blast of cold air with him.

He surprised her when he came right over to her, put his hands on her face and tipped it up to receive a kiss that was so fast, it was over before it started. "You're the best. We all appreciated the meal more than you'll ever know."

"I'm glad there was something I could do to help."

117

"It was a big help. And there's enough left over for tomorrow, too."

"That was the plan."

"Incredibly thoughtful of you."

"I wish there was more I could do."

"I wish we could hang out by ourselves tonight," he said in a suggestive tone that indicated what *hanging out* might've entailed.

"There's always tomorrow."

He smiled, and she melted. That smile was rare but potent, and when he unleashed it on her, she was almost powerless to resist him.

"I should, um, be heading home, I guess." She gathered up the serving spoons she'd brought in case he didn't have them. "Are you working tomorrow?"

"I'll be there in the morning to get the guys started before I head to the hospital. Did everything go okay today?"

"Yes, it was fine."

"I can't believe I didn't even ask before now."

"You have other things on your mind."

"I have a lot of things on my mind," he said, again in that meaningful way that sent shivers down her spine.

He wasn't even trying to hide that he wanted her and made her forget her worries about getting sucked into another "situation" with a man who had the power to hurt her. Noah made it easy to forget about what'd happened in the past and to be hopeful that not all men were capable of the kind of wreckage Rem had left in her life.

"Are you okay?" Noah asked, his brows furrowed with concern.

"Yeah, I'm fine. Just tired. I'll see you in the morning?"

"I'll walk you out."

"You don't have to do that. It's freezing out there."

"I want to." He followed her into the mudroom, where they

both donned coats and boots before heading into the frigid night.

"I've never been colder in my entire life than I am here," she said as she burrowed deeper into her coat.

"You get used to it after a while."

"How long of a while? Several months in, and I'm not used to it."

"Might take a year or two."

"I'd never make it."

"If you had someone to keep you warm, you might get used to it quicker."

"I should look into that."

He pinched her ass, making her startle and then laugh.

"Oh, were you volunteering for the job?"

"I was, in fact, and you hurt my feelings."

Brianna laughed at the indignant retort. "My heartfelt apologies."

"You're not even kinda sorry."

She couldn't stop laughing until he angled her, pressing her against the car so he could kiss her far more intently than he had inside. Her bag dropped to the ground with a clatter, and she wrapped her arms around his neck, opening her mouth to his tongue. She wondered if they were visible from inside the house until his hands landed on her ass, drawing her in tight against his erection. At that point, she couldn't bring herself to care if his siblings were watching them.

"Wanted to do that for two hours," he whispered against her lips before going back for more.

It couldn't be more than ten degrees, but every part of her was on fire for him.

"Wish we could pick up where we left off the other day."

"Your sisters are probably watching us."

He glanced toward the house. "I don't think so. The blinds are closed."

"I should go before we freeze to death."

"I'm not even slightly cold."

Her laughter formed a cloud of breath that disappeared in the icy cold. "I'd invite you to my place, but I have a feeling you'd take some heat from your houseguests if you left."

"You'd be correct about that, and normally, I wouldn't care, but I don't need them all up in my grill about you."

"They'll probably be on you, anyway, wanting to know who this woman is who brought you dinner."

"She's a friend. A very *good* friend." He pushed his erection against her belly, and even with multiple layers of clothing between them, the shocking burst of desire took her breath away. "With benefits they don't need to know about."

Brianna realized she had his coat fisted in both hands. She released him slowly. "I'll see you in the morning."

"You want me to bring you coffee and breakfast from the diner?"

"Sure, that sounds good."

"Least I can do after you cooked for my entire family."

"Hope you can get some sleep."

He held the door and waited for her to get settled before leaning in for one more kiss. Then he pulled away but stared at her for a long moment, making her wonder what he was thinking. "Drive carefully and watch out for moose in the road."

She swallowed hard at the thought of crashing into a moose. "I will."

Noah stood upright and closed the car door. He waved as she drove off.

Brianna drove slowly through town, watching for moose as she went, nervous about the icy roads as much as the possibility of crashing into a massive animal. If she lived here forever, she'd probably never get used to the bone-deep cold, the moose or the other hazards of mountain life.

But she sure as hell could get used to being kissed by Noah Coleman.

CHAPTER TWELVE

"You can victimize yourself by
wallowing around in your own past."
—Wayne Dyer

oah hung his coat in the mudroom and sat on the bench to untie his boots. He wanted to follow Brianna home and spend the night with her, but she was right that his family would be all over him if he did that. The Colemans were awfully good at minding each other's business, especially when they were sleeping under the same roof.

He went into the kitchen, where Nessa was pouring herself a glass of wine.

"She seems nice," Nessa said.

"Who?" He knew who she meant but wasn't going to make it easy for his sister to pry into his business.

"You know who. Don't be obtuse, Noah. Brianna seems very nice."

"She is."

"Didn't I hear somewhere that you don't get along with her?"

"We've had our challenges at work, but it's no big deal."

"Hmmm."

"What do you want to say, Nessa?"

"Just that I'm glad to see you smiling again, brother. It's been too long. If your architect friend is making you smile, then I like her."

Sarah came shuffling into the kitchen, sliding over the floor in her socks and coming to a stop right next to him. "Did you get the scoop on lasagna lady?" she asked Nessa.

"There's no scoop to get," Noah told his youngest sister. "We're *friends*, and that's it."

"Really?" Sarah asked. "Because I picked up on a vibe."

"What vibe?"

"The I-want-to-rip-your-clothes-off kind of vibe."

Noah rolled his eyes, unnerved by his sister's insight. "You picked that up while we were eating lasagna with her?"

"Yep."

"I sorta picked up the same thing," Nessa said. "There were all these veiled looks and yearning."

"Yes!" Sarah said. "Exactly."

"You people are insane. I'm going to bed. Help yourself to whatever you need."

Sarah grabbed his arm. "Noah, wait. I'm sorry. I didn't mean to run you out. I just wanted to say that it's nice to see you having fun again. We've all been worried about you."

"What she said." Nessa used her thumb to point to Sarah. "We don't know what happened a few years ago, and we don't need to know. We're just thankful to see you coming back to life."

Moved by their sweetness, he kissed them both on the forehead and left them to ponder the status of his private life without him there to hear it. He said good night to Ally and Henry in the living room and went upstairs to shower. One of his siblings had built up the fire in the woodstove, so he didn't have to worry about that for once.

Standing under the hot water, he thought about kissing Brianna in the cold and how much he wished she could've stayed with him tonight.

After how crazy she'd made him at work for months, it was amazing how one wild night had changed everything between them. Now all he could think about was how long he had to wait to be alone with her again.

After his shower, he got dressed in a long-sleeved thermal T-shirt and flannel pajama pants. He got in bed and reached for the bedside phone to call the number she'd given him earlier.

"Didn't I just leave you?" she asked, sounding as if she'd run for the phone.

"Just making sure you didn't encounter Fred the moose on the way home."

"No moose sightings, and no near misses on icy roads either."

"That's good news."

"It's nice of you to check on me."

"You can't be too careful driving in the mountains, especially in the winter."

"It's kind of scary to know someone like your sister, who grew up here, can end up off the road."

"She probably hit ice. That's the one thing you can't learn how to control, no matter how many winters you spend in Vermont."

"That's terrifying."

"Thankfully, it doesn't happen all that often." He didn't think she needed to know how many times his firefighter-paramedic cousins rescued people in similar crashes each year. "You just have to be careful and take it slow."

"I can do that. I enjoyed meeting your family."

"That's not even all of them. You haven't met Gray, Izzy or Jackson, or Gray's fiancée, Emma, and her daughter, Simone."

"That's a lot of siblings. Your brother is getting a ready-made family when he gets married, huh?"

"Yeah, but he's crazy about Simone. Her father has never been in her life, so they're both enjoying having the other one around. They're very cute together. In fact, she's the one who suggested he ask out her mother."

"That's adorable! How old is she?"

"Ten or eleven. I forget, and she's very cute. They met at my cousin Hunter's wedding, and from what Gray told me, Simone gave him a push in her mother's direction, not that he needed much of a push. He was already intrigued by her. Emma's sister, Lucy, is married to my cousin Colton. And Ray is Emma and Lucy's dad."

"I'm going to need a chart that shows how everyone is related."

"I can do that for you." He tugged the quilt up. "I wish you hadn't left."

"It's probably for the best. We don't want things to get…"

"What?"

"Complicated. While we're working together."

"Complicated happened a couple of nights ago."

"That was a fun night, and I'm glad it happened, but I just… I don't know, Noah. I'm still such a mess over everything with my ex. I don't trust myself or my judgment."

"You can't let him do that to you. There's nothing wrong with your judgment. He was the problem. You know that."

"I do, but I ignored some things that I now see should've been red flags. I was so in love with being in love that I let it make me stupid."

"You're wiser now. You'd never make those mistakes again, and besides, I'm kind of a what-you-see-is-what-you-get sort of guy. I'm not big on games or drama or nonsense."

"Are you trying to talk me into something more than a one-night stand?"

"Maybe."

"Is that what you want?"

"Maybe."

"Noah!" she said, laughing. "Quit with the one-word answers."

"Sorry." He chuckled at her outrage. "I'm not sure what I want. I just know I had more fun with you the other night than

I've had with anyone in years, and I didn't want you to leave earlier. Beyond that, I don't know."

"I had fun, too," she said softly. "You made me feel good about myself, which is a pretty big deal after feeling like shit for a year."

"You shouldn't let anyone make you feel like shit, Bri. You're a smart, beautiful, accomplished woman who doesn't have to take any crap from anyone."

"Even you?"

He could hear the smile in her voice. "Especially me. But not from anyone, least of all a man who didn't deserve you."

"He didn't. I loved him so much. So, *so* much. And the whole thing was just a big game to him. He never loved me at all, because the only one he's capable of loving is himself."

"Can you see how there's nothing you could've done to change the outcome with him?"

"Yeah, I can with hindsight, but I still feel like a fool for being so easily taken for a ride."

"Does that mean you're never again going to take a chance with someone else?"

"No, it doesn't mean that. It just means I'm not sure I'm ready for that yet."

"Fair enough." For someone who'd made it his mission to remain uninvolved with other people, Noah was far more disappointed than he ought to have been. "Believe it or not, I get it."

"I'm sorry, Noah."

"Don't be. Nothing says we can't be friends as well as colleagues."

"I'd like very much to be your friend."

"Consider it done. Get some sleep."

"You, too."

"I'll see you in the morning."

"See you then."

Noah pressed the button to end the call and put the phone back on the bedside charger. He shut off the light and settled into bed. He stared up at the ceiling for a long time, processing their conversation and the overwhelming disappointment. She didn't want anything more than a friendship and working relationship with him, which was a huge bummer.

She'd ignited something in him that he'd assumed died forever when his marriage ended, and he'd liked it.

However, she wasn't ready for anything more than friendship, and he had to respect her wishes.

Even if it totally sucked.

PAIN WAS IZZY'S CONSTANT COMPANION. THEY'D GIVEN HER A morphine pump that she could use whenever it got bad, but she could only have so much. The medicine dulled the pain but didn't eradicate it, which made it hard to sleep. She'd sent her mother home to rest, but now that she was facing a sleepless, painful night, she wished she hadn't done that.

She also wished the room had a TV or something she could do to while away the time until morning, but the ICU room had nothing but a bed, chair and tons of beeping equipment that could drive a sane person crazy.

How in the heck had she ended up in the ICU in the first place? One minute, she was driving home from St. Johnsbury, and the next, she was in an ambulance, or that's how it had seemed to her. She had no memory of the accident itself, which was a blessing.

She pressed the morphine button, hoping enough time had elapsed to allow her another dose, but the machine beeped to let her know that wasn't the case.

Gritting her teeth, she tried to find a more comfortable position in the bed and instantly regretted the movement.

"Izzy."

The familiar voice had her turning toward the door and wondering if she was hallucinating from all the meds she was on. Was that *Cabot*? In her hospital room? And was he coming toward her with concern and affection and dismay in his expression?

"Cabot."

"I got here as soon as I could. I was in New Jersey when Linc and Mia called me." He came to her bedside, took hold of the hand on her uninjured arm and kissed the back of it, being careful to avoid the IV needle. With his other hand, he swept the hair back from her face. "You gave us such a scare, my sweet girl."

"Sorry."

"Don't be sorry. I'm just so glad you're okay, or that you will be."

"Hurts."

"I'm sure it does. Can't they give you anything for that?"

She held up the morphine pump. "I'm maxed out for now."

"What can I do for you?"

Before she could answer that question, a nurse came into the room. "I'm sorry, sir, but visiting hours are over."

"I drove six hours to see her," Cabot said.

"Please let him stay. I'm wide awake and in pain. I could use the company."

"I won't be any trouble," Cabot said with the same charming smile that had turned Izzy's head at her cousin Wade's wedding.

Like her, the nurse was powerless to resist him. "I want her to rest."

"She will. I promise."

"He's a charmer, this one, isn't he?" the nurse asked Izzy.

"You have no idea." Izzy had been thoroughly charmed by him at the wedding and had hoped something more might come of their flirtation, but to her disappointment, she hadn't heard from him in weeks.

"I'm going to check in with the doctor about your pain management," the nurse said. "I'll be back shortly."

"Thank you," Izzy said.

Cabot walked around her bed and sat in the chair her mother had occupied all day. "Phew, I'm glad she let me stay."

"I am, too, but I have to admit I'm surprised you're here. I didn't think you were, you know, interested in me." The medication had loosened her lips and her inhibitions. Normally, she'd never say such a thing to a man. She liked to let *them* chase *her*, not the other way around.

"I'm interested in you, Izzy, even if I've done a poor job of showing you that."

"I thought I might hear from you after the last time we saw each other." In October, she'd been in Boston to shoot a friend's wedding and had called to invite him to dinner. They'd had a wonderful evening that had ended in him walking her back to her hotel and leaving her with a chaste kiss on the cheek. She hadn't heard from him since.

"I'd planned to call you. I thought of you every day. I'm just..."

"What, Cabot? I hope you know you can talk to me about anything." They'd had the best conversations at the wedding and the night they had dinner in Boston. That'd been the thing she liked best about him, how they could talk for hours about anything and everything and never run out of things they needed to tell each other.

"I do know that, and I appreciate it so much. More than you could ever know."

"Then what's the problem?"

"It's me."

Izzy rolled her eyes. "If I had a dollar for every time I've heard a guy say, 'it's not you, it's me.'"

His brows lifted in surprise. "Men say that to *you*?"

"More often than you'd think. I'm starting to believe it might be me."

"It's not you. You're... You're beautiful and funny and talented and sweet and so sexy, you make my heart beat fast."

"I do?"

He reached for her hand and placed it on his chest. "You do."

She could feel the fast gallop of his heart under her palm. "Even when I look like I got hit by a truck?"

"Even then, and PS, you don't look like you got hit by a truck."

"You're silly. I look terrible."

He shook his head. "You look beautiful, as always."

"All this flattery could go to a girl's head. She might start to get ideas about the man who says such lovely things to her." Funny how the pain had subsided since he arrived and gave her something else to think about.

"She probably shouldn't do that," he said, his smile dimming. "He's kind of a mess underneath it all."

"He is not."

"He is. You see, once upon a time, he married a woman he loved with all his heart. They had a beautiful little girl who was the best thing to ever happen to him. And then one day, he came home to find them gone. He never saw either of them again until he finally found his precious daughter, who was now an amazing woman married to a wonderful guy. He missed everything with her, and his bitterness and resentment toward her mother are deeper than the ocean."

Of course, she knew the story of how Mia had found her long-lost father by accident when she joined the family business, and Hunter discovered her Social Security number was a fake. Her mother's scheme had come unraveled after that, and Mia had learned her father had been looking for her the entire time she'd been "missing."

"You see," he said, "it wouldn't be fair to burden someone as special as you are with all that bitterness and resentment."

"Well, at least now I understand why I didn't hear from you when I was so sure I would."

"I'm sorry for that. I've wanted to call you. So many times, I thought of something I wanted to tell you or a funny thing that happened that I wanted to share with you. I wish you knew how much I've thought of you."

"I've thought of you, too."

"And when I heard you were hurt, getting to you as quickly as I possibly could was my top priority."

"That's very sweet of you."

The nurse came in and injected something into Izzy's IV that had an immediate calming effect. "That ought to help you get some rest tonight, honey."

"Thank you so much."

"I'll be back to check on you in a bit."

After she left the room, Cabot picked up the thread of their conversation. "I'm sorry it took me so long to get here. I left as soon as I could get free of the meeting I was there for."

"I can't help but wonder…"

"What do you wonder?" he asked as he ran his fingers through her hair as if he couldn't resist touching her in some way.

"If you're nothing but bitterness and resentment, why was seeing me your top priority?"

His slow smile unfolded across his handsome face. He was twelve years older than her but didn't look it. His hair had gone gray early, but everything else about him was youthful, except, it seemed, the heart that'd been broken decades ago by the woman who'd left him and taken his beloved daughter. "I'm not sure why. It just was."

"Hmmm." Izzy couldn't keep her eyes open. Whatever the nurse had given her had finally dulled the pain. Thank God.

Cabot's fingers skimmed her forehead as he continued to stroke her hair.

She wanted to ask him what it meant that he was there, that he'd needed to get to her as fast as he could, that he was stroking her hair. But her questions would have to wait.

For now, anyway.

CHAPTER THIRTEEN

"If we aren't capable of being hurt we aren't capable of feeling joy."
—Madeleine L'Engle

*C*abot watched her drop off, finally able to rest thanks to whatever magic potion the nurse had put into her IV. He'd had to hide his shock from her when he first saw the bruises on her face, the bulky cast on her arm and her fragile state. She'd had a close call, and the thought of how close he'd come to losing her had sparked something fierce and terrifying in him.

She was terrifying. She had been since last June when he met the groom's cousin at his daughter's wedding and had been truly interested in a woman for the first time since his long-ago marriage ended in disaster.

Since then, he'd lived almost like a monk, barely dating at all and hardly ever having anything to do with women. It was like that part of his life ended the day his wife left him and took the daughter he loved more than life itself. She'd kept Mia from him for more than twenty-five endless, horrible years during which he'd tried to go on with his life while nursing the gaping wound in his heart that'd never healed.

The wound was still there, even after the miracle of Mia uncovering what her mother had done and coming to see him that same day.

His beautiful daughter had been back in his life for a year now, but she'd left as a little girl and returned a fully grown adult. Thus, the boiling cauldron of bitterness and resentment he'd mentioned to Izzy. He was so *angry* over what he'd missed with his only child. That anger was a constant, tangible presence in his everyday life, so much a part of who he was, he couldn't imagine himself without it.

He loved every minute he'd gotten to spend with Mia and her wonderful husband, Wade. He adored Wade's family and all the new people who'd come into his life along with his sweet daughter. Mia had bent over backward to accommodate him in every way she possibly could. She'd even come to Boston the week before Christmas—her busiest time at the warehouse she helped run for Wade's family business. He'd wanted her to attend his annual holiday party and meet more of the people who'd kept him going during the rough years.

She did anything he asked of her, and he knew it was because she genuinely cared for him. The bond they'd shared when she was little was still there after the long years of separation. But he knew she also felt guilty over what her mother had put him through and was trying to make amends. Not that she owed him anything. She hadn't known he existed until Wade's brother had discovered her Social Security number was a fake.

Thank God for Hunter Abbott and his obsessive attention to detail.

That was a thought Cabot had every day since that miraculous day last winter when his daughter suddenly reappeared in his life.

What if Hunter hadn't run her SSN? He might never have seen her again, which was another part of the angry cocktail of emotions that constantly swirled in him.

That was why he'd kept his distance from Izzy, even though

he thought of her constantly. He'd wondered where her work was taking her and if or when he'd ever see her again. Sure, he was permanently attached to her family, but that didn't mean their paths would cross with any regularity. Unless they made that happen, and he'd had no intention of making it happen until he'd gotten a call from Lincoln Abbott about the accident as well as a message from Mia to call her as soon as he could.

He'd emerged from day-long meetings and had panicked when he got Linc's message. He returned Mia's call immediately, hoping she had more information. She'd told him Izzy was in ICU and that they hadn't been sure he'd want to know.

Hell yes, he wanted to know.

After getting that call and the details Mia had available—which weren't nearly enough for him—he'd cut short his business, rented a car and driven to Vermont, breaking every speed limit to get to her as fast as he possibly could. His assistant in Boston had done the math for him and determined driving would get him to her faster than flying. He'd missed the last shuttle to Burlington, which would've been two hours from her once he got to Vermont.

Six of the longest hours of his life later, he was by her side and wondering what the hell he was doing there. He couldn't explain it. He just needed to see for himself that she was all right and offer whatever comfort he could while she recovered.

Since she was asleep, he pulled out his phone and sent a text to his assistant. *Clear my schedule for the next little while.*

Even though it was nearly eleven p.m., she responded right away. *Define next little while.*

In deference to Izzy's significant injuries, he responded with, *Two weeks.*

She came back with bug-eyed emojis and question marks.

A close friend has been in a bad accident. I need to be with her while she recovers. As he typed those words into his phone, he had no idea if he'd be welcome in Izzy's recovery or if he had any business making plans that included her. Despite those reservations, he didn't change his directive to his assistant.

I'll do what I can. What about the council?

I'll let them know I'm going to be away for a bit. I might need you to get with my sister to send me some clothes and stuff.

Is it okay to ask if you've lost what's left of your mind?

Cabot laughed. Rachel was fantastic and always spoke her mind to him, which he appreciated. While looking for his missing daughter, he'd kept himself frantically busy and over-scheduled to the point of madness. That'd been intentional, to try to keep his mind off the nightmare that was so much a part of him, no matter how busy he was. Having Mia back in his life hadn't changed the pace at which he lived. It was no wonder Rachel was astounded at his directive to clear his formidable schedule.

It's okay to ask, as you know. I appreciate your help with this. I'll be in touch.

Um, you'd better be!

Next, Cabot texted his sister, Emily, who'd been his staunchest supporter during the long search for Mia. *Hey, sorry to text so late. I wanted you to know I'm going to be in VT for a couple of weeks. My friend Izzy was in a bad accident, and I want to be here for her. It will be nice to spend some time with Mia and Wade, too. I might need you to send me some stuff from the house.*

Emily wrote right back. *So sorry to hear about Izzy. Is she going to be okay?*

Yes, in time, but she's pretty banged up.

Glad she'll be all right, and let me know what you need from the house. Happy to send it. So um, you're in Vermont with your "friend" Izzy. What's that about?

I have no idea.

She responded with laughing emojis. *You're funny, Cabot. It's okay to LIKE Izzy, you know.*

Is it?

YES

I like Izzy, but...

No buts. Put the past where it belongs and start looking toward the future. That's all you can do.

I hear you. Maybe by supporting my friend Izzy as she recovers, I can start to figure out a way forward.

Maybe so. What happened to you was the worst thing that's ever happened to anyone I know. It was a fucking CRIME. But if you deny yourself the chance to be happy again, she wins. Don't let that bitch win. Do you hear me?

He smiled at the intensity that came through in her text. Sometimes he thought she hated what Mia's mother had done more than he did. *I hear you.*

Enjoy the time in Vermont, Cab. If anyone has earned the right to enjoy himself, you have.

Thank you. You're the best. I'll text you tomorrow.

Give Izzy my best and xoxo to you.

Will do. Xo back to you.

He was so thankful to Emily and his brothers, who'd stood by him through every devastating twist and turn of his desperate search for Mia. They'd held him up when the burden became too much to bear and had celebrated with him when Mia had turned up out of the blue and made him the happiest dad who ever lived.

Cabot hoped that in time he could contend with the residual bitterness. Mia had no idea how deeply that bitterness ran through him. He went out of his way to hide that from her. What'd happened between her parents wasn't her burden to bear, and he was always mindful of that.

He dashed off a text to his beloved daughter, still thrilled to be able to talk to her any time he wanted. She and Wade lived in a farmhouse they were renovating just outside the Butler cell phone blackout zone, so she could receive texts there with and without Wi-Fi. *I'm at the hospital with Izzy. I have no idea what I'm doing here, but I'm staying for a bit. Just wanted you to know.*

When she didn't reply, he suspected she was already asleep

and would get back to him in the morning. Waiting to hear from her gave him something else to look forward to. He loved every text, call, FaceTime and visit they got to have. She probably thought he was a freak show for the way he hung on her every word, soaking up the joy of her presence like a starving man who'd just stumbled upon an all-you-can-eat buffet.

Thankfully, she didn't seem to mind that he was a mess where she was concerned.

Law enforcement had given him the choice of whether to have her mother criminally charged for the ordeal she'd put him and his family through. Out of respect for his daughter, he'd declined to press charges. But Jesus Christ alive, he'd *wanted* to. He'd wanted to ruin her life the same way she'd destroyed his.

Emily had helped him see that revenge wasn't in his daughter's best interest. An ugly, protracted legal proceeding that held her mother accountable for what she'd done would devastate Mia, and in the end, he just couldn't be part of something that would hurt the daughter he loved more than anything. So, he'd let it go, and that's when the bitterness had set in.

He'd thought about suing her, but had scuttled that idea, too.

A year later, he was still working on living with the outrage of it all, which was why he hadn't pursued a relationship with the lovely, talented, delightful Isabella Coleman. She deserved a man who could be fully available in the present. Not someone mired so deeply in the past that he had no space for anything new.

But then he'd heard from Lincoln Abbott that Izzy had been badly hurt in a car accident. Getting to her as fast as he possibly could had been his only thought. He had no idea what that meant. All he knew was that he intended to be there for as long as she needed him.

NOAH'S FIRST ALARM ROUSED HIM OUT OF A DREAM THAT HAD LEFT him hard and reaching for Brianna, who wasn't there. Of course she wasn't there. They'd had a one-night thing, and it wasn't going to be anything more than that. In the gloomy morning light, he stared up at the ceiling as he tried to settle himself after the arousing dream.

He couldn't be dreaming about her. That was just ridiculous. A week ago, he'd wished he never had to see her again because she drove him so crazy. He'd wanted her even when they were constantly fighting. No, he hadn't thought of her *that way* until their night at the Pig's Belly.

That's not true, a random voice from deep inside him shouted. *You thought she was hot the first time you ever saw her.*

That's your voice, idiot, and it's telling you the truth. You've thought she was hot from the get-go, and the only reason you were so antagonistic is because you were having trouble remembering why you had to keep your hands to yourself around her.

For once, he was out of bed before the second alarm went off, too agitated to put up the usual morning fight against the clocks. He turned off the other alarm and headed for the shower, hoping some cold water could put out the fire burning inside him for a woman who'd told him just last night that she didn't want him that way.

How funny was that? For the first time in three years of hell, he'd halfway fallen for a woman who wasn't available. He'd laugh at the irony if it didn't make him feel so shitty to have to accept that he and Brianna were going to have only one incredible night together.

With the electricians starting today, he didn't have time for distractions like this. They were rewiring the entire place to bring it up to the current code. He needed to be on his game to supervise the subcontractors he'd hired, not obsessing about getting the architect and project manager back in a bed with him as soon as possible.

He got out of the shower and wrapped a towel around his waist while he shaved.

"That's not going to happen." Staring at his reflection in the mirror, he ran a razor over his face. "Just keep it cool and do the damned job. She'll be headed home to Boston soon enough, and you can get back to normal."

"Uh, are you talking to yourself?" Nessa asked as she appeared in the open bathroom door.

Embarrassed to have been caught, he said, "Maybe a little."

She thrust a mug at him. "I heard your alarm go off and thought you might want some coffee."

"Thanks." He took a sip of the coffee. "And I talk to myself because I'm usually here by myself."

"All you need is a couple of cats, and you'll officially be a crazy cat lady who talks to herself and her cats."

"Very funny. You're up early."

"Couldn't sleep. Worried about Izzy and my job situation and a million other things."

"Like what?"

"Such as who's keeping an eye on the polar bears and penguins as the ice cap melts, and what we're going to do about all the trash in the ocean."

Noah went to her, put his hand on her shoulder and squeezed it. "I thought the anxiety had been better lately."

"It had been until I had to quit my job and my sister nearly died in a car crash."

"You still taking the meds?" he asked gently.

"Every day. Most days, they do the trick. Other days..." She shrugged. "You know how it goes."

His father's departure had affected them all in different ways. Nessa struggled with debilitating anxiety.

"I called the nurse's station," Vanessa said. "Izzy had a good night. Her 'friend' Cabot was with her all night."

"Well, that's an interesting development."

"I knew something was going on there, even if she wouldn't admit it."

Noah was more worried about Vanessa after hearing the anxiety was bad again. "What can I do for you?"

"Being here with you guys helps."

"Stay as long as you want, indefinitely if you want. My home is your home."

"That's very sweet of you, but I know how you like your space. I can stay at Mom's after everyone else leaves."

"Stay here. It's fine." He kissed her forehead. "I promise."

"Can I say something else?"

"Can I stop you?"

She smiled. "It was nice to see you with Brianna last night. I can tell you like her."

"I do, but she tells me it's not happening."

Nessa tilted her head to the side. "Why is that?"

"She went through some rough shit with her ex."

"So did you. At least I assume you did."

"I did."

"That should make you two perfect for each other because you get it."

"You'd think, but she says she's not ready. She doesn't trust herself or her judgment." Even as he said the words, Noah acknowledged that talking to one of his siblings about his personal life was unprecedented. However, he needed someone else's insight, and Nessa had always been good about keeping his secrets.

"He must've done a number on her."

"It was pretty bad." He wanted to tell her more, but he couldn't betray Brianna's confidences, even with his sister. "Brutal, in fact."

Nessa shook her head and grimaced. "Why do people do that stuff to the people they supposedly love?"

The question was the story of their lives. "I wish I knew."

"You're going to have to prove yourself to her. That you're

exactly what you appear to be—a nice, decent, if often grumpy, guy who she can count on."

He play-punched her chin, making her laugh. "Had to add the grumpy part, huh?"

"Am I wrong?"

"Nah, you're not wrong."

"Show up for her, Noah. Be there for her as a friend and colleague. That'll matter to her, and maybe it'll lead to what you want, too."

"I'm not sure what I want. She lives in Boston. That's a long way from here, and she hates how cold it is in Vermont. She's not about to move here, and I can't live anywhere else with my business and everything."

When he finally stopped talking long enough to look at his sister, he found her giving him an odd look. "What?"

"You like this woman, don't you?"

"Yeah," he said on a deep exhale. "More than I should."

"You want to know what the good news is?"

"There's good news?"

Nessa nodded. "You like someone new. For a while, after you broke up with what's-her-name, we worried you might never try again with anyone else, because you were so upset about whatever *she* did."

"She slept with my best friend and foreman."

Nessa's eyes bugged. "She slept with *Miguel*? Is that why he doesn't work for you anymore? Fuck, Noah."

"Yes and yes."

"God, I'm so sorry. What a bitch. I never liked her."

"Really? I thought you did."

"Nope. I never thought she was good enough for you. I usually like to be right, but in this case, I'm sorry I was right about her."

He shrugged it off as if they weren't talking about one of the most painful things to ever happen to him. "It was a long time ago. I'm over it."

"No, you're not. That's something you never really get over. You just find a way to live with it."

He gazed at his younger sister with all-new appreciation. "When did you get so wise?"

"I've always been wise. You're just noticing it."

Smiling, he hugged her. "Thanks for listening, and do me a favor and keep the details about what's-her-name between us, okay?"

"No problem. Remember what I said about how to handle Brianna. Be her friend, her champion, her supporter. That'll matter to her."

"I'll give it a whirl."

"She'd be crazy not to give you a whirl."

Noah laughed. "I'll let her know you think so."

She started to walk away, but looked over her shoulder and said, "You might want to keep that part to yourself for a while."

CHAPTER FOURTEEN

*"Never allow someone to be your priority while
allowing yourself to be their option."*
—Mark Twain

eeling better after the chat with his sister, Noah got dressed in the layers necessary to survive working in the elements. He left the house ten minutes later and headed to the diner. As he parked in front, he was surprised to see his grandfather's truck. He went inside and noticed Elmer sitting alone at the counter with a cup of coffee in front of him.

"Morning, Noah," Megan said. "I'll have your order ready in a few."

"Could you please make it a double today? Hold the bacon on the second one."

She gave him an odd look. "Sure."

He never, ever, *ever* changed up his routine, so naturally, the people he saw every day would notice any minor difference.

Noah took a seat next to his grandfather. "Morning."

"Who are you buying breakfast for?" Elmer asked with a mischievous grin that had Noah laughing.

"Wouldn't you like to know?"

"Yes, I would."

"Damn, I've got myself cornered by the expert."

"If I had to guess, I'd think it was that gorgeous architect you're working with on the inn."

"Maybe. Maybe not."

"How was your night at the Pig's Belly?" Elmer asked nonchalantly.

"What night at the Pig's Belly?"

Elmer rolled his eyes. "The one you and Brianna had after Mrs. H sent you there with a coupon."

"Did that coupon come from you? Tell me the truth."

"Not until you answer the question."

"I may or may not have gone to the Pig's Belly with Brianna after Mrs. H—and you—gave me a coupon and an order to work things out with her."

"And how'd that go?"

"Fine."

Elmer released an exasperated sound. "You and your one-word answers. You'd drive a man to drink."

"That's the second time I've heard that in two days."

"About driving someone to drink? Not surprised you hear that from people."

"No, the part about the one-word answers."

Noah loved any chance he got to spend time with his grandfather, even when the older man was trying to get information from him that Noah wasn't inclined to give him. Not that he cared if Elmer knew what was going on with him. Stonewalling him was so much fun.

"Wasn't that the night of the storm and Izzy's accident?"

"It was."

"How'd you get home with the road closed?"

"We didn't."

Elmer sat up straighter. "Is that right?"

"That's right."

"Heard they've got some guest rooms upstairs. Must've been

filled to the rafters with the road closed."

"I think they were. I didn't ask about the occupancy."

Megan put two to-go coffees on the counter.

"Thank you." Noah fixed one the way he liked it and gave his grandfather the side-eye. "So, was that your coupon and your idea about the Pig's Belly?"

"Maybe. Maybe not."

Noah snorted out a laugh. "And you wonder where I get it from."

"I don't wonder. I was a lot like you back in the day. I never liked having people up in my business. I get it."

"But that doesn't stop you from meddling in our lives."

"What you call meddling, I call *support*. Did you have a good time with the pretty architect?"

Noah shrugged. "It was okay."

"You are so full of shit."

"Gramps! You're swearing."

"You drive me to it with your stonewalling. I'm an old man, Noah. Not going to live forever. Don't you want me to go to my eternal reward knowing that each of my precious grandbabies is happily settled with someone who'll care for them when I no longer can?"

Megan's snort of laughter drew a smile from Noah.

"I think he actually believes that nonsense," Noah said to her.

"His track record is quite impressive."

"Yes, it is," Elmer said. "You and your husband are one of my favorite success stories, my dear."

"We are rather thankful for your meddling, Elmer," Megan said as she put the bag containing Noah's order on the counter.

"See?" he said to Noah. "She's *thankful*. Her husband is *thankful*. You should consider yourself *lucky* to have someone with my skills interfering in your life."

"At least you acknowledge that it's interference," Noah said, endlessly amused by his adorable grandfather.

Before Elmer could respond with yet another witty comeback, Megan gasped and reached for the countertop with one hand while placing the other on her hugely pregnant belly.

"What is it?" Elmer asked, jumping to his feet.

"Just a weird pain."

"Noah, run across the street and get Hunter, will you, son?"

Elmer's tone was dead serious, and Noah was out the door before he could ask his grandfather whether it would be quicker to call his cousin than to get him. He crossed Elm Street, entered the store through the back door and went right up the stairs to the executive offices, where the light was on only in Hunter's office.

His cousin heard him coming. "What's up, Noah?"

"Megan is having a weird pain. Gramps told me to come get you."

Hunter was up and out of his seat before Noah finished talking. He ran out of the office without bothering with the coat that hung on a hook inside his office.

Noah grabbed it for him and followed his cousin across the street, where Elmer was standing over Megan, seated on one of the stools at the counter.

She looked pale and frightened.

Hunter went right to her. "Do we need to go?"

"I'm not sure we have time."

"*What do you mean?*" Hunter asked with a hysterical edge to his voice.

"The baby. I don't know. I think it's coming."

"*How is that possible?*"

"How should I know? I've never had one before!"

"Noah, call for the paramedics," Elmer said, maintaining his post next to Megan, hand on her shoulder.

Noah went to make the call. In Butler, when you called for rescue, you called the local firehouse, so he wasn't surprised when one of his cousins answered.

"Butler Fire Department, Lieutenant Abbott speaking."

"This is Noah. I'm at the diner with Megan, and we think she might be in labor."

"On our way."

The phone line went dead.

"They're coming."

"Breathe, honey," Hunter said, his voice higher than usual.

"I am breathing."

"The way they taught us in the class."

"Screw the class. This freaking *hurts.*"

Poor Hunter was wild-eyed and panic-stricken as he watched his wife writhe in pain. "Where the hell are they?"

"Any minute now, son," Elmer said. "Stay calm for your wife. That's what she needs."

"I need a freaking epidural," Megan said through gritted teeth.

Noah wanted to ask if it was customary for labor to come on this fast, but he wasn't about to say or do anything to interfere.

A customer came through the door and stopped short at the sight of Megan surrounded by overwrought men.

"We're closed today," Elmer said. "Noah, flip the sign, will you?"

Thankful to have something to do, Noah went to the door and turned the sign from Open to Closed. There'd be a lot of disappointed patrons.

Megan was panting and making other sounds that had Noah wanting to grab his order and get the hell out of there, but he couldn't do that until he was sure she was all right. She was his friend in addition to being his cousin's wife, and he was deeply concerned for her and their baby.

Elmer continued to speak to Megan in a soft, reassuring voice that she seemed to cling to as the pains came fast and furious.

Hunter wasn't much good to her as he was trying to keep from coming unglued.

Noah had always thought he might like to have kids someday. After witnessing this, he was probably all set.

The ambulance finally arrived a few minutes later. Noah's cousin Lucas was the first one through the door. Two other firefighters followed, bringing a gurney with them.

Lucas crouched to speak to Megan. "Do we have time to get you to the hospital?"

She shook her head.

"Seriously?" Hunter cried.

To his teammates, Lucas said, "Let's get her on the gurney and take a look."

"Wait a minute! You're not *looking* at my wife!"

"Elmer, do something with him, and hurry up about it," Megan said, her voice more of a growl at this point.

Elmer took Hunter by the arm and hauled him off to the side so the paramedics could tend to Megan.

"This baby is coming," Lucas declared after he examined Megan. "Right now."

"I, um, I think I'll get out of the way," Noah said, grabbing his bag and the tray of coffees from the counter.

"Take Hunter with you," Megan said through gritted teeth.

"He needs to be here with you. I'll, ah, check on you later." Noah hurried out the door before he could see something that couldn't be unseen.

Holy shit, Megan was having her baby—at the diner!

THIS COULD NOT BE HAPPENING. HE AND MEGAN HAD A PLAN, a plan that included a hospital and a doctor, not one of his idiot younger brothers face-first in Megan's unmentionables. Hunter was having a full-on meltdown at the possibility of her giving birth in the freaking diner, of all places.

"Lucas, we need to get her to the hospital," Hunter said.

"No time, bro. This is happening right now." Lucas never looked up from what he was doing between Megan's legs—dear

God in heaven, Hunter wanted to *kill* him—as the other paramedics scurried about, getting him what he needed.

Lucas spoke calmly to Megan, telling her what he needed her to do on the next contraction.

"Hunter."

He heard his wife say his name. He understood that she wanted him to come to her. He couldn't move or breathe or think over fear so massive, it had overtaken every cell in his body. What if something went wrong and they were in a goddamned *diner* rather than a fucking hospital like they were supposed to be?

"Hunter!"

"Go, son," Elmer said. "Your wife needs you."

Hunter looked to his grandfather, the wisest man he knew. "What if…"

"*Go.*"

Elmer gave him a push that propelled him toward Megan, on a gurney, in the diner. The paramedics had cleared out tables and chairs to make room for them to work.

Megan reached for him, her hand digging into his arm like a claw. "Stop freaking out."

"I'm not."

"Yes, you are."

"My brother has his face in your hoo-ha. What do I have to freak out about?"

"My eyes are closed," Lucas said.

"*Open your goddamned eyes,*" Megan cried.

"Do *not* open your goddamned eyes," Hunter said.

"I'm going to *kill you* if you don't *shut up*, Hunter," his lovely wife said.

"You might want to listen to the lady, bro," Lucas said. "She's the boss here."

Hunter was going to kill *him*, the first chance he got after the baby had been safely delivered, of course.

"Okay, Megan, it's about to get real," Lucas said. "On the next contraction, I want you to push as hard as you can and hold it for as long as you can, all right?"

"Yeah."

"Hunter, get behind her and support her back and shoulders." He directed the other firefighters to hold her legs open.

Hunter's head was about to explode at the thought of her on display for all these men they didn't even know—and one they knew all too well.

"Hunter!" Lucas's sharp tone snapped him out of his panic, and he moved into position behind his wife.

Right now, she was the only thing that mattered, as well as the baby they were so excited to welcome. He couldn't believe it was about to happen. Finally. He just wished it had gone according to plan and they were in a freaking hospital. "Lucas."

"It's fine, Hunter. She's doing great. Babies are born every day in places other than hospitals."

Hunter clung to his brother's assurances with everything he had. If anything happened to her or the baby... The possibility of that was enough to suck him down so deep, he'd never resurface. He shook off those thoughts so he could focus on his beloved wife. "You're doing great, sweetheart. I'm so proud of you."

"I'm scared."

"What the hell is going on?"

Hunter turned toward the kitchen, where their longtime cook and friend Butch was standing in the doorway, staring at the goings-on with big eyes.

"The baby's coming," Hunter told him.

"*Here?*"

"Right here, and right now," Lucas said. "Come on, Megan. Give me a big push. Hard as you can."

She pushed while Hunter held her and comforted her as best he could while she shrieked from the pain of labor with nothing to take the edge off. He hated that she was suffering.

"You're doing great, Meg," Lucas said between severe

contractions. "You're almost there." He gestured for one of the other firefighters to come closer to him and whispered something to him.

The guy took off out of the diner.

"What's wrong?" Hunter asked his brother.

"Nothing. It's all good."

Megan was whimpering through the start of another contraction that quickly intensified, requiring everyone's full attention. She pushed so hard, screaming the entire time, but the baby still didn't come. A half hour later, the firefighter who'd left returned with a woman Hunter recognized from their doctor's practice.

She quickly moved into position with Lucas between Megan's legs, where the two of them whispered about something that had Hunter's blood pressure spiking into the danger zone.

"Is she all right?" he asked.

"Everything looks good," the doctor said. "But let's get this baby out on the next contraction."

Megan pushed harder than she had yet, her screams breaking Hunter's heart.

As he held her up through the worst contraction yet, he hated that she was in so much pain, that nothing had gone according to plan.

"That's it," Lucas said. "The baby's coming, Megan. Keep pushing."

After the longest minute of his life, Hunter saw the baby land in his brother's hands, slimy and red and beautiful.

"It's a boy," Lucas said. "Congratulations, Mom and Dad."

"Oh my God," Megan said between sobs. "It's a *boy*."

Hunter was so overcome with emotion he couldn't speak around the massive lump in his throat. They had a *son*.

"What's his name?" Lucas asked as he stepped aside to let the doctor tend to Megan, while he and the other paramedic took care of the baby.

"Carson," Hunter said softly. "Carson Elmer Abbott."

"I love that," Lucas said. "And it starts with a C. Mom and Dad will like that."

All his parents' grandchildren had names that began with a C or an S.

Hunter and Megan had considered many C and S names before they'd landed on Carson, which was also Megan's maternal grandmother's maiden name.

"Is the baby okay?" Megan asked. "Why is he so quiet?"

"He's perfect," the other paramedic said as she handed the baby to Megan.

Hunter's eyes were so full of tears, he could barely see the tiny little face with the big eyes that stared up at the two people who'd love him more than anyone else. He'd read that babies couldn't see much of anything at first, but Hunter hoped his son knew how very much they loved him.

"Look at him," Megan whispered, sounding equally awestruck. "He's so beautiful."

"He looks just like his gorgeous mother," Hunter said.

"No, he looks like you. Elmer, come see him. Tell us who he looks like."

Hunter had almost forgotten his grandfather was there.

Elmer came for a closer look at his newest great-grandchild. "I agree with Megan. He's you all over again, Hunter."

"Poor kid," Lucas said with a chuckle.

Hunter ignored his brother and the predictable comment to focus on his family. He had a *family*.

"Are we transporting, Doc?" Lucas asked.

"I don't think we need to. Both mom and baby are in great shape. I think they could safely go home. I'd be happy to stop by and check on you later."

"What do you think, sweetheart?" Hunter asked his wife. "Should we take our son home?"

"Absolutely."

CHAPTER FIFTEEN

"The heart was made to be broken."
—Oscar Wilde

*B*efore he drove across the street to the inn, Noah stayed outside the diner until he heard that Megan and her newborn son were okay. While he'd waited for word about the delivery, he'd eaten his breakfast and kept the sandwich he'd bought for Brianna warm by putting the bag on top of the heating vent on the dashboard of his truck.

At the inn, his entire crew was already there and working, as was Brianna in her cute white hard hat and the Carhartt coat that hid all her most delicious curves.

But he knew they were there.

He handed the sandwich labeled "no bacon" to her along with a coffee.

"Thank you," she said. "What's going on across the street?"

"My cousin and his wife just had their baby."

Brianna's eyes bugged. *"In the diner?"*

"Yep. Her labor came on fast, and by the time the paramedics arrived, it was already too late. The baby was coming."

"I can't believe that's even possible. How does anyone have a baby knowing that can happen?"

"Judging from the way my cousin came unglued, I suspect they had no clue it could happen that way. But all's well that ends well. Baby Carson Elmer Abbott has arrived."

"I love that name."

"All the Abbott grandchildren have C or S names."

"Your family sure does keep things interesting."

"I guess we do. Stuff like this is so 'normal' for us that I barely notice it."

"Stuff like having a baby in a diner?"

Noah smiled at her retort. "Well, not that specifically, but it's always something between the Abbotts and Colemans."

"You're lucky. That sounds fun, even when babies arrive at diners."

"It's pretty fun, for the most part."

"Noah," Carlo called to him. "Electricians are here."

"Duty calls," he said to Brianna.

"Thanks for breakfast."

"My pleasure." He left her with a smile and went to supervise the electricians. As he worked, he thought of the advice his sister had given him to be a friend to Brianna, to be there for her, to show her he was worth taking a risk on.

And did he want that? Did he want her taking a risk on him?

Yeah, he did. He was sick of being a grumpy asshole loner. He was tired of his own company, of lonely nights and endless weekends spent alone. Being with her the other night had shown him something much better, and he wanted more of that feeling—and of her.

As he worked with the electricians and answered a million questions, he kept half an eye on the sexy architect who had him so captivated. Maybe he'd been better off when they'd been fighting all the time. Allowing himself to get caught up in a woman again opened him to all the things that went with it, up to and including heartbreak.

But he had a good feeling about Brianna. She certainly understood heartbreak, and he couldn't imagine her hurting someone the way she had been. But then again, Noah hadn't expected his wife to devastate him the way she had.

If you'd asked him before that dreadful day when he'd caught Melinda with Miguel, he would've said she loved him as much as he loved her. They'd been happy together, or so he thought. Three years later, and hours upon hours spent rehashing every second, looking for clues that hadn't been there, he still didn't understand what had gone so wrong between them that she'd take up with his friend and employee.

Maybe Brianna was right, and it was better that their fling was a one-and-done. What business did he have wishing it could be more than that when he still couldn't say how or why his marriage had reached the point where his wife would sleep with someone else? Shouldn't he have the answer to that question before he started something new?

That thought stayed with him throughout the day as he worked alongside his team and the electricians and prepared for the next stages that would include plumbing, flooring and drywall. Keeping things moving, ensuring the workers had what they needed for each step and sticking to the schedule was his primary role.

He was finishing up with the electricians for the day when one of his men came to find him.

"There's a guy here looking for Brianna. Seems kind of sketchy. Figured I should let you know."

"Thanks, Mark. I saw her go upstairs about half an hour ago." What did it say about him that he knew where she was at any given moment? That he was keeping tabs on her without even realizing it. "Will you run up and get her?"

"Sure thing, boss."

Noah took off his work gloves and stashed them in his coat pockets as he walked toward the Elm Street entrance to the inn.

Sure enough, a jittery young man was outside the door. "Help you?"

"I'm here for Brianna Esposito?"

The kid still had acne, and his nervous disposition put Noah on edge. "What's your business with her?"

"I need to speak to her."

"About what?"

"I'm afraid that's none of your business."

Noah was about to tell the guy to get lost when Brianna appeared beside him.

"You're looking for me?" she asked.

The man thrust an envelope at her, giving her no choice but to take it or be knocked over by the force at which it came at her. "You've been served."

As Noah reached for Brianna to stop her from falling backward, the man took off and jumped into a running car at the curb.

"What the hell?" she asked when she'd recovered her equilibrium.

"Someone is suing you."

"Seriously?" She ripped the envelope open and quickly reviewed the documents inside, her expression conveying her growing horror. "*Are you fucking kidding me?* He is *suing me* for slander that ruined his reputation and made it impossible for him to gain meaningful employment after I went public calling him a sociopath."

"Let's go see my brother."

She looked up at him, her eyes on fire with rage. "Your brother?"

"He's a lawyer. He'll know what you should do."

"I, um, well… Okay."

To Carlo, who was now lurking in the framed hallway behind them, Noah said, "Finish up here, and lock up for the night."

"Will do. Everything okay?"

"It will be." He'd make sure of it. There was no way that son of a bitch was going to get away with this. Grayson would know what to do. He always knew what to do. That was something Noah had counted on for most of his life.

He escorted Brianna to his truck and held the passenger door for her, mindful that their coworkers were watching. He couldn't care less if their colleagues saw them leaving together in his truck. What would've been inconceivable this time last week was now as natural to him as breathing.

She was in trouble and needed help. He was going to help her. End of story.

～

THAT MOTHERFUCKING SON OF A SCUM-SUCKING *BITCH*! BRIANNA had never been more furious in her entire life. His audacity knew no bounds. *He* was suing *her*? After the hell he'd put her through.

"Talk to me," Noah said as he drove them out of the downtown area, such as it was. "What're you thinking?"

"How dare he come at me this way when he knows exactly what he did to me? He lied to me about *everything*. He practically bankrupted me by spending money like we were printing it and then sticking me with most of the debt while he was off having full-blown relationships with other women and telling me I was the only one he'd ever want or love."

"Just tell Gray all that. He'll figure this out."

"I should call my lawyer in Boston."

"Gray can do that, too. Between the two of them, they'll figure this out. Try not to worry."

"He's suing me for *four million dollars*, Noah."

"Fuck."

"How can he do this to me after what he's already done?"

Noah reached for her hand.

Brianna held on tight, thankful for his support. *Four million dollars.* If she sold everything she owned, she couldn't raise a fraction of that.

"Try not to panic. You're on the side of truth here, and that will count for something."

"Except he has no relationship whatsoever with the truth. There's only his perception of things and how he tries to gaslight everyone else into believing his side. It's hard to understand how manipulative he is if you haven't experienced it firsthand."

"I assume you have proof of everything he did?"

"Every single fucking thing. I have receipts, videos, social media posts. You name it. I have it."

"Then you're going to be fine," he said, sounding relieved to hear she had proof. "The truth might mean nothing to him, but it will to the courts. You've got the proof, Bri. That's all you need. This is him trying to strike back because he knows you have everything you need to destroy him."

She loved the way her nickname sounded coming from him. "Maybe so, but it's a nightmare that refuses to end. He won't sign the divorce agreement, and now this. Sometimes I wonder if I'll ever be free of him."

"You will. It might take time, but you'll get rid of him."

"I hope you're right, because I'm not sure how much more of his shit I can handle. Just when I start to feel like I'm moving on and recovering from it all, he does something else that starts it up again."

Noah parked in the driveway of an adorable home that had once been a church. She couldn't wait to see the inside of it.

"My brother is here, so that's good news." Noah turned to look at her, his gaze intense, concerned and deeply involved. That wasn't supposed to have happened, but she couldn't remember why, exactly. "Don't let this take you backward. It's a desperate move by a desperate man. In his fucked-up mind, he's probably thinking he put a lot of effort into you. He's making sure that investment pays off, even though he doesn't have a chance in hell of winning any lawsuit against you."

She took a deep breath and released it slowly, comforted by his words. "You're right. That's very true. He knows I've got him nailed. That's why he's refusing to sign the divorce agreement. Because he gets nothing, except the debt he ran up while we were married."

"The lawsuit is a fundraising attempt that will *fail*, Bri. He doesn't have a leg to stand on."

His certainty filled her with a determination that she deeply appreciated. "No, he doesn't." She smiled. "Thank you for talking me off the ledge."

"No problem. Let's go see what Gray has to say about it."

Brianna followed Noah up the driveway and into the mudroom, which he entered without knocking. They took off their boots and hung their coats on hooks. In the kitchen, they found Ray at the table with an adorable redheaded girl. They had mugs of hot chocolate and, judging by the smell, freshly baked cookies.

"Hey, Ray," Noah said. "You remember Brianna."

"I do," Ray said. "Nice to see you again. This is my grand-daughter, Simone. Simone, say hi to Noah's friend Brianna."

"Hi." Simone raised the plate of cookies to offer them one. "Pop makes the best cookies."

Noah and Brianna each took one.

She took a bite of the gooey goodness. "You made these, Ray? I'm impressed."

"My sweetie Simone likes warm cookies after school," Ray said, his cheeks flushing with embarrassment.

"Don't do anything to mess with our arrangement," Simone said.

Noah laughed at the cute face she made at them. "Someone has you very firmly wrapped around her little finger, Ray."

"She sure does. The only thing she can't get me to do for her is her homework."

"I've even tried bribing him," Simone said.

"How do you know about bribery?" Noah asked.

"They learned about it in school," Ray said, sounding amused. "And now she's trying to practice what she learned on me."

"He won't budge," Simone said with a cute pout.

"I assume you've come to see your brother?" Ray asked.

"We have, but the cookies and the bribery made for a nice extra," Noah said.

"He's in the office. You know the way, right?"

"I do." Noah ruffled Simone's hair as he went by her. "Good luck with the bribery."

"Thanks. I'm gonna need it."

"They're adorable," Brianna said as she followed Noah through the living room in what had once been the central part of the church. "And this house is amazing."

"Yes, they are, and isn't it great? It was already like this when Grayson and Emma bought it, but it's one of my favorite houses in Butler. I'd love to do more of this type of renovation."

"Why don't you?"

He shrugged. "There's more money in the big stuff."

"Not if you had a few of them going at the same time and sold them all at a profit. You should think about that."

"Maybe."

"Gray's office is behind these French doors," Noah said as he knocked.

"Come in, Simone, but only if you're bringing cookies."

Noah opened the door and stuck his head in. "Sorry to disappoint. I'm not a cute redhead, and I have no cookies."

His brother laughed. "That's okay. You can come in anyway."

"I brought a potential client. This is Brianna Esposito. Bri, my brother Grayson."

Grayson stood to reach across his desk to shake her hand. His coloring was like Noah's, but he had a more refined way about him. He wore a dress shirt under a navy V-neck sweater and dark jeans. "Nice to meet you."

"You, too," Brianna said.

"Have you seen Iz today?" Noah asked his brother.

"Not yet. Emma and I are going tonight. What about you?"

"Going after this. Anyway, Brianna is the architect working on the inn with me."

Gray gave his brother a curious look. "Oh right. You were at a meeting the day I came to visit."

"Sorry I missed you," Brianna said.

"Her asshole ex-husband is trying to sue her after he made her life a living hell. I thought you might be able to help her."

"If you have time," Brianna said. "We didn't even ask if you were busy."

"I've got time. Any friend of Noah's is a friend of mine."

"Your family is very sweet."

"Just us," Gray said, smiling. "The rest of them not so much."

Brianna laughed. "If you say so."

"She met most of them last night," Noah said. "She brought us dinner after the hospital."

Grayson seemed intrigued to hear that news considering Noah's reclusiveness lately. "So, what's up with the ex?"

"It's kind of a long story."

"Start from the beginning. Tell me everything, and then I'll look at the lawsuit and see what I can do to help you."

Over the next hour, Brianna told him everything about what'd happened with Rem, giving him details she'd left out of the retelling to Noah the other night. While she talked, she felt Noah watching her in that intent, unblinking way of his. It was intriguing to her that his brother was every bit as attractive as Noah, maybe even more so, but Brianna had no interest in him. She was, however, incredibly aware of Noah sitting as close to her as he dared with his older brother watching their every move.

Grayson took notes as she told her story. When she got to the part about how Rem's frequent disappearances had led her to start tracking his credit card, Grayson looked up from his notebook. "Did you keep everything you uncovered?"

"Every single thing."

"That's good."

"Even before I understood the full scope of what was happening, I had the foresight to know I might need to document it all. Especially when the money in our joint account started to disappear." Her heart ached whenever she thought of those frantic early days when she'd first begun to put pieces together that added up to a nightmare.

"Did you figure out what he was spending it on?"

"Mostly other women and hotel rooms right in Boston. He didn't even try to cover his trail. He thought he had me so wrapped up in love for him that I'd never question what he was doing or who he was doing it with."

"Did you?"

"I confronted him with proof of multiple affairs. He said I was crazy, that he'd been working and had never been with anyone but me. I even had photos of various times I'd followed him and seen him with other women. He said it wasn't him. I had the wrong guy, and how dare I accuse him of cheating on me when I knew full well that I was the only woman he'd ever love."

"Unreal," Noah muttered.

"I'll take a look at the lawsuit," Gray said.

Brianna handed him the envelope, and as he read the opening pages, she fought the urge to fidget as nervous energy ran through her like nuclear power.

Noah reached over to put his warm hand on top of the freezing hands she had clutched in her lap. "Keep breathing."

Having him there and so clearly on her side helped tremendously. Later, when they had a minute to themselves, she'd tell him so.

"Talk to me about where the word 'sociopath' came from," Gray said.

"My therapist. She said that she could tell he had all the hall-marks of a sociopath without even meeting him. For one thing, he lacks a conscience. Without that, there's no hope of having any kind of meaningful relationship with him."

"I have some experience with antisocial personality disorder. I handled a case for my former firm in which a woman left an estate to her grandchildren. One of them was a sociopath who gaslighted the others out of their inheritance. They sued him, and we represented his siblings and cousins. From what you've told me, I'd have to agree with your therapist's assessment."

"He's a textbook sociopath with one caveat. Whereas most sociopaths are antisocial, Rem was very social, thus the fact that he could juggle five other women in addition to his wife. My therapist believed he was part sociopath, part narcissist."

"A delightful combination," Gray said with a hint of humor.

"Indeed. While my ex was lying, cheating and manipulating me into basically thinking I was losing my mind—which was intentional—he was pursuing grandiose, expensive endeavors that were mostly about feeding his ego. He used the savings we'd been growing to buy a house to open a restaurant he named for himself—Remington's. When I found out where that money had gone, the restaurant was already closed because he'd run out of money before it could open. His business partner in the restaurant sued him for breach of contract, and I was named a code-fendant because the partner knew I was the only one making any money. I was able to prove I had no knowledge of or involvement in the restaurant and was dropped from the suit, but not before it cost me ten thousand in legal fees to get free of it."

"This just gets worse and worse," Noah said.

"And we've only scratched the surface," Brianna replied.

"How did he find out you were referring to him as a sociopath?" Gray asked.

"I told some of our mutual friends that I'd come to believe he had antisocial personality disorder, which is the official term for sociopathy. I explained what that means and gave them examples of things that'd happened to make my case. They were as shocked as I had been initially. I think some of them didn't believe most of what I was telling them, because it seemed so farfetched that it couldn't have happened."

"You can't honestly think he has a case against her when she can prove he did all this shit?" Noah asked, sounding as agitated as Brianna felt.

"My concern would be that Brianna isn't a trained therapist or psychiatrist, so she doesn't have the authority to diagnose him," Gray said.

"That diagnosis came from a trained therapist," Brianna said.

"Who has never met your ex-husband in person, correct?" Gray asked.

"Correct."

"The diagnosis was made from anecdotes you provided, not from a complete evaluation of him."

A sinking feeling overtook Brianna. "What does this mean?"

"He may have a case if the info you gave your mutual friends impacted his ability to make a living."

She wanted to howl from the sheer injustice of it all. That Rem could treat her like he had, lie, cheat and steal from her and then sue her and possibly *win*? That couldn't happen. It just couldn't. "What should I do?"

"I'd suggest countersuing him for damages, focusing on the things he did before you split. We'll toss in pain and suffering and generally throw the book at him."

"How fast can we do that?"

"I can put something together this week. Do you know where to find him?"

"I think so."

"Work on nailing that down so we can have him served. Often, suits and countersuits tend to cancel each other out when the rubber meets the road, so try not to worry."

"How much will it cost to countersue him?"

"I'll give you the friends and family discount wherever I can, but about ten thousand to start with."

"To start with."

"If the two suits don't cancel each other out, it could get costly to defend yourself against his."

"Even though she can prove all the shit he did?" Noah asked.

"Even though. He may have a case that your accusations hurt his reputation."

"Even if they're true?" Brianna asked.

"Even if."

She'd known for some time now that life wasn't fair, but this was almost too much to handle.

Grayson got up and went to his file cabinet, returning with a sheet of paper he handed to Brianna. "My engagement agreement. If you sign this, I can get started for you right away."

Since she needed his help so badly, she took the form and signed it, resigned to fighting back no matter how much it cost her.

"With your permission, I'd like to retain a private investigator I've worked with before in Boston to do some groundwork for us. He's excellent, and if there's new dirt, he'll find it."

"Go ahead," Brianna said, anticipating another costly, protracted battle to rid herself of the man she'd once loved so much.

"I know it's easy for me to say try not to worry, but I honestly believe we'll be able to reach a settlement with him that won't break the bank. He's going to have to deal with our suit, and at the end of the day, he'll probably see it's easier to let his go than to have to defend against ours."

"You don't know him. He won't give up until he's completely ruined me."

"That's not going to happen," Noah said, reaching for her hand and holding on tight. He didn't seem to notice the subtle lift of his brother's eyebrows.

But she saw it.

"We won't let that happen, Bri. You heard what Gray said. It's going to be okay."

"I've got a lot of experience in this kind of thing," Gray said. "I'll do everything I can for you, Brianna."

Did he have a lot of experience dealing with sociopaths? Had he ever come up against someone so devoid of basic human emotions that he would do to someone what Rem had done to her? She doubted it, but he'd find out soon enough who he was dealing with.

CHAPTER SIXTEEN

*"We are afraid to care too much, for fear that
the other person does not care at all."*
—Eleanor Roosevelt

*N*oah couldn't believe Bri's ex might have a possible case against her after all the shit he'd done to her. He'd never thought of himself as a violent person, but he'd love ten minutes alone with that son of a bitch.

"I'm sorry you're so upset."

He looked over at her. "Don't worry about me. This isn't about me."

"Thank you for taking me to see your brother. I'd be losing it if I hadn't been able to do *something* after being served."

"I'm sorry he wasn't more outraged."

"He's just doing his job, and it's not helpful to me if he doesn't give it to me straight."

"I guess… It just makes me so fucking mad."

"You're very cute when you're mad."

He looked over at her, seeming stunned before he had to return his attention to the road. "I must be fucking adorable, then."

"You are, and I appreciate it, Noah. It helps to have a friend right now."

"I'm glad. It's total bullshit, and I have to believe that any judge in the world will see right through him and his bullshit lawsuit."

"I hope so."

"I hate that he's going to cost you even more money than he already has. If you don't have it, I can help you out."

Later, she would probably look back and realize that was the exact moment when she began to have genuine feelings for Noah Coleman, the kind of feelings that could be complicated and wonderful and life changing. "That's very kind of you to offer, but I've got some savings left. I just don't want to spend it on him."

"Try to think of it as spending it on yourself. It's an investment in a future that doesn't include him."

"That makes it a little less painful."

"I need to go see my sister. You feel like going for the ride?"

If she went home, she'd do nothing but stew about the latest nightmare with Rem. "Sure, I'd like that."

"Good." He reached across for her hand. "I don't want you sitting home alone freaking out about this."

Smiling, she glanced over at him as she wrapped her hand around his. "That's what I would've done."

"I know. I get it. I've been there. This kind of stress is all-consuming."

"It's the worst. That first month, after I realized our entire life was nothing but a house of cards…" She felt sick as she remembered the trauma of that dreadful time. "The worst thing I've ever been through in my life."

"It's in the past now, even if you still have to deal with this shit. He can never get near you again unless you let him, and you're not going to let him. You got me?"

"Yes, Noah," she said, smiling again. "I've got you. It helps to have you on my side."

"I'm on your side."

"Remember when we used to fight about everything?"

"I remember, and that was completely your fault for making me want you."

Stunned by his confession, she said, "*How* was that my fault?"

"You were beautiful and sexy and smart and didn't put up with my shit. I wanted you from the first day I ever met you—and I didn't *want* to want you. I was very busy being a miserable loner. The last thing in the world I wanted was to be attracted to you."

She couldn't stop the laughter that gurgled up from deep inside her.

"It's not funny!"

"Yes, it is."

"No, it isn't."

"Is."

"Isn't.

"And we're back to fighting."

"This isn't fighting," Noah said with a sexy little grin that made her wish they were going somewhere they could be alone. "Aren't you going to admit you were into me, too?"

"I wasn't."

"Oh, *please*. You were, too."

"Full of yourself much?"

"I knew you were digging me. I could tell by the way your eyes would throw fire at me when we were arguing about why I'd done something I shouldn't have."

"I was throwing fire at you, hoping you'd disappear."

"Nah, baby, I knew you wanted me."

Brianna sputtered with outrage as she tried to pull her hand free of his.

"Stop fighting it."

"I was starting to like you."

"Let's go back to that, then, shall we? After you admit you were digging me all that time you wanted me to go away."

"You're very exasperating sometimes."

"Maybe so, but you're not thinking about that other thing anymore, are you?"

"For a minute there, I was thinking of all the reasons I used to dislike you so much."

Noah laughed. "It took a full minute to think of them all?"

"There were a lot."

"But all that time you disliked me, you also wanted me, right?"

"You can keep trying, but you'll never get me to admit that."

"Oh, I do so love a challenge."

"Thanks," she said softly, glancing at him. He was too good-looking for her own good, and yes, she'd thought that from the beginning. But she would never tell him so.

"For what?"

"Taking me to see your brother, bickering with me, asking me to go to the hospital with you. You're keeping me from a trip to the dark side, and it means a lot to me. Even if you are a pompous fool with a large opinion of yourself."

"She gives and then takes away, all in the same sentence."

"Gotta keep you humble, Coleman."

"You do, Esposito. You're very tough on my ego."

"Your ego could use some humility."

They were still going back and forth with the insults when he drove into the hospital parking lot twenty minutes later.

After he'd parked and shut off the engine, he turned to her. "Kiss me."

"I'm not sure I want to after all your nonsense."

"What nonsense?"

"You know what I'm talking about."

His smile lit up his entire face, and dear God, she was powerless to resist him. That smile completely transformed his face. He bore no resemblance whatsoever to the man who'd driven her *mad* for weeks.

"You know you want to."

Because she did want to, Brianna leaned across the center console to give him a chaste kiss on the lips.

"That was cheap. I know you can do better."

"Maybe later. If you're good." She pulled free of his grip and was out of the car before he realized she was gone.

"That was mean," he said as he followed her to the hospital's main entrance.

"You'll get over it."

"I'm not sure I will."

She couldn't believe she was having fun after being served with that damned lawsuit. Under normal circumstances, she'd be losing her shit, but being with Noah had given her a welcome and entertaining distraction.

Inside, he asked if his sister was still in the ICU.

"No," the woman working the info desk said. "She's in four eighteen now."

"That's good news. Thanks."

"How do you people stand to live without cell phones?" Brianna asked as they walked to the elevator. "In any other universe, you'd already know she was out of the ICU."

"Vermont is unlike any other universe."

"You can say that again."

"You can admit it. It's a very *attractive* place." In the elevator, he hit the button for the fourth floor. "It has many *attractions*."

Brianna rolled her eyes. "Give it a rest."

"Not until you admit the truth."

When they arrived on the fourth floor, they found a room full of Colemans, including one she hadn't met yet.

"Brianna, my brother Jackson. Jack, meet Bri."

Jackson, who had darker hair and eyes than Noah, shook her hand. He had the kind of perfect dark stubble on his jaw that models had to work to get just right. "Nice to meet the lasagna lady. I hear it was epic."

"It was and is," Noah said. "Leftovers are in my fridge."

"I'll be hitting that up later."

"Leave some for me," Noah said.

"Nice to meet you, too," Brianna said. "I'll wait here while you see Izzy."

"I won't be long," Noah said.

"Take your time." As he walked away, she took a seat facing Sarah, Vanessa and Ally with Jackson to her right.

"So," Ally said. "You're here with Noah."

"That's right." Brianna bit her lip to keep from laughing at her shameless quest for info.

"They've been talking about that lasagna all day," Jackson said.

"I'm glad everyone enjoyed it."

"We *loved* it," Nessa said, "but you know what we love even more?"

Brianna had her suspicions, but she played a little dumb. "What's that?"

"Seeing Noah with you," Sarah said. "He seems happy when you're with him."

"We've been worried about him for years," Nessa added.

"I don't remember when we weren't worried about him," Jackson said. "Been a long time."

"He's lucky to have you guys on his side," Brianna said.

"We're always on his side," Ally said. "We don't know what went down with *her*, but she'd better hope we never run into her. His loner stage began right after she departed. It doesn't take a rocket scientist to realize that two plus two adds up to her doing him wrong."

Brianna felt a little guilty that she knew more than his siblings did about how Noah's marriage ended. "You should just ask him what happened. He'd probably tell you."

"We don't want to push him away by prying," Sarah said. "It's a fine line."

"I can certainly understand," Brianna said.

"Sorry if we're making you uncomfortable," Nessa said. "It's just so nice to see him smiling and laughing and joking around again. We've missed that guy."

"You're not making me uncomfortable," Brianna said. "I'm glad to hear Noah seems happier than he's been."

"He's much happier, and that seems to be related to you," Sarah said.

Brianna felt her face heat with embarrassment.

"Now we're making her uncomfortable," Ally said. "Back off, ladies."

"It's okay," Brianna said. "It's nice how concerned you guys are about him. Your family is sweet."

"Not always," Jackson said. "We can get into it with the best of them."

"Not so much anymore," Ally said to her brother. "Well, except for Henry and Sarah. They fight like cats and dogs."

"Noah likes to fight, too," Brianna said.

Sarah scoffed. "Noah *wishes* he could fight like me."

"No one wishes they were like you," Ally said.

The two of them took it from there, and Brianna just watched the show, thankful they had stopped trying to get info from her about Noah.

For now, anyway.

~

"TELL ME ABOUT LASAGNA GIRL," IZZY SAID.

"Not until you tell me why Cabot spent the night here."

Cabot had gone with their mother to get coffee in the cafeteria, leaving Noah and Izzy alone.

"You first," Izzy said. "I'm injured, so I'm in charge."

"Jeez, are you going to milk being injured?" Noah was thrilled to see her looking much better than she had yesterday, although the bruises on her face were turning an angry shade of purple.

"If it gets me some info. Spill it."

"Nothing to spill. We're friends."

"*You*, Noah Coleman, do not have *friends* who are women."

"Yes, I do!"

"Who?"

The only one he could think of was his friend with benefits, and Izzy didn't know about her, nor did she need to. "People you don't know."

"Try that shit with someone who doesn't know you as well as I do. You've never had women who were friends unless you were dating them."

"I have, too! I had college friends who were women."

"And when was the last time you talked to any of them?"

"I don't know."

"Rather than arguing with me about your lack of female friends, tell me about lasagna girl. Everyone was saying she's pretty, nice and a great cook."

"She's all those things."

"And?"

"And nothing. We work together."

"If that's all it is, why did she make dinner for your very large family?"

"Because she felt bad when she heard my sister drove her car off the road and was in the ICU."

"I heard that in addition to the lasagna, there was dessert and salad and garlic bread."

"So?"

"As a woman myself, I'll tell you that most newer friends aren't going to go all out like that for someone they barely know unless there's a certain level of interest there."

"Do you charge for this kind of insight into the female psyche?"

"It's free for you. Family discount."

Noah chuckled. "It's good to see you feeling better, even if you're trying to psychoanalyze my friendship with a colleague. Now let's analyze you. What's Cabot doing here?"

"I'm not entirely sure. He showed up last night. Said he drove from New Jersey where he was when he heard I was in the hospital."

"That's nice for someone who isn't your boyfriend or significant other. He isn't, is he?"

"Nope. We're just friends."

"Huh, and he drove from New Jersey to northern Vermont for someone he's just friends with. That sounds like more than friends to me."

"What do you know about such things? You needed me to tell you that lasagna girl wouldn't be cooking for your entire family unless she was into you."

"You think you're so smart, don't you?"

"I know I am."

"Since you're clearly fine, I should go rescue her from the others in the waiting room."

"Wait a second! She's *here*? Get her. I want to meet her."

"You're sick. You need your rest."

"Go. Get. Her. *Now*."

Groaning, he started toward the door. "Me and my big mouth."

"Hey, Noah?"

"Yes, Izzy?"

"She wouldn't be visiting your sister in the hospital if she wasn't into you."

"She came along for the ride."

"She came because she is *into* you. Are you really this stupid? Wait, don't answer that. I'll answer for you—you're that stupid."

"I was glad you didn't die in that crash."

"And now?"

"I'm still glad. Kinda." He left her laughing and went to get Brianna, certain he was going to regret this.

She smiled when she saw him coming, and he started to wonder if maybe Izzy was right. While Brianna wouldn't admit to being into him, her actions were speaking loudly.

"How is she?" Brianna asked.

"Full of beans. And she wants to meet you."

"Were you talking about me in there?"

"No, she was. She heard about the lasagna. By the way, she's calling you lasagna girl."

"It was *good* lasagna," Ally said. "And PS, we were talking about you, Noah, while you were talking about her."

"What was I thinking bringing you here?" he asked Brianna.

"That's what we were wondering, too," Sarah said, grinning. "The Colemans are a hornet's nest at the best of times. We're even worse when we have nothing to do but sit around killing time."

"Looks like I'm getting you out of the hornet's nest just in time, then." Noah escorted Brianna from the waiting room and pointed her in the direction of Izzy's room.

"We're here all day," Nessa called after them. "You can come back and tell us more about Noah after you see Izzy."

"I didn't tell them a thing," Brianna said.

"I know you didn't."

"But you ought to. They've been worried about you since you broke up with *her*."

"Is that right?"

"Uh-huh."

"I'll take that under advisement."

CHAPTER SEVENTEEN

"Pain is what we're in most of the time.
And I think the bigger the pain, the more gods we need."
—John Lennon

oah held the door to Izzy's room and sent Brianna in ahead of him. "Izzy, this is Brianna. Bri, meet Izzy. I apologize in advance for anything she might have to say."

"Come closer so I can see you," Izzy said.

"She can see you just fine." Noah hadn't thoroughly thought out the consequences of bringing Brianna to the hospital or the conclusions his family would leap to if they saw them together two days in a row. He was jumping to some significant conclusions where she was concerned all on his own.

"I'm so glad you're doing better," Brianna said.

"Everything still hurts, but it's a tad bit better than it was yesterday."

"That's good."

"So, I hear you're one hell of a cook."

"I don't know about that."

"You've got my whole family talking about your lasagna."

"I'll make some for you when you get out of the hospital."

"I'll look forward to that."

"I've seen some of your work. There's a book about you at the house I'm renting. It's so impressive."

"Thanks. That's nice of you to say."

"I felt like I'd had a tour of Vermont after flipping through that book."

"Vermont is the gift that keeps on giving."

"It's beautiful. Especially the fall colors."

"You'll have to come back to visit next fall so you can see it for yourself."

"I'd love that."

"What's a nice girl like you doing hanging out with a degenerate like my brother?"

Brianna laughed at the face Noah made at her.

"She thinks she can get away with that crap because she almost died," Noah said, "but when she gets out of here, it's business as usual."

"They want to send me to a rehab place," Izzy said, frowning. "I can't be home alone."

"I'll stay with you," Cabot said from the doorway. "You don't need to go to rehab."

"Oh, um…"

Noah hadn't seen Izzy flustered very often. She was the most self-assured, confident woman he knew. "Someone has a boyfriend," he said in a soft singsong voice.

"Someone else has a girlfriend," Izzy said under her breath.

"Cabot, this is Brianna," Noah said. "Brianna, meet Cabot."

He shook her hand. "Nice to meet you, Brianna."

"You, too. There're so many of you. I'm going to need a cheat sheet."

"He's not technically part of the Coleman family," Noah said. "He's our cousin Wade's father-in-law."

"That's helpful," Brianna said.

"My daughter, Mia, is married to their cousin Wade," Cabot

said. "I met Izzy and the other Colemans at Mia and Wade's wedding last June."

"Ah, I see."

"There's no need for you to go to rehab," Cabot said to Izzy. "I can take care of you at home."

"You have work. And stuff."

"Nothing I can't do from here."

Noah found it interesting that Izzy seemed extremely flummoxed by Cabot's offer. If only he knew Cabot a little better. Noah might've given her a taste of her own ridiculous medicine. But he didn't want to embarrass Cabot, even though it would be fun to tease his sister. She deserved it after the crap she threw at him before.

"We ought to go," Noah said. "We'll let you guys talk."

"You don't have to go," Izzy said, seeming almost frantic to keep them there.

What was that about?

His mother came in, carrying a coffee cup. "Oh hey, Noah. I heard you were here with Brianna. Nice to see you again, Brianna."

"You, too, Hannah."

"We were just going to head out." Noah leaned over to kiss his sister's cheek. "I'll come by tomorrow."

"But things are just getting interesting," Izzy said. "You brought a date to visit me at the hospital. This is huge news."

"We're not on a date, you nitwit. We were taking care of some other business and came here after. Tell her, Bri. It's not a date."

"I thought it was a date."

Noah stared at her, shocked, which was how he saw her crack up laughing.

"Oh my God, your face," Brianna said, wiping laughter tears from her eyes.

His mother snorted with laughter. "Well played, Brianna."

"I really, *really* like this woman," Izzy said. "I like her a whole lot."

He liked her, too, even if she was busting his balls. "Now that you ladies have had your fun at my expense, we'll be leaving."

"Come see me again soon, Brianna," Izzy said.

"I'll do that."

"I will, too," Noah said.

"Only if you bring her. Otherwise, don't bother."

Brianna was still laughing when they left the room. "I wish I'd had a picture of your face when I said we were on a date. Not that I'll ever forget your expression. Priceless. And PS, your family is awesome."

"I can't stand them."

"Can't stand who?" Ally asked when she approached them from the direction of the vending area, holding a bottle of Diet Coke.

"You and your sisters and most of your brothers, too. Gray is okay. The rest of you are a pain in my ass."

"I take it Izzy gave you shit about coming here with Brianna?"

"Yes, and Brianna was mean to me."

"I was not! I was joking!"

Noah shrugged and pretended to be hurt, when really, her immediate groove with Izzy and the others pleased him. The Colemans could be a tough crowd. Brianna fit right in. Her delicious lasagna had helped pave the way, but she'd held her own, and he admired that.

Ally took Brianna by the arm. "You have to tell me what you said."

Noah steered her out of his sister's clutches and walked them toward the elevator. "We're leaving now. Get the dirt from Izzy."

"Oh, we will. See you at home, Noah!"

"Freaking pains in my ass," he muttered on the ride to the lobby.

"You love them."

"Sometimes."

"All the time."

"If you say so."

"I say so." She glanced over at him. "I'm sorry if I took your sister's side against you."

"You are *so* not sorry!"

"I'm really not," she said, laughing again. "Your face... Hysterical."

He held the passenger door for her. "Get in the truck and shut it."

"Hey, Noah?"

He held on to the doorframe. "Yes, Brianna?"

"Thanks for making me laugh. A few hours ago, I never would've believed it was possible to laugh tonight."

"I'm happy to have been the victim of your little joke if it took your mind off other things."

"It did."

"Good."

Giving him a cute side-eye, she said, "So the little joke was funny, right?"

She was adorable, and he liked her more with every passing minute. "Nope."

"Yes!"

"Not even kinda."

"Oh, come on!"

Grinning, he said, "That's my final answer." He shut the door to make his point and walked around the truck to get into the driver's side, dismayed to realize it was snowing a lot harder than he'd thought when they first came outside. He'd have to take it slow going home, which was fine. That gave him more time with her.

And that was what he wanted—more time with her. As much time with her as he could get. Soon enough, she'd be done at the inn and would head back to her life in Boston. The thought of her leaving and him going back to the austere existence he'd been leading before he met her made him feel panicked.

He held the wheel a little tighter, mindful of the slippery roads, not to mention the slippery path he was heading down as his feelings for her blossomed into something completely unexpected. A few days ago, he would've said he didn't even like her, but that wasn't true even then. He hadn't liked how she made him feel—off his game, edgy and aroused at work, which was the last freaking thing he'd needed with the biggest job of his career underway.

So, he'd argued with her nonstop, hoping if he annoyed her enough—and vice versa—he wouldn't be tempted to act on the unreasonable attraction. She had him so preoccupied, he could barely concentrate on the thousands of details that were his responsibility.

Then Mrs. H had intervened, probably with the assistance of his grandfather, and everything had changed. Last night, Brianna had said she didn't want this thing between them to be anything more than friends and colleagues. He'd gone along with that, but maybe he ought to tell her what *he* wanted.

You sure about that, pal? You could say nothing and keep things the way they've been. We were fine before she came along, and we'll be fine after she goes. But isn't this better? Isn't laughing with her and having her laugh at me better than being alone all the time? Sure, but don't forget what can happen when you give someone else the power to hurt you. Brianna wouldn't do what Mel did. She's had that done to her. She'd never do that to someone who cared about her. Okay, so maybe she wouldn't cheat on you, but that doesn't mean it won't end badly.

"Noah."

He snapped out of the conversation he was having with himself to realize she'd been talking to him. "Sorry, what did you say?"

"I asked if there's any chance we might drive off this road."

"Nope. There's a guardrail on this one."

"Why wasn't there one on the road where Izzy had her accident?"

"There used to be, but so many people hit it that it fell off. I think the plan was to replace it in the spring."

"Is there some kind of map or something that shows all the places where you can easily plunge to your death around here?"

Noah laughed. "Not that I know of, but I can give you a tour of the hot spots."

"That'd be good. What's the story with Izzy and Cabot?"

"I'm not sure, to be honest. They had fun together at the wedding, but I wasn't sure if it was anything more than that."

"Seven months later, he's camped out in her hospital room and offering to stay with her when she gets home. Sounds like something more."

"Maybe so."

"Do you like him?"

"I don't know him very well, but he seems like a nice guy. You won't believe the story of him and his daughter." Noah told her about how Mia had discovered her long-lost father. "Needless to say, he was elated to have her back in his life. He threw the most incredible wedding for her and Wade."

"What an unbelievably shitty thing his ex-wife did to him and their daughter."

"Seriously fucked-up."

"Tell me they charged her with something."

"Cabot declined to press charges because he didn't want to put Mia through that, but I can't imagine how deeply the anger must run through him."

"I'd be a raving lunatic if someone ever did that to me. I say all the time how thankful I am that Rem and I didn't have kids. Not for lack of trying, but for all I know, he'd had a vasectomy or something. I can't even imagine an innocent child caught in the nightmare our marriage became."

"I hear you. I thought I wanted kids with *her*, but I'm so glad that never happened."

"Were you trying?"

"I thought so, but like you said, who knows? She was probably on the pill, or some other birth control, the whole time while pretending to be disappointed we never got pregnant. Considering how things ended, it was a blessing that she never conceived."

"I just keep wondering why people have to be so shitty to the ones who love them. It's so rare to find true love, and to treat it so callously... It'll never make sense to me."

"I've asked myself that a lot, especially after my dad left my mom with eight kids to finish raising on her own."

"Speaking of shitty."

"It was pretty bad. My dad was the one who made most of the money. It was rough without his income."

"And no one made him contribute?"

"The court did, but only the minimum required. Nowhere near enough for a family of nine. Gray, Izzy, Nessa and I were working when we were far too young to be concerned about things like food on the table and younger siblings who grew out of shoes and clothes so quickly."

"What a terrible thing he did."

"We think he had some sort of mental health issue. We'll probably never know for sure. And get this—a year or so ago, I ran into him out of the blue, and he told me he was planning to reach out to us."

"Did you believe him?"

"I did because he was sick and needed a bone marrow transplant. He wanted us to get tested."

She spun around in her seat to stare at him. "Are you *serious*? I hope you all told him to fuck off."

"We wanted to, but more than that, we didn't want his death on our consciences. Gray ended up matching to him and donated. We haven't heard much from him since then except that he's in remission."

"Wow. It takes some kind of balls to reach out to kids you abandoned to ask for such a thing."

"Yep. Everyone was upset about it. I was the one who said we ought to do it and move on. That way, we wouldn't have to feel bad if he died."

"You're a bigger person than most would've been under those circumstances."

"He's still our father, even if we want nothing to do with him."

"Did you call him about Izzy?"

"We did. He said he wanted to see her, but I guess he hasn't shown up yet. I would've heard about it if he had."

"I hope he's filled with shame over what he did to you and your family. I hope he doesn't have a minute of peace. And in case you were wondering, I never would've said something like that about *anyone* until it happened to me."

"I get it. Believe me."

"It helps to talk to someone who understands. It's been weird at home. My family loved Rem and couldn't believe what I was telling them could be true. His parents were in a total state of disbelief until I was able to prove that he stole from them."

"How'd you do that?"

"He was on one of their accounts. They'd put each of their children on various things so someone would have access if anything happened to them. I logged in as him and was able to prove he'd been withdrawing money from the account for years. Small amounts that wouldn't trigger any kind of suspicion, but it added up to more than twenty-five thousand. After that, they were completely on Team Brianna."

"He stole from his parents. What a dirtbag."

"That was the least of what he did. The worst part was the gaslighting, him making me believe I was seeing things when it came to him cheating and lying and stealing from me. 'Come on, baby,' he'd say, 'you know me. You know how much I love you. I'd never do anything to hurt you.' I wanted to believe it so badly that I started to question the black-and-white evidence staring me in the face that confirmed he was full of shit. Being made to feel like I was crazy was worse than anything."

Noah listened to what she was saying, but he kept his eyes on the road so they wouldn't end up in the hospital with Izzy. "That had to be so awful."

"It was, and I'm not even sure why I'm talking about it to you again. You must be tired of hearing the many ways my ex did me wrong."

"I don't mind listening, and I'm sorry for all the ways your ex did you wrong. I hope he's regretting what he lost."

"He's not capable of regret. That's one of the hallmarks of his condition. He has no care for anyone but himself. Anyway, enough of that. I'm good at bringing down the mood, huh?"

"You're fine. I don't want you ever to feel like you can't talk to me about what you went through with him, what you're continuing to go through. I can't believe he dares to sue you after what he did."

"I know but being with you and your family helped me this afternoon, Noah. I'd be a disaster if I'd gone straight home to spend the evening alone with my disturbing thoughts."

"Glad we were able to help."

"The Colemans are a great distraction."

"How hard did my sisters pump you for info?"

"They were pretty crafty, but I was craftier. I dodged them."

"Well done. That's not easy to do."

"They worry about you."

"I wish they wouldn't. I'm fine."

"Are you, though? Are any of us fine?"

"I've been a lot finer this week than I've been in months."

"Is that so?"

He pulled into her driveway and put the truck in Park before looking over at her. "That's very much so."

"Me, too."

"It's funny, isn't it, how we found a kindred spirit in the least likely of people."

"It is, and it's proof that we need to take the time to get to know people before we judge them."

Noah grinned at her. "Had you judged me?"

"Rather harshly."

He laughed. "I deserved it. The minute I heard Mrs. H was bringing in an architect from Boston, I wanted off the job."

"You did? Seriously?"

"Dead seriously. Architects are always such a royal pain in my ass, and this time was no exception."

She sputtered with outrage. "*You* were the royal pain! Not me."

"Nope, you were. So precise with your rolls of plans and your detailed instructions. Not to mention your forked tongue."

"As I recall, you quite liked my tongue the other night."

And just that quickly, he was hard as a rock for her. "I've come around on the subject of your tongue."

She laughed softly. "You want to come in?"

He really ought to go home. If he didn't, his siblings would be all over them both even more than they already were. But the last thing in the world he wanted to do, when she was offering the opportunity for him to spend more time with her, was go home.

"Yeah," he said. "I want to."

CHAPTER EIGHTEEN

"The heart will break, but broken live on."
—Lord Byron

*H*unter couldn't stop staring at the tiny face that had captured his heart from the second he first saw his son.

Carson.

He had a son named *Carson.*

He'd been an emotional mess all day, from the minute Noah had appeared in his office until now, hours later when Megan and Carson were safely home, and they were settling into their new life as a family.

"He's beautiful, son," Hunter's dad, Lincoln, said. "He looks just like you did as a baby."

"Poor little bugger," Hunter's twin sister, Hannah, said.

"Don't talk crap about my handsome husband," Megan said from the sofa.

"If I can't talk crap about him, who can?" Hannah asked.

His sister had come running the minute Hunter had called to tell her about the baby being born at the diner, of all places. He'd never get over that. All their careful planning had been for naught. Their son had had his own plan, and Hunter was already learning that the little guy was now in charge. He'd taken over their lives in one eventful day.

"I can't wait to introduce Callie to Carson," Hannah said.

"You could've brought her over tonight," Hunter said.

"She was in a mood today, and she's had the sniffles. We'll wait until we're sure she's not sick before we bring her for a visit."

"How in the world did you do this ten times, Molly?" Megan asked.

"Technically, I only did it eight times."

"*Eight*." Megan groaned as she tried to find a comfortable position. "I have a whole new appreciation for two sets of twins. I bow down to you."

"I'm sure the next seven won't be this difficult," Hunter said, grinning at his wife. He'd never loved her more than he did on the day she'd given him his beautiful son.

"Bite your tongue," Megan said. "Carson will be lucky to get one sibling, let alone nine of them."

"You'll forget," Molly said. "In a week or two, when you're feeling much better, you won't be thinking about the birth anymore."

"I'll have to take your word for that."

"It's true." Hannah was due with her second child next month. "I'm so obsessed with my little Callie that I rarely think about the day she was born. Although, I seem to remember it more as baby number two gets ready to make an appearance."

"Do you want to hold him, Gramps?" Hunter asked Elmer.

"I'd love to." Elmer took a seat and received the baby from Hunter. "Hi there, my little friend. How're things going on your first day on the outside?"

"Let us know what he has to say," Megan said. "We'll record it for the baby book."

"So far, he's quite pleased with the accommodations and the beverage service," Elmer said.

Hunter, who'd sat next to his wife, squeezed her hand and smiled. His face hurt from smiling so much. Megan's doctor had come by earlier and had declared her and the baby robustly healthy after their big day, which was such a huge relief. He'd worried they might regret the decision to forgo the hospital. Hours after the birth, he'd finally begun to relax and release the anxiety that had spiked after Noah came to tell him Megan needed him.

When Noah had called to check on them late that afternoon, Hunter had thanked him for his help and told him he'd always be part of the story of Carson's birth. Noah had liked that. For the first time since he'd run out of the office that morning, Hunter wondered if anyone had shut off his computer. Ah, what did he care? He'd done the payroll first thing, so everyone would get paid. Beyond that, he wasn't going to worry about work for a few days. He had much better things to do.

Molly had offered to spend the night, but he and Megan felt like they had things under control. He hoped they didn't regret that decision.

"I'm just a phone call away if you need me," Molly said, kissing the three of them. "Don't hesitate to call."

"Thanks, Mom." Hunter walked them to the door and waited until they'd driven away before he shut off the outside lights and locked up.

"Poor Horace doesn't know what to make of Carson." Megan cuddled the baby in one arm while she scratched Horace between his ears.

The dog had been sad since the minute they arrived home with the baby. Hannah and their brother Will had advised them to let the dog smell and lick the baby and not push him away so he wouldn't resent Carson for bumping him down a notch in the family pecking order.

"He's used to being an only child," Hunter said. "He'll adjust. Are you ready to go up to bed?"

"So ready."

"Let me take him up, and then I'll come back for you." He accepted the baby from her and went upstairs to put him in the bedside bassinet he and his siblings had used. Moving quickly, he went back downstairs for Megan.

He helped her up from the sofa, going slow in deference to how sore she was.

"Everything hurts."

"I'm so sorry, honey. I hate that for you."

"It's a small price to pay for our sweet little boy."

"Hold on to me." He carefully picked her up and settled her into his arms for the ride upstairs. The second he put her down in the bathroom, she said, "Check on him."

Hunter went around the bed to look at the baby, focusing on the rise and fall of his tiny chest. "He's good."

Megan came out of the bathroom a few minutes later, grimacing with every step she took.

Hunter helped settle her in bed and then moved the bassinet so it was next to her. "Do people sleep after they have a baby?" he asked.

"I believe they do."

"How do they do it? I'm afraid to close my eyes. What if something happens to him?"

"He'll be fine."

"How do you know that?"

"Because I'm his mother, and I know things. Get in bed, and let's get some rest while we can. He'll be up again soon."

Hunter went to use the bathroom and brush his teeth. He got in bed carefully so he wouldn't jostle Megan.

"Come here," she said, reaching for him.

"I don't want to hurt you."

"You'll hurt me if you don't come here."

He snuggled up to her, putting an arm around her—carefully.

"Much better."

He kissed the top of her head. "I'm so, so proud of you, sweetheart. You were amazing today."

"I can't believe he was born at the diner."

Hunter chuckled. "Which is kind of fitting, in a way. He's going to spend a lot of time there."

"He's already spent a lot of time there. I'm surprised he didn't smell like fried onions when he came out."

Laughing, Hunter kissed her cheek and then her lips. "Thank you so much for our beautiful son."

"Thank *you* for him. Couldn't have done it without you."

"We did it together. Our best project yet."

Izzy wasn't sure what to make of Cabot. He'd barely left her room all day, except to shower and change at a nearby hotel room earlier in the day. Cabot had returned less than an hour later with a milkshake for her and coffee for himself. He'd been there ever since, chatting with her mom and Ray, her siblings as they came and went, and with the nurses, who found him charming.

"I'm sure you must have things you need to do," Izzy said.

"It's all good. I've got a great team who can cover for me."

"What is it exactly that you do?"

"I'm involved in numerous businesses in Boston and elsewhere."

"What kind of businesses?"

"Restaurants, hotels, a marina, a boatyard, to name a few. I'm also a city councilman in Boston."

"That's a lot."

"It keeps me busy and out of trouble."

"I need to do something about my schedule." That had been her most significant concern since she realized the extent of her injuries. "I'm booked solid for the next year, starting next month. I suppose I need to start notifying people that I won't be available." She hated to do that. Over the last decade, she'd built her business from a hobby to a viable living doing the thing she loved most. "The downside of being a sole proprietor is there's no backup plan for sickness or injuries."

"What can I do to help?"

"Do you feel like sending a few texts for me?" The bulky cast on her left arm made it impossible for her to manage her phone.

"Of course." Cabot got the phone off the charger and took a seat next to Izzy's bed.

Over the next hour, while she dictated, he sent texts to her upcoming clients, notifying them of her accident and inability to keep her immediate commitments.

Responses flooded in, which Cabot read and then responded for her.

"Nothing but good wishes for a speedy recovery," he said.

"That's a relief. All these years to build a business, and all it takes is one accident to mess it up."

"Listen to what this lady said: 'You're Isabella Coleman. You're worth the wait!' I couldn't agree more with her. Your photographs are breathtaking. They'd be crazy not to wait for you."

"Thanks. I'm glad you like them."

"I love them. I ordered your book after you told me about it. I look at it all the time."

Izzy was more confused than ever. He was acting like a man who was seriously interested in her, and yet he'd not done a thing about that until she was injured. Now he'd offered to disrupt his entire life to help care for her when she went home from the hospital. At some point, they were going to have to talk about that and what it all meant.

Not now. But soon.

～

NOAH FOLLOWED BRIANNA INTO HER HOUSE, HAPPIER THAN HE probably should've been to get to spend more time with her.

"Drink?" she asked.

"What've you got?"

"Vodka, soda, water, coffee, hot chocolate."

"How about a vodka and soda, then?"

"I can do that."

Noah didn't usually drink vodka, but he was okay with making an exception if it meant hanging out with her. And when, exactly, had hanging out with her become such a big priority to him?

You know precisely when. Noah thought of their night at the Pig's Belly when she'd gone from being an annoying stranger to someone he wanted to know better.

She brought their drinks, each topped by a slice of lemon, to the sofa and sat next to him. "I'd offer to make a fire, but I haven't figured that out yet." A stack of wood sat next to a white brick fireplace.

"You want one? I'll do it for you."

"Sure, if you don't mind."

"I don't mind." He took a sip of the surprisingly refreshing drink, put it on the coffee table and got up to build her a fire. "This is one thing I remember learning from my dad. He told us if we were going to live in Vermont, we needed to learn how to build fires to stay warm in the winter. We kept a woodstove going six months a year in those days."

"You didn't have regular heat, too?"

"Nope, just the stove. It mostly heated the whole house. On the frigid nights, we 'camped' in the living room."

"I can't imagine living here in the winter without real heat."

"That was real heat. When it's all you've got, you make it work."

"I suppose so."

"I was splitting wood when I was eight. It's just a way of life around here." In a matter of minutes, he had a fire going and sat back to make sure it was going to take. Leaning in, he blew on the flames and watched them grow. Over his shoulder, he looked back at her. "Want me to show you how?"

"Yes, please." She got up and went to kneel next to him on the rug in front of the hearth.

Noah walked her through the steps, from opening and priming the flue to building a fire. "You want to start with kindling on the bottom and the larger logs on top. Tuck newspaper under the logs or get fire starters at the grocery store to make it easier. Once you have it going, blow on it until it starts to catch, and you should be good to go."

"You make it seem so easy. I'm always afraid of forgetting a step and burning the house down."

"You won't burn the house down, but you can smoke yourself out if you don't open the flue. My sisters used to forget that step sometimes."

"What did you do when that happened?"

"Opened windows. In the winter. In Vermont. It only happened a few times." Noah sat on the rug and wrapped his arms around his knees as he watched the flames dance. "Want to hear a secret?"

"Um, *yeah*…"

"I've always been a little obsessed with fire. I love to make fires and watch the flames and the way the fire devours the wood. I was a little pyromaniac when I was a kid, forever setting fires in places I shouldn't have. I got lucky that nothing ever got out of control, and no one got hurt. Me and fire, we go way back."

"Interesting that you're currently rebuilding an inn gutted by a fire."

"The irony isn't lost on me."

Brianna laughed as she settled on the rug next to him. "You're not some crazy fire-starting criminal, though, right?"

"Nah, my fire starting is contained to woodstoves and fireplaces these days."

"That's good. I'd hate to replace a sociopath with a pyromaniac."

Noah rested his chin on his forearm and looked at her. "Is that what you're doing? Replacing him with me?"

"I don't know what I'm doing. I was joking about replacing one deficiency with another."

"You have nothing to worry about where I'm concerned."

"I know."

"Do you?" He couldn't resist the need to reach out and touch her, to let one of her long curls wrap around his finger. "You've been fed a steady diet of bullshit in the past, so how are you supposed to know whether I mean what I say?"

"Something like that, but I know you're nothing like him. I know that for sure, Noah."

"I hope you do. If it's any consolation to you, I'd love nothing more than ten minutes alone in a room with your ex-husband so I can show him what happens to bullies who prey on sweet women and break their hearts."

"You'd do that for me?"

"I'd love to do that for you."

"I'd do it for you, too. I'd slap your ex right across the face and tell her how stupid she was to let such a good man get away."

He couldn't stop the smile that stretched across his face. "You really are cute when you're fierce."

"I'm not kidding! She's a fool."

"So was he." He scooted closer to her, put his arm around her and kissed the top of her head. "We've probably given them enough of our mental energy, especially when we have much better things to talk about than them."

"Like what?"

He raised her chin up to receive his kiss. "Like that." Tipping his head, he kissed her again, leaving his lips to linger for a moment this time. "And that."

"I like this conversation much better than the other one."

"Thought you might."

She placed her hand on his face and drew him into another

kiss that quickly had them both straining to get closer to each other. Her mouth opened, and her tongue dabbed against his bottom lip, making Noah groan.

They ended up stretched out on the floor in front of the fire, arms and legs intertwined, lips pressed together, kissing as if they had nothing but time to spend alone together. The real world would interfere soon enough, but for now, nothing was stopping them from having this.

In the back of his mind, the lingering concern about what she'd said the night before nagged at him. She'd said she wasn't ready for this, but it was happening anyway. In the past, he might've told that lingering concern to shut the fuck up and leave him alone to enjoy being with her.

In his postmarital meltdown present, he couldn't let it go.

CHAPTER NINETEEN

"Sometimes good things fall apart so better things can fall together."
—Marilyn Monroe

*N*oah withdrew slowly from the kiss but kept her tucked in tight against his aroused body.

"What's wrong?"

"Not a thing is wrong."

"Why'd you stop?"

Let it go, Noah. I can't. I want to, but I can't. "Last night, you said this wasn't what you wanted. I don't want to push you into something you're not ready for."

"I'm a mess, Noah. I'm a terrible bet."

He shook his head. "You're neither of those things."

"No, I am."

Kissing her, he whispered, "Not," against her lips. "You're so much stronger than you give yourself credit for."

"I'm not strong at all."

"Yes, you are. You're strong and ballsy and funny and sexy and smart. Don't you ever let anyone make you feel that you're not all those things and so much more."

"You think I'm all those things?"

"Hell yes. You come into the inn wearing that sexy white hard hat and have every guy in the place waiting to hear what you have to say because you're the boss, and we all work for you."

"They can't stand me because I'm a woman."

"That's not true. The workers respect you because you know what you're doing and because you're nice to everyone."

"Except you," she said with a bit of a smile that made her eyes twinkle.

"Except me, but I deserved your fury. I was pushing your buttons." He kissed along her jaw and down her neck, making her shiver. "You want to know why I pushed your buttons so much?"

"Yes, I want to know."

He shifted so he was on top of her and could press his erection against the V of her legs. "Because this happened every time I laid eyes on you from the second I first saw you."

"That's not true!"

"It is true, and it irritated the fuck out of me. I'm a contractor, Brianna. Architects are the bane of my existence. I couldn't be *attracted* to the architect."

Her snort of laughter was the cutest thing he'd ever heard. "You're gonna get drummed out of the contractor club when they hear about this."

"You can't tell anyone. You'll ruin me."

"How much is my silence worth to you?"

"A whole lot." He ensured her silence by kissing her with deep thrusts of his tongue into the heat of her mouth.

She tasted like lemons and honey and everything sweet.

Noah could've kissed her for hours and not wanted for anything more—until her hands worked their way under his multiple layers of clothes and landed on his back, sparking a desperate need to feel more of her skin against his. "Tell me to stop."

"No."

"This isn't what you want."

She curled her legs around his hips and pressed against his hard cock. "It *is* what I want."

"Just this or more?"

"Just this for now. The rest? I don't know."

Noah knew he ought to stop while he still could. At some point in the last few days, she had become a big deal to him. If they kept this up, he'd end up crushed—again—when she left. But damned if he could bring himself to do what he knew he should. Wrapped up in her, steeped in the delicious scent of her and with her lips still damp from his kisses, protecting himself was the least of his concerns.

He slid a hand under her sweater and lifted himself enough to slide it up and over her head. "I cannot believe you're wearing *that* under your Carhartt."

"This old thing?" She placed her hands on either side of her bra and pushed her breasts together.

"I'll be sporting wood every second we're at work knowing what you've got on under your work clothes."

"Wait until you see the bottom part."

"Yes, please." It was all he could do not to pant like a dog in heat as he pulled back to get the rest of her clothes off, nearly swallowing his tongue when he uncovered a scrap of fabric that left very little to the imagination.

Thankfully, his imagination was super fertile where she was concerned. He bent over her, pressing his lips to her core through the thin fabric and breathing in the rich, feminine scent of her desire.

"Noah."

"Yes, Brianna?" He pressed his tongue against her clit.

"I, uh… Ummmm."

"You were saying?"

"I don't know what I was saying."

Laughing, he pulled her panties down her legs and then went back to what he'd been doing, now with nothing between his tongue and her. God, she was so sweet and responsive and sexy. He could spend hours pleasuring her and never get tired of how she reacted to everything he did. But he desperately wanted to be inside her, to be joined with her.

And then he remembered he didn't have condoms. "Son of a bitch."

His harsh words startled her. "What's wrong?"

"No condoms."

"We don't need them."

"What?"

"I'm on long-term birth control, and I'm clean. I haven't been with anyone but you since my husband, and after that, I had all the tests."

"I'm clean, too. I got tested recently."

"Then we're good to go."

"Sex with you? Without a condom? I hope you're ready for this to be fast."

Her joyful giggle made him ache in the place where his heart had once lived before betrayal had caused it to shrivel up and die. But here with her, he felt it coming alive again. He teetered on the precipice of something new and vital. After what he'd been through, that ought to scare the shit out of him.

But he wasn't scared of her. He was thrilled, even if he understood that the highest highs could lead to the lowest lows. As much as he'd loved his wife—and he'd truly loved her—he'd always felt a little off-balance with her, as if it could all go wrong at any second. He hadn't had the sense of connection to her that he did with Brianna. And wasn't it ironic that the connection had come from their shared experience with betrayal?

Having her arms around him as he made love to her felt better than anything had in, well, forever. He'd never felt this good with any woman, even the one he'd married.

Brianna drew him into a kiss that cleared his mind of every thought but one: *I want to be with this woman, no matter what it takes.*

~

At lunchtime the next day, Noah left the inn and drove to Gray's house, hoping to catch his brother between clients. Gray answered the door holding a sandwich and gestured for him to come in.

"Hungry?"

"I was going to grab something on the way back to work."

"I made tenderloin last night. It melts in your mouth. Want a sandwich?"

"Uh, yeah."

Gray laughed as he made the sandwich. "The secret is in the au jus."

"I'm officially drooling."

"I almost like the sandwich the next day better than the initial meal." He put Noah's plate in the microwave for thirty seconds, ground some pepper on top and delivered it to him at the table along with a Coke and a bag of chips.

"Thanks. I wasn't expecting you to feed me."

"Happy to see you twice in two days. That has to be a record."

Noah felt guilty for being so absent the last few years and making his family worry about him. "Sorry about that." He took a bite of the sandwich and moaned. "Holy hell, that's fantastic."

"Right?" Gray took another bite and chased it with a drink of water. "You seem good. I can't help but wonder if your pretty architect friend might be the reason."

"She is," Noah said, taking his brother by surprise. It wasn't like him to be forthcoming about anything, especially his private life. "I like her a lot."

"I can see why. Although, the shit with Brianna's ex is a lot to take on."

"It's much worse than the shit I went through with mine, but that was pretty bad, too."

"Is that so?"

Noah nodded and forced himself to tell his brother why he'd come. "I caught her in bed with Miguel."

Gray's eyes widened, and his face froze with shock. "Miguel, as in your foreman Miguel, who was also one of your closest friends?"

"The one and only."

"Oh my God, Noah. I knew he left around the same time she did, but I never put that together."

"Neither did I. They made a total fool of me."

"And you *caught* them?"

Noah nodded. "After a night out with the search-and-rescue team. They were asleep in our bed."

"Ugh, Noah. I'm so sorry."

Noah shrugged off the predictable blast of pain that resurfaced any time he recalled that dreadful day.

"What'd you do?"

"I punched him in the face and fired him. And I told her to get the fuck out of my house and not to come back."

"I don't even know what to say to you. No wonder you've gone deep underground the last few years."

"It was what I needed to do to get past it. I focused on work and just said fuck it to everything else."

"I don't blame you, but I do wonder why you're telling me this now."

"I never got divorced, and suddenly that seems like something I need to do."

"Ah, shit, well, we can get that done. Do you know where she is?"

"No idea. I hoped you might have an investigator who could find her and get her out of my life."

"I've got someone I can put on it."

"I should've done this a long time ago. I just didn't have any good reason to."

"And now you do?"

"Maybe. I like Brianna. And I like that she gets what I've been through, because she's been there herself—even worse in her case."

"I couldn't believe the things she was saying he did. What a scumbag."

"Seriously. She'd told me some of it before, but I was still shocked by the new stuff that came out when she was talking to you."

"What happens when you finish the inn, and she goes back to Boston?"

"I have no idea. She's going to be done there before much longer. I guess we'll see what's what when it's time for her to go."

"It's nice to see you living again, Noah, but I'd hate to see you get your hopes up about her and then have them dashed when she leaves."

"Maybe I'll go with her."

"Really? Your whole life and your business are here."

"I could get a job there, and it'd be kind of nice not to have the responsibility of running the business anymore."

"You say that now, but you've been self-employed a long time. It'd be tough to go back to working for someone else."

"I'd hold out for a good fit, and I'm not saying it's going to happen. I'm just saying I wouldn't rule it out."

"I understand better than you might think. If Emma hadn't been into moving up here, I would've moved to New York to be with her and Simone. When it's right, it's right, and you should do whatever it takes to make it work."

"That's the plan, but first, I need to get divorced."

"I'll take care of that."

BRIANNA COULDN'T STOP THINKING ABOUT HER NIGHT WITH NOAH and how he'd stayed with her, even while knowing it would cause a stir with his siblings when they discovered he'd been out all night. Noah said he didn't care what they thought. Knowing how little he'd told them about his private life, that made her feel extra special. He didn't care if they knew he'd stayed with her.

And she was so glad he had.

She was falling for the sexy contractor, even as she continued to deal with the fallout of her last relationship. Part of her felt like maybe she ought to put this thing with Noah on hold out of fairness to him, but she couldn't bring herself to go back to where she'd been two nights ago when she'd told him she wasn't ready for what was happening between them—ready or not.

After last night, there was no going back to before everything had changed with him. There was only forward, hopefully *with* him.

He'd gone somewhere at lunchtime, saying he'd be back in an hour, and had been quiet and withdrawn since he returned.

The electricians were all over the place doing their work, which made it difficult to do much of anything else. Noah sent his crew home early with orders to be back at seven the following day.

Brianna found him in one of the guest bathrooms, measuring, making notes and talking to himself as he worked.

"Do you ever get an answer?"

Startled, he spun around, saw her leaning against the doorframe and smiled. "I'm capable of in-depth conversations with myself."

"You want to get out of here and take a walk or something? It's forty-five degrees, which is like summer around here."

"Haha, it gets much warmer than that in the summer."

"For what? Like, five days a year?"

"Easily six. Sometimes seven. And yes, I'd love to get out of here. Let me just finish this, and we can go for a hike."

"I said walk, not hike."

"A walk is a hike in Vermont."

"I'm not signing on for any treks up the side of a mountain or anything."

"So noted."

"Why are you remeasuring in here anyway? You should have all the measurements."

"Just double-checking."

"Haven't you learned to trust me on these things?"

Amusement danced in his gorgeous eyes as he surprised her with a kiss. "I trust you more than I've trusted anyone in a very long time."

Suddenly, she realized they were no longer talking about bathroom measurements but something much more important. "I trust you, too."

"That's a pretty big deal for both of us."

"Yes, it is."

"I want you to know that at lunchtime, I went to see Gray about something I should've taken care of years ago."

She was almost afraid to ask. "What's that?"

"I need to get divorced."

"Noah! You never got *divorced*?"

"Nope. That would've required me to contact her, and that was the last fucking thing I wanted to do."

"But still…"

"I know. I should've done it. I just didn't want to, and I had no reason to. Until now."

"Why now?"

He slid an arm around her waist and rested his forehead on hers. "After last night, you have to ask me that?"

"What do you see happening here?"

"I don't know. All I know is I like being with you. I like how I feel when you're around, and I want as much of that feeling as I can get for as long as I can have it."

"That's starting to sound like a pretty big deal."

"Could be."

She knew him well enough by now to understand that him saying even that much was the biggest deal of all.

"Does hearing that freak you out?"

"Not like it probably should." She looked up at him, a smile tugging at her sexy lips. "I'm being sued by my ex. My divorce isn't final. Your divorce hasn't even started. I live in Boston. You live here. I mean, what could go wrong?"

Noah grinned at her. "Our timing is horrible."

"The worst."

"And yet…" Leaning in so close, his lips a heartbeat away from hers, he made her breathless.

"And yet what?" she asked.

"This." He kissed her without seeming to care that one of the many electricians working in the building could catch them.

"Ah, that."

"Mmm, that. It's all I seem to think about." He tipped his head and kissed her again from another angle. "And this, too."

By the time he finished kissing her, she had fists full of his coat, and every part of her was on fire for him. "Maybe we should hike another day."

"What would you rather do instead?"

"This." She pressed against his erection as her hands encircled his waist and cupped his ass. "And some of that, too."

"You're killing me."

"Same."

"I wanted to take you somewhere, do something fun."

"Take me to my house. We'll have fun."

"I meant fun that isn't the sexy kind."

"Can't we have both?"

He held her close, nuzzling her neck until her hard hat fell off with a loud *whack* that made them laugh. "We absolutely can have both, but first, we're going to hike."

She moaned when he withdrew from her. "That's just mean."

"How so?"

"You got me all… interested."

"I assume you'll still be interested later."

"If I don't fall off any cliffs."

"I won't let you get anywhere near any cliffs."

"You say that now."

Noah cuffed her chin playfully. "I'm already standing at the edge of a cliff with you. It wouldn't take much for me to take a pretty serious fall."

Amazed to hear him admit such a thing, Brianna could only stare at him for the longest time.

"Am I standing on that edge by myself?"

She swallowed hard and shook her head. "Not at all. I'm right there with you."

"Look, I know the timing stinks, and lots of things are a mess for both of us, but this..." He rested his hands on her hips and kissed her. "This is..."

"It's good. Very, very good."

"Yeah."

"And maybe," she said, "after everything that's happened to both of us, we deserve to feel good."

"We do deserve it. Let's stay focused on things that make us feel good while we deal with the shit that doesn't, okay?"

"I can do that."

"Before we hike, I need to get you a good pair of hiking boots."

"I can get my own hiking boots."

He guided her out ahead of him toward the stairs. "I insist. My treat."

"No way. You're not buying me boots."

"I get a family discount, and I'm not sharing it with you unless you let me get them for you."

"How much is the discount?"

"Forty percent."

"Fine, then you can buy them, but I'm buying dinner."

"Fine."

"Fine."

He grabbed her ass and squeezed it. "Yes, you certainly are."

"Knock it off, Noah. I'm busy fighting with you." Lately, she loved fighting with him. It was the most fun she'd had since her life went sideways. He was right about focusing on the stuff that made them feel good while dealing with the crap that didn't.

Noah asked the lead electrician to lock up when they finished for the day.

"Will do," the man said.

"I never leave when subs are still working," he said. "But I've been doing business with him for years, and he's fine on his own."

"It's nice to have people you can count on."

"Indeed, it is."

CHAPTER TWENTY

*"A broken heart is just the growing pains necessary so that you can love
more completely when the real thing comes along."*
—J.S.B. Morse

*A*s they left the inn, his sister Ally was coming toward
them from the parking lot. "Ah, just the duo I was
hoping to find."

"Is Izzy okay?" Noah asked.

"She's fine. They're hoping to send her home in a day or two."

"That's good news."

"I came to find you to tell you that Nessa is cooking Mexican
for dinner, and you're both invited."

"I'm invited to my own house?" Noah asked, smiling.

"After much debate, we decided to invite you. Brianna was at
the top of the guest list."

"I see how things work around here," Noah said.

Ally grinned at her brother. "We already like her better than
you."

"It was the lasagna, wasn't it?" Brianna asked.

"That certainly didn't hurt anything. Dinner is at seven, and
Nessa said don't be late."

"We'll be there," Noah said.

"What can we bring?" Brianna asked.

"Not a thing. Nessa said to tell you that. She said for you to bring beer, Noah."

"Will do. We're going for a little hike before the sun disappears. We'll be there afterward."

"See you then."

Brianna and Noah walked to his family's store across the parking lot from the inn.

"Have I told you before that this is my favorite store in the entire world?" Brianna asked him.

"You might've mentioned something about that."

"It's magical. I come in here almost every day just to poke around, and every time, I see something I haven't seen before."

"It was my favorite place in the world when I was a kid."

"I can see why. I love how it's a family business that's been passed through the generations.

"It is, and like I said, everyone still speaks to each other, which is a big accomplishment in a family business."

"That's so true! The brothers I work for are always at each other's throats about something. It's so stressful."

"That has to suck."

"It's the worst. That, and the shit with Rem, were the reasons I couldn't say yes fast enough to the job up here."

"I'm glad you said yes to the job up here."

"Are you?"

He put an arm around her waist. "Uh-huh, very glad indeed."

"Noah?"

His arm fell from her back. "Hey, Charley and Ella. How's it going?"

"Good," the darker-haired woman said. "How are you?"

"I'm hanging in there. Busy next door."

"It's looking great and going up fast," the one with lighter hair said, glancing at Brianna with curiosity.

"Brianna, these are my cousins Ella and Charley. Ladies, this is Brianna Esposito, the architect working on the inn."

"Oh," Charley said. "The architect. I thought you two did nothing but fight."

"That was so last week," Brianna said, making them laugh.

"Brianna needs hiking boots," Noah said.

"We just got some new ones in," Charley said. "I can help you find the right size."

"That'd be great," Noah said. "How's the new baby doing?"

"He's adorable," Ella said. "We were over there at lunchtime, and he's settling right in. Even slept for a few hours during the night."

"Glad to hear it. That was pretty crazy doings at the diner yesterday."

"We heard you were there when it happened!" Charley said.

"I was. I thought Hunter was going to implode, but he held it together for Megan. How's she feeling?"

"Sore but thrilled to have her little guy finally here," Ella said as she followed them through housewares to the shoe department.

"And how's Sarah doing?" To Brianna, he said, "Ella's daughter was born right before Christmas."

"Oh, congratulations. I told Noah I'm going to need a map to understand your family."

"Don't feel bad," Charley said. "My partner, Tyler, has been around for a while now, and I'm still drawing pictures for him."

"That makes me feel a little better."

"To answer your question, Noah, my Sarah is lovely and delightful and already has her Mommy and Daddy completely in love with her."

"Happy for you, cousin," Noah said.

"Thank you. Stop by to meet your cousin any time."

"I'll do that."

With Charley and Ella's expert assistance, they had Brianna outfitted in new hiking boots twenty minutes later.

"Do we still have that awesome silk long underwear that keeps people super warm?" Noah asked.

"We do," Charley said.

"Can I get some for Brianna in what, medium?"

"Medium is good," Brianna said.

"Coming right up."

Charley went to get the long underwear and returned with three colors—off-white, light pink and black.

Brianna took a good look at each of them. "I'll take the black, please."

"Put them on my tab, please," Noah said.

"Wait, I was supposed to buy you dinner in exchange for the boots, but now your sister is making dinner," Brianna said. "And you're not buying me silk underwear."

"You can buy dinner tomorrow night," Noah said. "And it's *long* underwear, which doesn't even count as underwear, so stuff it."

His cousins watched their exchange with interest.

"So are you guys… like…"

"Hush, Charley," Ella said. "It's none of our business what they're doing."

"Yes, it is our business," Charley said. "Everything in this family is our business, just like it was when you started seeing Gavin and I started seeing Tyler, and everyone was up in our crap."

"That's true," Ella said. "So, what gives?"

"We're hanging out," Noah said. "Having fun and going hiking before we lose the daylight. So as nice as it's been to see you ladies, I'm afraid we have to go." With his hand on Brianna's back, he moved her toward the exit.

"Thank you for your help," Brianna said to his cousins.

"Pleasure to meet you," Ella called after them.

"Phew, we escaped their clutches," Noah said.

"They were very nice."

"They're great, but they would've stayed there all day trying to get the scoop on us."

"It's so cool how you run into family everywhere you go in this town."

"I love my family, but I like my privacy, too, and that's hard to come by with a relative on every street corner."

Brianna laughed at how he said that as if he had family members planted on every corner. "I think it's an awesome way to live, surrounded by people who love you and want the best for you."

"It's pretty awesome. Between siblings and cousins, we always had lots of friends to play with—and fight with—as kids."

"Your moms must've had the patience of saints with eighteen kids between them."

"They were pretty chill. Charley says there was vodka in their coffee cups when we were all young and used to spend time together."

"Who could blame them for drinking with that many kids to oversee?"

"Not me."

"Do you want kids?"

The question took him by surprise as he held the door to his truck and gave her a hand up. "I used to."

"Not anymore?"

He shrugged and closed the door.

Brianna hoped she hadn't struck a painful nerve with the question. When he got in the driver's side, she said, "Sorry if I shouldn't have asked that."

"It's fine. You can ask me anything. You know that." He started the truck and headed for Elm Street, taking a right turn out of the lot. "I figured I'd have a few by now. I didn't want eight, but three or four, maybe. But we all know why that didn't happen."

"It hasn't happened *yet*."

"I'm getting old."

"You are not."

"Yes, I am. I'm going to be thirty-six. I never wanted to be sixty and sending kids off to college, but that's where I'm at if I have kids now."

"Sixty is the new forty."

"Maybe so, but I'd like to be able to retire at some point, and college is expensive. Even with a scholarship, I had to take loans to live. I just finished paying them off two years ago."

"Congratulations. That's a huge accomplishment. At this rate, I'll never pay off mine, especially when I have to deal with lawsuits."

"That lawsuit doesn't have a snowball's chance in hell of going anywhere."

She appreciated his certainty. "I still have to pay to defend and countersue, and I'm paying for the divorce, too, for all the good that's done me. My cousin's husband has done what he can, but I'm still married almost a year after I filed."

"I know it doesn't seem like it now, but someday after it's all resolved, it'll be nothing but a distant bad memory. It won't always loom as large as it does right now."

"I hope you're right, but something tells me that he plans to make my life as miserable as he can for as long as he can."

"You ought to let Gray look at the divorce situation, too. He's good at what he does. He might be able to get both those things resolved for you."

"I'll ask him about the divorce. It's all ridiculous."

"It's beyond ridiculous, but try not to worry. You've got the truth on your side."

"For all the good that's done me."

"I have to believe that still matters, Bri. You can prove he stole and lied and gaslighted you. That's going to mean something in the end. I know it will."

"Thanks. It helps to hear that. You know more about what Rem did than anyone else in my life, even my cousin, who knows most of it. I was so embarrassed by it all that I only told people enough so they'd understand why I wasn't with him anymore."

"I'm glad you told me, and I'm here any time you need to talk about it."

"I'm sick of talking about it. How can you not be sick of listening?"

"I like talking to you. I don't care what we're talking about."

"Even my psycho ex?"

"Even him. I have one, too, don't forget."

"I haven't forgotten, and I need to ask you how you feel about asking Gray to find her and start divorce proceedings."

"I don't feel anything about it. I feel nothing for her, except a sudden, burning desire to be free of her."

"Any particular reason?"

"There's this other woman."

"Anyone I know?"

"Nah, you haven't met her."

She gave him a playful shove that had him laughing as the truck swerved and nearly connected with the moose standing in the middle of the road.

Noah slammed on the brakes, and the truck fishtailed wildly but came to a stop three feet from where Fred stood, staring at them like they were the problem.

"Holy. *Shit.*"

"Brianna, meet Fred, the Butler town moose."

"Stop it right now. *That* is Fred, the town moose?"

"That's him, in the flesh."

"He's *massive.*" She turned to look behind them. "Back up before he comes at us."

"He won't. Fred's a pussycat."

He was out of his mind. "*What?* Seriously, Noah, let's get out of here."

But instead of getting out of there, Noah lowered the window and stuck his head out. "Hey, Fred. How's it hanging?"

"Moo."

Brianna nearly levitated out of the car at the loudest *moo* in recorded history. "Noah…"

"You're freaking out my friend, Freddie boy. She's new around here and isn't used to friends like you."

"This is the craziest place I've ever been. Are you *talking* to a *moose?*"

"I'm talking to Fred. I've known him most of my life. We go way back."

"I can't with this. I just cannot."

Laughing, Noah said to Fred, "Can you maybe move your ass so we can go by before my friend has a stroke?"

"I think I might've already had one."

Fred let out another loud moo that made Brianna startle before he strode off into the woods to continue on his way.

"So that was Fred."

"I can't talk. I'm still hyperventilating."

"You could come face-to-face with him in town, and he'd never hurt you. He's super gentle. My cousin Hannah is raising a baby moose named Dexter at her house. Fred comes by for play-dates with him every day. I can take you to meet Dex if you'd like."

"Is this place for real? Your cousin is raising a baby moose. At her house."

"Yep, and she even convinced her husband, Nolan, to let him into the house. We're not sure how she pulled that off, but Dex has a bed by the fire now."

"When I go back to Boston and tell people about what goes on up here, they aren't going to believe me. They're going to say I'm making up the fact that my friend Noah's cousin has a baby moose *sleeping in her house.*"

"Hannah is a moose whisperer."

"Come on."

"No, really. You should see the way she gets Fred to do what-ever she tells him to. It's kind of amazing. The best part, though, is watching Nolan have a complete meltdown about his pregnant wife talking to a full-grown bull moose like he's the next-door neighbor."

"It's comforting to hear that someone in this town has a lick of sense."

"Aw, come on, don't tell me this place isn't growing on you."

"What's not to like? No cell service, gigantic moose roaming the streets, baby moose sleeping inside houses, cold that makes your lungs ache from breathing, cars that fall off mountain roads. Have I forgotten anything?"

Grinning at her litany, he said, "Breathtaking scenery, interesting people who make sure you're never bored, so much snow that you have no choice but to snuggle by the fire for months on end. It doesn't all suck."

"I hope you don't think I'm saying that it does. Vermont is beautiful, even with the gigantic moose that stands in the middle of the road."

"That moose led my cousin to his wife."

"I can't believe she stayed in town after hitting the moose. I would've run for the hills."

"Well, she couldn't really because she stepped out of the car into shin-deep mud. Did I mention Vermont has a mud season?"

"It just gets more charming by the minute."

"I know, right? But our incredible foliage season makes up for the mud."

"I'll have to take your word on that."

"You should stick around up here so you get the full picture before you make any final judgments. You've only seen the worst part, although some of us think winter is the best season because of the skiing and other winter sports."

"You would think that because you're all certifiable up here. I think the cold has gotten to you and pickled your brains or something. You think talking to a moose is normal."

"It is normal."

"It's not."

"Is."

"Isn't." She had more fun with him than she'd had with any man—ever. Even the one she'd married and thought she'd love forever.

Noah turned onto her street so she could change before their hike and slowed the truck when he saw a Vermont State Police SUV parked outside her house. "What the hell?"

Brianna's stomach dropped. She wanted to tell Noah to keep driving so she wouldn't have to deal with whatever fresh hell had come to find her.

He pulled into the driveway, turned off the truck and looked over at her. "Whatever this is, I'm here, and it's going to be fine."

Brianna had begun to believe that nothing would ever be "fine" again for her. She had to force herself to get out of the truck to meet Noah and the state police officer in the driveway.

"I'm Officer Brinkman with the Vermont State Police. Are you Brianna Denning?"

"That was my married name. I've gone back to Esposito since my marriage ended. What's this about?"

"I didn't realize you were no longer married. You are listed as next of kin for Remington Denning."

"We're not technically divorced yet, but we haven't been together in more than a year. I'm not sure why I'm his next of kin."

"What do you need with her, Officer?"

"And you are?"

"Noah Coleman. A friend."

"I'm sorry to have to tell you that your ex-husband has been murdered."

The words landed like a roar in her ears as her knees gave way. Only Noah's arm around her waist kept her from falling.

Rem was dead.

CHAPTER TWENTY-ONE

*"I wish I were a little girl again because skinned
knees are easier to fix than a broken heart."*
—Julia Roberts

fter the nightmare Rem had put her through, Brianna shouldn't have cared that he was dead. Hell, she ought to be relieved and happy that he was out of her life forever. But the part of her that'd once loved him with all her heart refused to be ignored. "Wh-what happened?"

"He was found in the Boston Public Garden. He'd been stabbed multiple times."

Noah squeezed her shoulder, letting her know he was there.

Brianna leaned into him as she processed what the officer was telling her. She refused to cry over the man who'd put her through hell. She would *not* cry. "Ha-have his parents been told?"

"Yes, ma'am. They told us where we could find you. They asked that you call them when you're able to."

Brianna processed that information along with the fact that Rem was dead. Someone had murdered him. She knew she ought to be surprised, but she wasn't. Not like she should've been. When you treated people the way he'd treated her—and no doubt others—eventually, it caught up to you.

"The Mass State Police are interested in speaking with you. They've asked us to transport you to the Massachusetts state line, where they'll meet you."

"Why do they want to speak with me? I haven't seen or talked to him in more than a year."

"I'm not privy to the why, ma'am. I only have the request to transport you."

"Is she a suspect?" Noah asked.

"I'm sorry that I don't have that information."

"We'd like to know more about what they want with her before she goes anywhere," Noah said. "And her attorney will want to be there."

Thank God he had his wits about him, because her brain wasn't functioning after hearing the news that Rem was dead. That he'd been *murdered.*

"Let me call them," the officer said.

"We're going inside to wait for her attorney to get here. She'd be happy to talk to them from here with her attorney present."

"Are you a lawyer?" the officer asked.

"No, but my brother is, and I know just enough about how these things work to know that she's not going anywhere with you or talking to the police until he's here. We'll be inside." He put his hand around her arm and directed her toward the back door. "Come on, Bri. Let's go in and call Gray." Outside the door, he said, "Keys?"

She handed him her keys. "What is happening, Noah?"

"I don't know, but we're going to figure it out. Don't worry."

Don't worry. Right. Hysteria bubbled up inside Brianna, threatening to spill out at any second. When they were inside, Noah went straight to the phone on the counter and called his brother. She could hear him saying words, but none of them registered with her. She was thankful for his ability to function while she was too shocked to do anything more than sit on the sofa and try not to be sick.

The minute she'd learned the full extent of Rem's deception, the love she'd once felt for him had died a quick but painful death. Love had turned to hatred in three surreal days in which all the hopes and dreams she'd had tied up in him had disappeared in a haze of grief and disbelief that she'd only recently started to emerge from.

But hearing he was dead, that he'd been murdered...

She was going to be sick. Bolting for the bathroom, she made it just in time to lean over the toilet and throw up as she broke down into sobs that shook her entire body.

Noah suddenly materialized to hold back her hair. "It's okay, sweetheart. You're okay."

No. Brianna shook her head. She'd never be okay again if she felt actual heartbreak at hearing the man who'd ruined her life was dead. What the hell was wrong with her that he could still do this to her?

"Yes." After wiping her face with a towel, Noah sat with her on the bathroom floor, keeping his arms around her as she cried it out. "You're going to be just fine. I promise."

Brianna had no idea how long they were there before she heard Grayson come in and call for them.

Noah kissed the top of her head and got up. "Come out when you're ready."

"Noah..."

"I'm here, Brianna, and I'm not going anywhere."

He'd never know what his steady presence meant to her at that moment. "Thank you."

Noah left the bathroom and went to meet Gray, rattled by her reaction to the news of her ex-husband's death. He hated to see her so upset.

"Thanks for coming," he said to Grayson.

"No problem. Is she okay?"

"Not at all, and we have no clue what the Mass State Police want with her."

"Let's find out, shall we?" Grayson went to the door and signaled for the state trooper to come in. "I'm Grayson Coleman."

The officer shook hands with Gray. "Officer Brinkman. I've spoken with Mass State Police, and they're willing to talk to her on the phone but reserve the right to request that she come in for a formal interview."

"They're going to need to give us grounds for that."

"They're aware of that."

"Let me see if she's up for talking." Noah returned to the bathroom to find Brianna right where he'd left her. Her new hiking boots reminded him how quickly their plans had gone to shit. "Gray is here. Are you up for talking to the police, sweetheart?"

"I don't get what they want with me. I don't know anything."

"You just need to tell them that." He helped her up and kept his hands on her hips while she brushed her teeth and hair.

"Sorry to be such a mess."

"Don't be. It's a shock to hear that kind of news."

"I don't get why I'm so upset. After everything he did…"

"At one time, you loved him. That's why you're upset. Despite what he did, you still care."

"I don't, though. I don't care about him."

"Not like you once did, but anyone would be upset after hearing about the murder of someone they once loved."

"It's all very confusing."

"I know, honey, but let's talk to the cops and get rid of them. We can talk about all of it when they're gone."

"Okay."

Noah took her by the hand and led her to the living room.

Gray and the officer were seated in chairs, leaving the sofa for them.

"I've got Detective Mercer with the Mass State Police on the phone," Brinkman said. "He's working with Boston Police on this case. Detective Mercer, Brianna Esposito is here along with her attorney, Grayson Coleman, and his brother Noah, who's a friend of hers."

"Grayson Coleman. Why do I know that name?"

"Our paths crossed a few times when I worked in Boston."

"Ah, right. Well, thanks for getting on a call with us. Ms. Esposito, I'm sorry for your loss."

"It's not my loss. I split with him more than a year ago."

"When was the last time you saw or talked to him?"

"Last Christmas Eve, when I confronted him about being involved with multiple other women and how he'd stolen from our joint bank account. Since then, I've only spoken to him through lawyers."

"And seen him?"

"Also that day. Not since then."

"Not even in court?"

"We haven't been to court because he refuses to engage in the divorce proceeding." Brianna caught herself when she remembered he was dead. "I guess I should say he refused. Past tense." She was no longer married, and under any other circumstances, that would be cause for celebration. But under these circumstances, she didn't feel much like celebrating.

"I'm going to be honest with you, Ms. Esposito. Your ex-husband told several people that if anything happened to him, they needed to tell the police to speak to you."

After everything she'd learned about the man she'd married, Brianna knew she shouldn't be shocked to hear such a thing. But she was shocked speechless. It took a full minute for her to recover her senses enough to realize they expected her to reply.

"Ms. Esposito? Do you know why he might've said that?"

"Because he wanted to hurt me," she said softly.

"Are you aware that Mr. Denning had antisocial personality disorder?" Grayson asked.

"I wasn't," the detective said. "He had an actual diagnosis?"

"I can't say that for certain," Brianna said, "because I wasn't privy to his medical or mental health records. But I can tell you that his behavior and actions are indicative of a textbook case. His parents would tell you that. I can put you in touch with the therapist I saw in Boston until recently and give her the authority to tell you anything you want to know about what I endured with him."

"That would help," the detective said.

"Let me get my phone so I can give you her number." Brianna got up and walked into the bedroom, her legs unsteady beneath her. Rem had been murdered, and he'd set her up to take the fall. Would the nightmare ever end? She got the phone off the charger and returned to the living room, scrolling through her contacts until she found the one she needed. "You can tell her I gave you her number, and I'll text her to let her know she'll hear from you."

"Thank you. Can you tell me where you've been for the last forty-eight hours?"

"Right here with me," Noah said. "Around the clock."

He never hesitated, even if that meant telling his brother they were sleeping together.

"We work together," Noah added. "And we're together outside of work." He reached for her hand and held on tight, the heat of his hand making her realize how cold hers was. "She hasn't left Vermont in more than two months."

"That's helpful information," the detective said. "Do you have any idea why your ex-husband would've told people to look at you if anything happened to him?"

"Because he's a psycho! It would take me twelve hours to tell you the full extent of the nightmare he put me through. He just served me with a lawsuit yesterday, and now this."

"What was the lawsuit about?"

"He's seeking damages for me telling people he's a sociopath, which he is." Brianna needed to change the *is* to *was*, but hadn't fully processed that he was dead. "No doubt there were a lot of people who wanted him dead. He lied and cheated and schemed and had zero remorse toward the people he hurt. His parents can tell you how he was. They know."

"We have detectives interviewing them later today. I think we have what we need from you. Since you have an alibi, we won't take any more of your time, but we ask that you stay available in case we need more information."

"Th-that's fine," Brianna said, her nerves shredded.

"Can you think of anyone else we should talk to, any close friends or business associates?"

Brianna named a few people. "But that was more than a year ago. He tended to go through friends once they figured out his racket. I have no idea if any of them are still in his life. I've spoken with his parents a few times, but other than that, I've had no contact with anyone else in his group."

"That's helpful. Thank you."

"I want to clarify that my client is not, in any way, a suspect in this case," Grayson said.

"She's not a suspect at this time," the detective replied. "We reserve the right to interview her again, should the need arise."

"Understood," Grayson said.

"Thank you again for your time, Ms. Esposito."

Officer Brinkman ended the call and put the portable phone on the coffee table. "We appreciate your cooperation. I won't take any more of your time."

Grayson got up to walk him out and returned a minute later, taking the seat across from them. "I don't think you have anything to worry about, Brianna. That was a formality so they could rule you out."

Noah kept his arm around her, infusing her with his heat and support. "What can we do for you, Bri?"

"I don't know. I just don't know what to think of this or how to feel or anything."

"No matter how things ended with him or the hell you've been through at his hands, it's still a shock to hear he was murdered," Grayson said.

"Yes, it is," she said with a sigh. "Even if it solves a lot of problems for me." She glanced at Noah. "At least one of us isn't married anymore, not that I'd want it to happen this way. As much as I hated him for what he did to me, I didn't want him to die."

"We know that, sweetheart," Noah said. "Of course you didn't."

"Is it okay to speak freely about your situation in front of Brianna?" Grayson asked.

"Yes," Noah said.

"My guy thinks he's located her outside of Burlington. He's going there tomorrow to check it out."

"That was fast," Noah said.

"He's good. That's why I use him. I'll let you know when I hear from him, and I'll get the paperwork started in the meantime."

"Thanks, Gray, and thanks for coming when I called you."

"No problem."

"Yes, thank you, Grayson," Brianna said. "I appreciate you being here and having my back."

"We've got you covered," Gray said. "I know it's easy for me to say, but try not to worry. You've got the truth on your side."

"The truth..." Brianna shook her head, filled with dismay. "It's amazing how people manipulate the truth. Rem was a master at that. He could make you believe you were losing it when he'd rewrite history or say something didn't happen the way you know it did. I used to think people were essentially good. He showed me otherwise."

"The deficiency was on him, Brianna, not you," Grayson said.

"All you did was love the guy. I'm going to get out of your hair so you can get some rest. Call me if there's anything else I can do."

"You're the best," Brianna said. "Thanks again."

"Happy to do what I can to help."

Noah got up to walk him out, and the two men embraced. She'd enjoyed watching the bond that Noah shared with his siblings, despite his professed loner tendencies.

That was when she remembered his sisters had invited them to dinner. "You should call to let your sisters know why we're not there for dinner."

"Oh crap. I'd forgotten. I'll do that now. Is it okay to tell them what happened?"

"Sure."

Noah reached for the phone on the table and placed the call to his house.

Brianna could hear loud music in the background when one of them answered the phone.

"Hey, it's me," Noah said. "Brianna just found out that her ex-husband was murdered in Boston. We had to deal with cops and stuff, so we're not going to make it over there."

She couldn't hear the other side of the conversation.

"No, I don't think she'd be up for that tonight."

"Up for what?" Brianna asked.

"They want to bring dinner over here."

"It's fine. They can."

"Are you sure?"

Brianna nodded. "I could use the distraction."

"All right, then. Bri says to come on over, but don't come in hot, you hear me?" Noah gave the address to Brianna's house and ended the call. "I apologize in advance for the chaos they're going to bring."

"I'm looking forward to it. They're fun, and it'll help to be surrounded by friends tonight."

"You are surrounded by friends. I hope you know that."

"I'm glad you're here. Once again, you're helping me through a very rough day just by being here and holding my hand."

"Your hand is my favorite hand to hold." He brought it to his lips and kissed the back of it. "You're going to be okay. Tell me you know that."

"I know."

"You've had a terrible shock, and your feelings are understandably all over the place."

"They are. If you told me earlier today that I could still feel anything other than disgust for him, I would've laughed. But when I heard what'd happened to him…"

"That's perfectly normal, Bri. Once upon a time, you loved the guy more than anything. It's natural to feel sad that he's dead."

"I feel sad to know that he probably crossed someone who wasn't having his shit, that his condition most likely led to his death. He never had a chance because there's no cure for antisocial personality disorder. He wasn't going to suddenly develop the compassion for others that the rest of us take for granted. He just wasn't capable."

"The whole thing is sad. When they said Boston Public Garden, I thought of being there last June at my cousin Wade's wedding. They took pictures in the garden."

"Rem hated it there. He was allergic to everything." And then she was sobbing again, her heart breaking for the man she'd thought he was, only to find out that man had been an illusion, a figment of her imagination, a con man of the highest order.

Noah held her close to him, rubbing her back in soothing circles.

"I have no idea why I'm crying."

"It doesn't matter why. Just let it out."

"I need to call his parents," she said ten minutes later.

"Do you want to do that now and get it out of the way?"

"I suppose so."

Noah reached for the phone and handed it to her.

Brianna held it in her hand for a long time before she dialed the number from memory.

He stood watch over her, wishing he could spare her from the pain this news had caused her.

"Hi, it's Brianna." Tears rolled down her face. "I'm… I'm sorry for your loss."

Noah could hear the muffled sound of the voice on the other end of the call, but not what they were saying.

"Yes, the police were here. I told them what I know, which isn't much. I hadn't seen him in a long time."

She talked to them for a few more minutes, expressed her condolences again and then paused to listen to what they were saying as more tears fell from her eyes. "Thank you," she said softly. "I'll be in touch." With a deep sigh, she said, "I need to call my parents, too, so they don't hear this news from someone else."

"Go ahead. Get it over with."

After the emotional exchange with her parents, Noah took the phone from her and turned it off, placing it on the coffee table. "Are you okay?"

"I have no idea what I am. His parents were so nice. They said that no matter how it ended, they believed with all their hearts that Rem loved me as much as he possibly could."

"That might be something to hold on to, you know? That he loved you the best way he knew how."

"Maybe. I don't know. It's all so confusing. How can I feel the way I do about him most of the time, but still be crushed to hear he's dead?"

"Because you're a good person, and part of you still loved the person you thought he was. And believe me, I get that. It's a fucked-up jumble of emotions that makes no sense whatsoever."

"No, it doesn't. My mother cried when she heard the news. That's the dichotomy of Rem. They hate what he did to me, but a part of them still loves the person we all thought he was."

"Strangely enough, that makes sense to me."

"I'm glad it does to you. For me, it's just hard to figure out what exactly I'm supposed to feel."

"You will, honey. Just keep breathing."

They were still huddled together on the sofa when his sisters arrived, carrying pans and trays, and one of them even had a blender. They got busy in the kitchen and left her and Noah alone until they were ready to join the group. And then each of them hugged Brianna and expressed condolences as Sarah handed her a margarita.

"Thank you, guys. This is very nice of you."

"We're sorry for your loss," Nessa said.

"I feel guilty accepting condolences for someone I would've liked to have stabbed myself at times."

"You're allowed to feel crappy that someone you used to love has died this way," Sarah said.

"Thank you. What did you guys make? It smells amazing."

"Enchiladas," Ally said, "including some with just grilled veggies for you."

Brianna teared up again at their thoughtfulness. "That's really nice of you and to relocate dinner over here."

"Happy to," Nessa said. "Now, have a seat and let us take care of you."

Brianna did as she was told, sat at the table and let them take over. She'd never had sisters, but she could certainly get used to having these ladies in her life.

CHAPTER TWENTY-TWO

*"One day you're going to remember me and how much I loved you...
then you're gonna hate yourself for letting me go."*
—Drake

$\mathcal{W}$atching Brianna interact with his sisters, Noah felt out of sorts and off-balance. Something had changed for him, something big and vital. He loved her. After his marriage blew up in his face, he'd promised himself he'd never go *there* again. *There* was a place where you gave another person control over your heart and your emotions. *There* was a place he never wanted to be again, until Brianna blasted into his life and turned everything upside down.

The discovery had him spinning and his stomach dropping as if he'd fallen into a bottomless pit.

He loved her.

He cared about her.

He hated to see her upset over a man who'd never deserved her.

He wanted her in his life.

And none of that was supposed to have happened. His goal had been to avoid anything that required a commitment or having to place trust in strangers. But she wasn't a stranger. Not anymore, and regardless of his goal to avoid such things, he trusted her.

"What's wrong?" Brianna asked him quietly.

When he looked at her, he noticed that her eyes were red and puffy. "Nothing."

"I'm sorry to be such a mess over him. That's not how I wanted to spend this afternoon and evening."

"It's not your fault, and I don't blame you at all. I can only imagine how I'd feel if something had happened to *her*. I'd be upset with myself for being upset about her."

"That's it, exactly. It helps that you understand, but that doesn't tell me what's got you wound up."

"It's nothing. Just thinking about some stuff."

"Will you tell me later?"

He couldn't tell her he loved her. Not yet and certainly not tonight. That couldn't happen the same night she found out her ex was dead. But he could tell her he was having feelings and get a sense of whether they were on the same page. And if they were? What then? "Yeah," he said in response to her question. "We'll talk later."

"I'm looking forward to later."

Ugh, that little smile, those pretty eyes, that face, the curls... He was crazy about her, and it was getting worse by the minute.

The girls were unusually thoughtful. They cleaned the entire kitchen, did all the dishes and got ready to leave shortly after dinner, each of them hugging Brianna and letting her know they cared and were close by if she needed friends.

"I'm heading back to Boston tomorrow for school," Sarah said, hugging Noah. "Keep me posted on what goes on here, okay?"

"I will."

She whispered in his ear, "I like her. Don't mess it up."

Noah laughed and gave her a playful shove. "Get out of here. And drive carefully tomorrow."

"Yes, Dad."

"Speaking of Dad, no sign of him this week?"

"Not that we heard, and we would've," Nessa said. "Is anyone shocked that he's a no-show?"

"Nope," Ally and Noah said in stereo.

"Who cares?" Ally said as she put her coat on and pulled her long hair out of the collar. "Izzy doesn't need him. She has us. And Cabot, who's been there for days now."

"What's up with that?" Noah asked.

"I don't think even Izzy knows," Sarah said, laughing, "but she hasn't kicked him out, so that's something."

If Izzy didn't want him there, he wouldn't be. That was for sure.

"Any word on when she's coming home?" Noah asked.

"They said maybe the day after tomorrow," Nessa said, "and Cabot is planning to stay with her to help for as long as she needs it."

"Has Izzy figured out that he has a massive crush on her?" Brianna asked.

"She's not sure that he does," Ally said. "She's as surprised as we are that he's planning to stick around."

"Very interesting," Noah said. "Thanks again for dinner, you guys."

"Make sure you're home by curfew." Sarah smiled at Brianna. "He used to *love* saying that to us."

"Because not one of you ever made it, and I had to listen to Mom rant about where you were and what you were doing."

Ally winked. "Wouldn't you like to know?"

"Actually, no, I wouldn't."

Brianna laughed at their antics, which made him thankful for his sisters and the lightness they'd brought to this difficult evening.

He walked them out and waved as they drove off. Back inside, he shut off the outside lights and locked the door before wondering if Brianna wanted him to stay. Maybe she'd rather be alone. He ought to at least ask her.

She'd curled up on the sofa with a blanket over her lap.

Noah sat next to her. "What can I do?"

"You've already done so much. Thanks for being here. You and your sisters make it easy to forget my troubles."

"Do you want to be alone?"

"No," she said quickly. "Unless you'd rather go home."

"I'd rather be with you."

"Are you going to tell me what you were thinking about earlier when you looked weird in the eyes?"

"Did I?"

"You did."

"Tonight isn't about me. It's about you and whatever you need."

"I'm talked out on that topic. Let's talk about something else."

"What I was thinking would be better discussed at a time when there's nothing else weighing on us."

Her brows furrowed adorably. "This sounds serious."

"It's serious in a good way."

She tipped her head, studying him so intently, he wondered if he had something on his face. "What're you saying, Noah?"

"Nothing yet, Brianna, because you've had a rough day."

"Let's pretend today was any other day. What would you say to me then?"

"In that case, I might say that I find myself wondering what's going to happen when you're done here and have to go back to Boston. I might tell you I've been thinking about maybe going with you because I can't imagine being here without you. I might say something like that."

Her lips parted, and her eyes widened. "You would come to Boston with me?"

He shrugged. "Maybe."

"But your business and your family… Your whole life is here."

"If you're there, my whole life isn't here."

"Noah…"

"See what I mean? Not the right time for this."

"Yes, it is. It's the perfect time to remind me that the past doesn't define me."

"It doesn't. You're amazing, and I just want to be with you. If you need to be in Boston, then that's what we'll do. If you want me there, that is."

"Yes," she said on a long exhale, "I want you there, Noah. I want you here, there, everywhere."

As he reached for her and wrapped his arms around her, he was overwhelmed with relief to know there'd be more. There might be upheaval and big decisions to be made, but he'd put her on notice that he didn't want her to get away. "I didn't want anything like this, ever again. I was quite determined to avoid it until this sexy, infuriating architect showed up and made herself essential to me."

"I'm essential to you?"

"Hell yes," he said, kissing her. "You make me not want to be a cranky loner anymore. You make me want to rejoin my family and live fully again instead of burrowing into my misery. Do you have any idea how miraculous that is when I honestly believed I was going to live that way for the rest of my life?"

"You have too much to give to live like that. I wish you could see how your sisters look at you with so much love and admiration. They're so happy to have you back."

"How do you know?"

"They told me. Every one of them has said something about it this week. That they've missed you and hurt for you and wanted to help but didn't know how."

"They're delightful, even if they drive me bonkers sometimes."

"They love you."

"And I love them." He linked their fingers and looked down at their joined hands. "There's just one other thing I have to say about all these big things we're talking about."

"What's that?"

"It's the biggest of big things."

"Okay…"

"If we do this, if we make some sort of commitment to each other, I need to be certain we're both in it for keeps. I can't go through what I did before again, and I'm sure you feel the same way."

"I do, but I'm not sure I'm ready to say *this is it* for the rest of my life. After everything that's happened, I don't trust my judgment the way I used to. And while I know you're nothing at all like him, I thought he was perfect for a long time. Until I realized how wrong I was about that, and now…"

"Now you don't know what to believe."

"Something like that."

"I get it. All I can do is continue to prove you can trust me with the hope that maybe, at some point, you might decide to believe in me."

"I already do. I just need to be sure I'm not making another bad decision."

"The good news is we have a few weeks left before you head home, and that gives us plenty of time to spend together to get to know each other." It would also give him time to show her he was just what she needed. How he would do that, he wasn't quite sure yet, but he'd wage a campaign to keep her in his life if that's what it took.

Brianna snuggled up to Noah in bed. He was always so warm, like her own personal heating pad, and during a Vermont winter, that was a nice thing to have. He'd been so sweet earlier, telling her he'd move to Boston if that would keep them together after she had to leave.

She was beginning to wonder if she wanted to leave. Her life in Boston had changed dramatically after her marriage ended.

Everywhere she looked was a painful memory of something she'd done with Rem, back before she knew their entire relationship was a big lie. The friends who'd been so supportive of her when things first went bad with him had continued with their lives, their marriages, their children, while she had to wonder how her life had gone so wrong.

Her cousin, Dominique, was the only one there she'd truly miss if she didn't go back, but Dom was so busy with her own life and family that they rarely saw each other.

Adding to her woes in Boston were the always-fighting brothers she worked for who made each day so stressful that she'd jumped at the chance to work in Vermont—primarily outside in the winter—just to get away from them for a few months. She'd been thinking about looking for a new job long before the inn project had bought her a reprieve. If she went back, she didn't want to return to that firm.

If she went back...

Since when was that even a question?

She smiled in the dark. It'd become a question when Noah told her he wanted her in his life, but only if she was there to stay.

Of course, she understood why he'd want those assurances. Neither of them ever again wanted to be in the place they'd been before, but Brianna was wise enough now to know that all the assurances in the world didn't guarantee that things wouldn't still go sideways.

"What're you thinking about?" he muttered, his voice hoarse and sleepy sounding.

"You."

"What about me?"

"The things you said earlier."

"I don't want you awake worrying about any of that."

"I'm not worrying. I'm thinking."

"Talk to me. Tell me what's on your mind."

"I like that you keep me warm at night."

He tightened his arms around her. "I've never liked sleeping like this until you wrapped your sexy self around me, and now I love sleeping wrapped up in you."

"You didn't sleep like this with your wife?"

"Nope. She didn't like anything touching her while she slept."

Brianna kissed his neck and breathed him in. "That was most definitely her loss."

"Is that right?" he asked on a low chuckle.

"Oh yeah." She took a minute to enjoy the warm, safe feeling that came with being wrapped up in him. "I want you to know…"

"What, honey? What do you want me to know?"

"If I were going to have faith in anyone, I'd want to have faith in you."

"I saw what my father did to his wife and children and vowed as a teenager I'd never be that kind of man, the kind who left and disappointed the people who loved him. I may not be the best guy who ever lived, but I don't leave when things get hard. If Mel hadn't done what she did, I never would've left her, even if there were things about our marriage that didn't work for me."

"Like what?"

"She spent a lot of time with her friends—more time with them than she spent with me. She even traveled with them."

"Without you?"

"Yep. They didn't invite me. We did stuff together, too, but it bugged me that she spent so much time with other people, and they seemed to come first with her."

"Did you ever tell her that?"

"I tried to, but she didn't want to hear it. They were her ride-or-die girls, and they came first."

"That's not fair to you."

"I knew they were incredibly close before we got married. I just thought our relationship would come first after we got married, but nothing changed. I realized much later, after she was long gone, that I was lonely in our marriage. But I stuck it out because I committed to her. That mattered to me."

"She didn't deserve you."

"No, she didn't."

Brianna laughed. "We both deserve better than what we had before."

"We do, and that's why I believe that if we were to make a go of this, we'd know how to do it right. We know what *not* to do."

"For sure," she said with a sigh. "I also want you to know that I'd been thinking about making some other changes long before I came up here."

"Like what?"

"My job, for one thing. I hate it. I work for brothers who do nothing but scream at each other all day long, and I can't *stand* it. When they were looking for someone to take this job, I jumped at the chance to get the hell away from them, even if it was Vermont in the winter, and I hate being cold."

Noah slid his leg between hers. "But now you know the secret to staying warm in Vermont, and it doesn't seem so bad, right?"

"Everything about Vermont is different from what I expected."

"So, move up here and be part of my business."

Brianna raised her head off his chest. "What?"

"You heard me. I've had this idea running around in my mind for a while now, and you'd fit right into it."

"What idea?"

"The renovation idea. There're all these great old buildings all over Vermont that would make for unique homes. For instance, my aunt and uncle live in a restored barn that's the most incredible home I've ever seen. You'd have to see it to get the full picture. I'll take you over there tomorrow."

"Like Grayson's place, the restored church, which is amazing."

"Yes, exactly. I thought it might be a fun niche for the

company to buy the places, restore them and then sell them at what I hope would be a huge profit. People are always looking for ski houses up here. I think there'd be a real market for it."

"That's the most exciting idea I've ever heard."

He laughed. "That can't possibly be true."

"No, it is. It sounds so fun and interesting. My brain is exploding with ideas and thoughts, and well, I think it's a great idea."

"Even though I work for myself, there're so many daily demands from clients that I just get tired of it all. I feel like this way, I could truly work for myself, and I'd want you to be part of it."

"Really? You'd want to work with me when all we did was fight for weeks when we first worked together?"

"We only fought for weeks because we were both pretending we weren't attracted."

"I wasn't attracted."

"You're such a liar!"

Brianna lost it laughing.

"Everything is different now." He squeezed her ass for emphasis. "We'd be a great team. You'd do the design, and I'd do the work. While I was finishing one project, you could be preparing for the next one."

"I have goose bumps."

Noah ran his hand down her arm. "You do."

"You've given me so much to think about."

"I'm glad you're thinking about good things rather than things that hurt you."

With her hand on his face, she turned him to receive her kiss. "Thank you for giving me good things to think about."

"You've done the same for me."

"I just need a little more time to think. I hope you understand."

He kissed her. "I understand, and I'm not going anywhere. I'll be right here when you figure out what you want."

CHAPTER TWENTY-THREE

"In three words I can sum up everything I've learned about life:
it goes on."
—Robert Frost

The middle-of-the-night conversation had changed things between them—in a good way. Noah could tell she was giving careful consideration to his idea. They didn't talk about it again or anything more significant than what they should have for dinner and when would be a good time to visit Izzy, who was now at home with Cabot tending to her every need.

They were bringing dinner to Izzy's that night, two days after their late-night conversation.

Brianna had made some of her famous lasagna for Izzy, who was curious to try it after hearing about it from her siblings.

When Noah pulled into Izzy's driveway, he noticed Ray's truck parked in front of the house. "Mom and Ray are here, too."

"I made a ton, so there's plenty if they want to eat with us."

Noah leaned across the center console to kiss her. "Thanks for cooking for my family again."

"I love your family."

That was just another reason for Noah to love *her*. Mel had often been annoyed by his boisterous family, who were always asking them to do something. She usually had something else she'd rather be doing when he spent time with his immediate family and his Abbott cousins. "Too many people," she'd say, dismissing whatever invitation they'd received.

"I'm glad you love them," Noah said to Brianna. "Let me come around to help you carry that."

He circled the truck and opened the passenger door to take the heavy pan from her. After she retrieved another bag from behind the seat, she followed him up the walkway to Izzy's adorable Craftsman-style house.

"I love this house."

"She does, too. She did most of the work herself with a little help from her contractor brother. It took years."

"It's beautiful."

"I agree. She did a great job." The house was painted white with bright red trim that Noah had thought would look silly. But Izzy had been determined to go with the red, and he'd later had to admit it was perfect. In the summer, the porch was full of potted plants and comfortable furniture that he usually helped his sister move to the basement for the winter.

Cabot met them at the door and held it open for them to pass through with the food. "Something smells delicious."

"It's Brianna's famous lasagna," Noah said.

"I've been thinking about that all day," Cabot said.

"How's the patient?"

"She's much better today," Hannah said. "She even took a shower without any help. I was here on standby in case she needed me."

"Stay for dinner," Noah said. "Brianna made a ton."

"We don't want to crash your party," Hannah said.

"Don't be silly," Noah said. "We'd love to have you."

His mother gave him a curious look, but before he could ask her what was up, Brianna needed him to show her how to work

Izzy's fancy oven. Since he'd helped her install it and figure out how to use it, he was able to show Brianna.

"That's her pride and joy," Hannah said of the restaurant-quality oven and gas stove.

"After her cameras," Noah added.

"Are you guys talking about me?" Izzy asked as she came into the kitchen, moving slowly but looking better than she had.

Cabot was ready with a chair for her and an arm to hold as she lowered herself to sit in what seemed like a well-practiced routine.

Noah was intrigued by the way Cabot doted on his sister. He caught Izzy's eye, raised a brow, and she shrugged as if she didn't know any more than he did about what was going on with Cabot.

Brianna put a plate in front of Izzy with lasagna, salad and garlic bread.

"This looks fantastic," Izzy said. "Thank you. Everyone has brought the yummiest food. I'm going to be nine hundred pounds by the time I can move normally again."

"You need to relax and let your body heal," Hannah said as she brought her plate and Ray's to the table.

"That's easier said than done," Izzy said, frowning. "Being out of work is going to put me in a bind. The downside of self-employment. There's no one to fill in for me."

"You can file for disability," Hannah said.

"That'll take a while to kick in," Izzy said.

"I'll take care of whatever you need," Cabot said. "Don't worry about anything."

"You're not paying my bills, Cabot," Izzy said. "But it's sweet of you to offer."

"Why not? You need it. I have it. No big deal. Now eat your dinner, and we'll have that fight later."

She gave him a withering look that had helped to keep their younger siblings in line. Izzy could be scary when she wanted to be—not to Noah as the older and wiser brother, but to the younger ones for sure. They did what she told them to, and she'd been a huge help to their mother when the "kids," as they called them, became teens.

Cabot had no idea what he was in for after they left.

The thought of Izzy handing him his ass made Noah smile. He was so very thankful she'd survived the awful accident.

When the doorbell rang at the back door, Brianna got up to see who it was. "Come in, Gray."

"Sorry to interrupt your dinner," Grayson said, his gaze finding Noah.

"Everything okay?" Noah asked his brother.

"Could I speak to you in private?" Gray asked.

"What's going on, Grayson?" Hannah asked.

"I just... I need a minute with Noah."

Noah got up from the table and led the way into the living room.

Grayson followed him.

"Noah," he said in a low tone so only Noah could hear him, "we found Melinda where you thought she'd be."

"Not surprised. That's where she grew up."

"There's more."

"What?"

"There's a child—a boy. The investigator said he's about two to three. He took photos from a distance."

Noah's entire body had gone cold. "What the fuck are you saying, Gray?"

"Look, we can't prove anything with photos from a distance—"

"What the fuck are you saying?"

"He looks like you, Noah." Grayson showed him a photo on his phone, and right away, Noah could see the resemblance to a picture of himself that hung in the hallway at his mother's house.

The entire world tilted, and it was all he could do to remain standing. This could not be happening. *She wouldn't.*

And then he was screaming, oblivious to his mother, Ray, Cabot, Izzy and Brianna, all of whom came into the room and looked on with alarm.

"Noah, my God," Hannah said. "What is it?"

"I'm going to fucking kill her!"

Grayson held on to him so tightly that Noah couldn't move. He could only scream at the top of his lungs. It was the only thing he could do to keep from bawling his head off. How could she have done this to him? *How?* Once upon a time, she'd told him she'd love him forever.

When the tears came, he pulled loose from his brother's grasp and sank to the sofa, face buried in his hands.

Gray sat on one side, Brianna on the other. He knew she was there because he could smell the fresh scent of her hair.

"What's happened?" Hannah asked.

"You can tell them," Noah said.

Grayson filled them in.

"Are you kidding me?" Hannah asked in the tone that used to make her children quake.

"Noah." Brianna's soft voice and gentle touch shattered him.

Noah didn't want comfort from her or anyone. "I, uh... I have to go."

"Where're you going?" Grayson asked.

He had no idea. His house was full of siblings who'd want to talk about it. Noah didn't want to talk about it. "I don't know, but I've got to go."

"Stay with me," Brianna said. "We'll figure it out."

"No, we won't. We won't figure it out. We won't figure out anything."

Ignoring the stricken expression on her face and the pain it gave him to know he'd hurt her, he got up, grabbed his coat and left the house.

Grayson followed him, jumping into the passenger seat of his truck before Noah could drive off.

"Get out and go home, Gray," he said. "I'm not going to kill her. You don't need to babysit me."

"I'm not babysitting you. Your place is full of Colemans. Go to my house. The guest room is all yours if you need a minute to yourself. Emma and Simone are at a Girl Scout thing tonight."

After a long moment of silence, Noah asked his most pressing question. "How could she do this to me?"

"I don't know. It's an awful thing to do to anyone."

"She used to tell me she loved me so much, more than anything."

"It's complete and total bullshit, and we're going to get to the bottom of it, Noah. I promise."

"What does getting to the bottom of it even entail? I have a son I didn't know about for almost three years. How do I ever get back that time?"

"You don't, but you can go forward from here."

He sat staring blankly out the window for a long time before he noticed it was snowing. "Is she still with Miguel?"

"Yeah."

"Great, so he's raising my kid as his own. Just when I thought this situation couldn't be any more fucked-up than it already was." Rage made it almost impossible for Noah to process the implications. "She was never going to tell me."

"Probably not."

"She's a fucking monster, as bad as Brianna's ex-husband."

"Maybe even worse."

"How do you ever know that you're with someone who won't crush you?"

"When it's the right one, you know."

Noah shook his head. "I don't believe that."

"Don't do this, Noah. You've started something great with Brianna. We've all seen there's something special between the two of you. If you let Melinda ruin that for you, that's just another thing she will have taken from you."

Noah heard his brother's words and even agreed with them,

but he was so fucking furious that he couldn't imagine ever trusting anyone outside of his own family ever again.

Even Brianna.

"I DON'T KNOW WHAT TO DO FOR HIM," BRIANNA SAID, FEELING frantic after Noah left. Thankfully, Gray had gone after him. "What do we do?"

"We give him a minute to wrap his head around this news," Hannah said. "And once he does, we'll support him in the war he'll wage with her over what she did to him."

Cabot got up from the table and started clearing the dishes, taking them to the sink and rinsing them before loading the dishwasher. He made such a racket that they stopped talking to look at him.

"Cabot," Izzy said. When he didn't reply, she called to him again.

He stopped what he was doing and stood at the sink, shoulders bent forward, head down. "Sorry. Just brings it all back."

Izzy reached out to Brianna, who was sitting next to her. "Help me up."

Brianna stood and gave Izzy an arm up.

She moved slowly to where Cabot stood at the sink and put an arm around him.

"You shouldn't be on your feet."

"Shhh," Izzy said. "I'm fine."

He leaned into her, seeming to draw comfort from her presence.

Watching them, Brianna felt removed from what was happening right in front of her. All she could think about was Noah and how he'd stood by her through every rough moment she'd had in the last few days, not leaving her side for as long as she needed him. "Where would they go? Noah and Gray?"

"The kids are all at Noah's place," Hannah said.

"They'd go to Gray's," Izzy said. "He'd take Noah to his place."

"Will you take me there?" Brianna asked Ray and Hannah. "Please?"

"Of course, honey," Ray said. "Whatever you need."

"I need to be with Noah. He needs to know he's not alone. Not anymore."

"We'll take you," Hannah said.

"Go ahead and go," Cabot said. "I'll finish cleaning up."

"Are you sure?" Hannah asked, eyeing the dishes on the table.

"Positive. Take Brianna to Noah." To Brianna, Cabot said, "Don't let him push you away. Let him know you're there for him no matter what happens. That'll matter to him when the shock wears off."

"I will," Brianna said softly. "Thank you, Cabot."

Twelve minutes later, Ray pulled up to Grayson's house, where Noah's truck was in the driveway.

Brianna had never been more relieved to see a vehicle in her life.

Hannah turned to speak to her in the back seat. "He's going to try to push you away. That's what he does when things like this happen. He'll try to put up a wall around himself to keep the hurt out. Take Cabot's advice and don't let him push you away."

"I won't. Thank you both."

"We're rooting for you two, Brianna," Hannah said. "My son hadn't smiled in years. All he does is smile when you're around. He needs you, even if he tries to convince himself he doesn't."

"I need him, too. I won't give up. Don't worry." Bolstered by Hannah's words of encouragement, Brianna got out of the car and went up the shoveled walkway to the mudroom door they'd used the last time they were there. She rang the bell, aware of Ray and Hannah in the truck watching to make sure she got inside safely before they left. Or maybe they'd go to Ray's place over the garage in the back of Gray and Emma's. Thinking about what they might be doing was better than worrying about Noah sending her away.

Gray came to the door, seeming surprised to see her. "Come in."

Brianna waved to Ray and Hannah and then followed Grayson into the house. "I know he doesn't want me here, but he's not getting rid of me that easily."

"He's a bit of a bear."

Brianna kicked off her boots. "I'm not afraid of him."

Grayson smiled. "I knew I liked you. The guest room is to the left of the family room. First door on the right. Make yourself at home."

"Thank you, Gray. And tomorrow, we'll be petitioning the court for paternity or custody or whatever needs to happen, right?"

"First thing."

"Excellent." Brianna walked through the kitchen to the family room, taking a left and coming to a stop outside the first door on the right. She took a deep breath and let it out, squared her shoulders and gave a quick knock on the door before she walked in.

Noah stood at the window, staring out into the snowy darkness.

Brianna closed the door and leaned back against it. "I know you don't want me here, but I'm not leaving you alone with this, just like you wouldn't have left me alone with the news about Rem. Whether you want me here or not, I'm here and I'm staying. You don't have to do this yourself. A lot of people love you." She licked lips that'd gone dry. "Including me."

CHAPTER TWENTY-FOUR

"Sadness flies away on the wings of time."
—Jean de La Fontaine

*L*ong moments passed while Brianna stood out on the edge of a cliff all by herself, taking a gigantic leap forward that neither of them was ready to make. But there they were, on the cliff, teetering.

"I'm not fit for company, Bri."

That he called her by her nickname was somehow comforting. "That's okay. I'll just be here if you need me."

She took off her coat and brought it with her to the bed, where she sat on the mattress, still holding her coat. That wouldn't do. She looked like she was ready to leave at a moment's notice, and she wasn't going anywhere. Rising, she put the coat on an upholstered chair in the corner of the room and returned to the bed.

Was she prepared to stay there all night? If necessary. The room was chilly, and it didn't take long for her to be uncomfortably cold, so she got under the covers and sat propped against the pillows, watching over Noah, who never moved from his post by the window.

She had no idea how long they stayed like that, silent and separate, until he stood up a little straighter and cleared his throat.

"You know what I'd like to know?"

"What's that?" Brianna asked, relieved to hear him say something, anything.

"When did we go from 'I'll love you forever' to her sleeping with my best friend and giving birth to my kid and keeping that from me for *years*? When did that happen? Where was I the day it all changed? What was I doing? What did I miss that I should've seen?"

Brianna was up and out of the bed before he finished talking. She wrapped her arms around him from behind and held on tightly. "You didn't miss anything, Noah, because she kept it from you. She didn't want you to know things had changed."

"*Why?* Why would she do this to me? And to our child?"

"I don't know. We may never know why. But now you know your son is out there, and he's yours, and you can be part of his life."

"I'll be a stranger to him."

"At first, but over time, it won't be like that."

"I'm so fucking *angry*. I've never been this angry, even the day I caught her with Miguel. That was nothing compared to this."

"I can't begin to know how you must feel."

"I'm filled with rage. It's like a wildfire that wants to consume me."

"Don't let it, Noah. Fight it back. The rage won't help anything. It'll only make a difficult situation more so. I learned that lesson the hard way. Your only thought should be for your son and asserting your parental rights where he's concerned. She's nothing to you, except your soon-to-be ex-wife and your son's mother."

He took a deep breath and let it out. "I wanted them to *suffer* for what they did to me, and instead, they're out there living like a happy little family with *my* son. He's *mine*."

"Yes, he is, and he's going to know who his father is, Noah. He'll know that. Kids don't remember the first few years of their lives. You'll be such a big part of his life that he'll never know anything other than you as his father."

"I want custody of him."

"Let's see what Gray says about that."

"It's too much to ask of you, Brianna, especially when you have your own stuff going on."

"It's not too much."

"I wouldn't blame you if…"

"What? If I cut and run? That's not happening, Noah, so don't try to push me away. I'm not going anywhere. Did you hear what I said to you before? I love you. I didn't intend to love you when I first met you, and you drove me crazy every minute of every day, but that was *so* two weeks ago. And now…"

"What?" he asked gruffly.

"Now you're all I think about. You're all I want and need, and I already love your son because he's part of you. It's not too much."

With a moan that sounded an awful lot like surrender, Noah turned to her, enveloping her in his strong arms and burying his face in her hair, seeming to breathe her in. "I love you, too. How could I not? You're so sweet and smart and sexy and perfect for me because you understand my pain and would never cause me more of it—and vice versa. I'd never hurt you."

"That's about the best guarantee any girl with a recovering broken heart could hope to receive."

"We've both had enough of the bad stuff."

"Yes, we have."

"This thing with my son is apt to get ugly. I'll do my best to protect you from that."

"No, Noah, I'll do *my* best to protect *you* from that. We're going to get through all this shit and figure it out together. I promise."

"I'm afraid all this external crap will mess things up for us."

"It won't. We won't let it." She took him by the hand and led him to the bed, encouraging him to sit. Crouching in front of him, she untied his boots and removed them, tossing them aside. "Get under the covers."

"Are you coming with me?"

"You know it."

She went around the bed and got in next to him, snuggling up to him.

His arm came around her, and she rested her head on his chest.

"I've been thinking a lot about the restoration idea," she said.

"Have you?"

"Uh-huh, and the more I think about it, the more interested I am."

"Really?"

"Yep. Do you have some properties identified yet?"

"I've found ten that interest me."

"That's so exciting."

"Um, Brianna?"

"Yes, Noah?"

"You do realize if you stay up here and become my partner in the restoration business, that means you'll live in Butler, Vermont, with no cell service and nine months a year of cold. You don't like being cold."

"No, I don't, but you bought me that jazzy long underwear that'll keep me warm, and I'll probably spend most of my time in our home office doing design work while you manage the construction. Would you build me a fire before you left for the day?"

"I'd build you the biggest fire ever so it would keep you toasty all day."

"And when you got home from work, would you snuggle with me in front of the fire and let me warm you up?"

"I would, and I'd keep you warm all night in bed."

"Then I suppose fall, winter and spring in Vermont would be more than tolerable."

"Are you serious about this?"

"If our life looked like the one we just discussed, then yes, I'm serious."

"You'd want to live with me?"

"Since we'll be together all the time, or at least I think we would be, it'd be dumb to pay for two places when we only need one."

"That's true."

"And PS, yes, I want to live with you and be with you all the time. But only if you want that, too."

"A few weeks ago, I would've said no way, but I've been dreading the end of the job at the inn and you going back to Boston."

"You didn't tell me that."

"I didn't want to make you feel bad about going back to your life there."

"I have no life there. Not anymore. All I do is work for three men I can't stand and then go home alone. Even my closest friends got tired of me being such a sad sack and stopped asking me to do stuff I didn't want to do anyway. It wasn't until I came up here and got away from everything that I realized my life there was nothing but a giant rut. Even before this happened with you, I knew I needed to make some changes. And the kind of changes we're talking about make me excited about the future for the first time in a very long time. I'll have to find another job until our business becomes profitable. I'm still paying off the debt that Rem left me."

"Work with me. I need so much help. I'm always a month behind on everything. I can pay you enough to cover any bills you have until the new business starts making money."

"You're not creating a job for me, are you?"

"It's something I've needed for a long time. Your project management skills will be a huge help to me."

"Then I accept your kind offer."

"I could be looking at an extended battle over my son."

"That's okay. We'll do whatever it takes to bring him into your life. Our life."

Noah was quiet for a long time, even as he ran his hand up and down her arm. "When I came here with Gray, I was a mess. I was so spun up and enraged and sad. I was so fucking sad. But then you came bombing into the room, and that's all it took for me to feel better. Just knowing you were here."

"Then you know how it is for me when I'm spinning, and you tell me it's all going to be okay."

Noah shifted them so he was on his side, facing her. "If you want that life you described for us, then I'm in."

"I want it. And you. And your son. And your wonderful family and this adorable town and your gigantic moose and nine months a year of cold. I want it all. But more than anything, I want *you*."

"Then how about we make that happen?"

"Let's do it."

NOAH WAS AWAKE ALL NIGHT, THINKING ABOUT BRIANNA AND how she'd pulled him back from the edge of disaster he'd been on when she arrived at Grayson's and how she'd forced him to let her be there for him. Not that he'd taken much convincing. At some point, she'd become necessary to him, and leaning on her felt natural, like loving her was something he'd been born to do.

He was sitting at the table in Gray's kitchen nursing a second cup of coffee when his brother came in, dressed in gray pants and a navy V-neck sweater over a dress shirt.

"You're all turned out for a Saturday," Noah said.

Gray poured himself a cup of coffee. "I'm going to Burlington."

"I'll go with you."

"Nope." Gray brought creamer with him when he sat at the table. "You're staying right here until I sort this out. The last thing we need is you storming in there hot."

"I'd let you do the talking."

"No, Noah. You're going to stay here, spend the day with Brianna and let me do what I do. That's what is in your best interest. Trust me."

"Now that I know about him, I don't want to wait another day to see him."

"I completely understand that—"

"Do you? Do you really? Did you just find out that your cheating bitch of an ex-wife hid your child from you for more than two fucking years?"

"No, I didn't, and I can only imagine how you must feel."

Noah exhaled a deep breath. "I'm sorry. I don't mean to take it out on you. I know you're trying to help."

"We're going to figure this out, and we're going to get your son into your life as soon as we possibly can. But we need to be careful about how we approach it. The last thing we want to do is cause her to take the child and run."

The thought of that sent fear rippling through him, especially knowing that was what'd happened to Cabot with Mia. No, he didn't want that. "What's the plan?"

"I'm going to go there, knock on her door, tell her we're aware there's a child, ask for a paternity test and a divorce. I'm going to tell her that unless she fails to cooperate, we have no intention of making a federal case out of the fact that she denied you your child for all this time. And I'll put her on notice that should the DNA prove the child is yours, you fully intend to file for joint custody."

"Why not full custody? That'd be a slam dunk after she hid him from me for all this time."

"Because that's not in *his* best interest. You'd be bringing him to live with people who are strangers to him."

"I'll never forgive her for this."

"And you don't have to, but you need to think of what's best for him and not what's best for you."

"Is it normal to feel like you're coming out of your skin when you hear something like this?"

"Absolutely. But keeping a calm head will make a big difference. I've got you covered, and I'm going to handle it. If you give me Brianna's cell phone number, I can text you the minute I know anything. I figure hers is charged, and yours probably isn't."

"You figure correctly."

"She'll have to keep her phone logged in to Wi-Fi to get the message."

"I'll make sure she does." Noah retrieved his wallet from his back pocket and got out the scrap of napkin bearing Brianna's numbers.

Gray put the cell number into his phone. "Got it."

"Thank you for this and everything you do for our family. I know it seems like we take you and all you do for us for granted—"

Grayson laid his hand on Noah's arm. "I never think that, and you know I'd do anything for you."

Damn if his brother wasn't going to make him bawl like a baby.

"Before all this happened last night," Gray said, "I was going to tell you that Dad called me to ask how Izzy's doing."

"I thought he was going to come to see her?"

"His doctor told him not to go to the hospital. He's still immunocompromised after the transplant. He said he's going to call her now that she's home and see if there's a time he can come by."

"Well, that's something anyway. So, the remission is holding?"

"That's what he said."

"That's good."

"Yep."

Nothing had changed between Mike Coleman and his eight children. He would always be the man who'd abandoned them and their mother.

"What he did... It makes it worse for me that I have a son out there I didn't know about. I never wanted to be the kind of father he was."

"Come on, Noah, there's no comparing what he did with this. You didn't know the child existed. He left eight children who not only knew him but loved him. This is in no way the same thing."

"Just the thought of my kid out there, not even knowing me... And being raised by the two people who betrayed me. It makes me sick."

"What she did is monstrous, and she knows it as well as we do."

"I want to see him. As soon as possible."

"I'll do everything I can to make that happen." Gray drank the last of his coffee. "I'm going to go so I can get there early before they leave for the day or whatever."

"And you'll text me the minute you know anything?"

"I will." He glanced toward the doorway. "Is Brianna still here?"

Noah nodded. "She stayed."

"She seems to care about you."

"She does."

"Are you letting her? Care, that is..."

"Yeah," Noah said with the first hint of a smile. "I'm letting her."

"I know that's a big deal for you."

"It is for her, too."

"You two are just what the other needs."

"That's how it's starting to seem. We're making some plans."

"That's good. I'm happy for you both."

"Thanks."

"Let me go see what I can do to resolve this situation in Burlington. It'll be four hours or so before I have any news. Take Brianna out to do something fun today to keep yourself busy."

"I will. Emma knows we're here, right?"

"She does and said to make yourselves at home."

"Thanks again, you know, for everything."

"No worries."

Grayson got himself together and departed a few minutes later, leaving Noah alone to contemplate how this day would transpire. What if she was hostile? What if she wouldn't even talk to Gray? What if he had to go through a protracted legal battle to see his child? Any of those possibilities was enough to make him feel exhausted and overwhelmed.

Just as he was on the verge of spinning himself up with worst-case scenarios, Brianna came shuffling into the kitchen. She looked adorably rumpled and sleepy. "I woke up and couldn't figure out where I was."

Noah held out his arms to her, and she came to him, settling on his lap as if she belonged there, which she did.

She caressed his face. "Did you sleep?"

"Not much. Gray just left to go to Burlington to talk to her."

"Oh, wow. Well… How're you feeling?"

"Resigned to a very long morning waiting to hear how it goes. I gave Gray your cell number. He said if you keep it logged in to Wi-Fi, he'll message us as soon as he talks to her."

"I'll keep it logged in. In the meantime, we'll have to find something to do."

"I thought we could stop by my aunt and uncle's so I can show you the incredible home they created from a falling-down barn."

"I'd love to see it—and meet them."

"And I thought you might like to meet the baby moose my cousin Hannah is raising."

"Is he as huge as Fred?"

259

"Nah, he's a little guy. Hannah babies him, so he's like a puppy."

"A puppy moose. Sounds like something I need to see. Whatever you want to do today, that's what we'll do."

"I don't want my thing to overtake your thing."

"My thing was shock at receiving the news and being questioned by cops. Now that I've processed it, I'm better. I'm sad for him and the people who loved him, but I've moved on from him. I refuse to let his death cause a massive setback for me. I've come too far to let that happen."

"I'm proud of you for being so strong."

"It took me a very long time to get to this place." She kissed his neck, his cheek and then his lips. "And I like it here."

"We like you here, too."

CHAPTER TWENTY-FIVE

"It is strange how often a heart must be broken
before the years can make it wise."
—Sara Teasdale

Being with Brianna, Emma and Simone helped Noah get through the morning. Brianna and Emma made pancakes and eggs while Simone supervised.

"Why did you stay at our house last night?" Simone asked Noah.

"Simone!" Emma said. "That's none of your business."

"It's fine," Noah said. "I was upset about something, and Grayson brought me here because my house is full of Colemans."

"Are you still upset?"

"I am, but Gray's helping me figure it out." Noah paused, not sure how much he should say to her. He deferred to her mother. "Is it okay if I tell Simone what's going on?"

"That's entirely up to you, but you're under no obligation."

"I don't mind telling her." Noah smiled his thanks to Emma for the fresh cup of coffee she placed in front of him, squeezing his shoulder before returning to the stove. "I was married, and it ended a few years ago. We never got divorced, so I asked Gray to find her so I could take care of that. The investigator he hired to find her discovered she has a child, and from the pictures the investigator took, we think he might be my son."

Simone's eyes went wide when she realized what he was telling her. "And you didn't *know?*"

"I had no idea."

"Wow, that's really mean for her not to tell you."

"It sure is."

"Gray will make her sorry she did that," Simone said. "He's an excellent lawyer."

Noah couldn't help but smile at her affection for his brother. "You're right. He's very good at what he does, and I'm confident he'll work things out."

"Will you get to see him? Your son?"

"That's the plan. I want to see him as soon as I possibly can."

"I'm sorry that happened to you."

"Thank you, sweetheart. But like you said, Gray will fix it for me, and you'll get a new cousin out of it."

"That's cool."

"Simone, go brush your teeth and get ready for dance class. We have to leave in fifteen minutes."

After she ran off, Noah glanced at Emma. "I hope that wasn't too much information for her."

"You handled it well. She'll have questions. I'll answer them."

"She's very mature for her age," Brianna said.

"Which is why we have to tell her the truth about things, even when they might be hard for her to understand," Emma said.

"We'll do the dishes and get out of your hair," Noah said.

"You're not in my hair. You're welcome here any time. You know that."

"Thanks. I appreciate the use of your guest room last night."

"If there's anything we can do, please don't hesitate to ask."

"Thanks, Emma. It's nice to have you and Gray on my side."

"We're completely on your side. What she did…"

Noah had never seen such a fierce look on Emma's sweet face. "I know. Believe me."

"I'd better go check on Simone."

Noah got up to do the dishes. He and Brianna left with Emma and Simone and stopped first at his house so he could shower and change. Ally, Nessa and Jackson were in the kitchen, sitting around the table with coffee and breakfast.

"We were just talking about you guys and wondering where you were," Nessa said.

"We stayed at Gray's last night," Noah said.

"Are you okay?" Ally asked, her eyes going from one of them to the other.

"I take it you heard about Mel—"

"Do not say her name in this house," Nessa said. "She's dead to us."

Noah looked to Brianna. "They've heard the news."

"What's being done?" Jackson asked.

"Gray is on his way to Burlington to see her."

"I hope he puts the screws to her," Ally said. "What a shitty thing to do."

"He's going to work it out so I can see my son and get a divorce. Those are my only goals here."

"You're not going to sue for full custody?" Jack asked.

"No," Noah said, his teeth gritted, "because that would be awful for the child, who'd end up living with strangers."

"It's so fucking *wrong*," Ally said.

"I agree," Noah said, "but all I can do now is everything I can to fix it and make him part of my life. I can't change the past."

"That's very evolved of you, bro," Jack said. "I'd be ripshit."

"Believe me, I am, but it's not about me. It's about my son and what's best for him."

"You have a *son*," Ally said. "We have a *nephew*."

"Yes, you do." He extended a hand to Brianna. "I'm going to run up and shower. We'll be back in a minute."

They went upstairs to Noah's room. "Make yourself comfortable. I'll be quick."

She stretched out on top of his bed. "Take your time."

Wanting to get back to her, he rushed through a shower and shave. He stepped out of the bathroom with a towel knotted around his waist.

Brianna's eyes heated at the sight of him, and she crooked her finger at him. "Bring that over here."

Smiling, Noah walked over to the bed and sat on the mattress next to her. "You rang?"

"I did." Brianna dragged her fingertip over the contours of his chest and abdomen. "I like looking at you."

"Likewise, my love."

"Your love," she said with a sigh. "This is really happening."

"It's happening." He tilted her chin up to receive his kiss. "It can happen right now, in fact."

"Not until I get to shower, too."

He took her hand and wrapped it around his hard cock. "You're going to let a world-class boner get away?"

"I'm afraid so. But something tells me it'll be back."

"Now, you're just being cocky."

She squeezed his erection. "Literally."

Noah laughed—hard. Looking down at her dark eyes, alight with mischief and happiness, he felt himself settle somewhat. As long as he had her around to entertain him and keep him sane, he could get through this very long day and whatever came next. "Thanks."

"For what?"

"Just for being here and making me laugh and keeping me from losing my mind."

"That's entirely my pleasure."

"Let's go to your place so you can take this shower you feel you need before we tend to your pleasure."

Her smile lit up her pretty face. "You're doing the same for me, you know," she said, tilting her head so he could kiss her neck. "You're keeping me from dwelling on the bad stuff."

"No more bad stuff. Only good stuff from here on out."

"I'm down with that."

Twenty minutes later, she came out of the bathroom at her house, wrapped in a towel.

Noah had made good use of the time she was in the shower to remove his clothes and get under the covers of her bed. "Bring that over here."

Brianna sat, just as he had, on the edge of the mattress. "You rang?"

"I did. Guess what?"

"What?"

"That boner you wasted at my house came back."

"He's a resilient fellow, isn't he?"

"Especially when he has you to inspire him." He tugged on the knot that held her towel together and invited her to join him under the covers.

She slid in next to him and wrapped herself around him, her skin warm and soft against his.

For the longest time, he only held her tight against him, breathing in the fragrance that was so uniquely hers. "I love you, Bri. I never thought I'd ever say that to anyone again, but then there you were, in my face, not taking my shit and making me want you so fiercely."

"I love you, too, and I never thought I'd ever say that again either until I met the infuriating contractor with the gorgeous eyes and face who made me rethink my vows to steer clear of all men forever."

"I'm happy you did." Noah kissed her, determined to keep her close to him for the rest of his life. He already knew that she'd never hurt him the way Melinda had and that he could trust Brianna with his life and his love. Everything about this was different, and he was thankful to have found her after his terrible ordeal had made him wise enough to know the difference.

She responded to him with eager enthusiasm, making him crazy when she wrapped her hand around his hard cock and pushed him onto his back. When she leaned over him and took him into her mouth, he had to hold his breath to keep from exploding the second her lips brushed against the sensitive head of his cock.

"Bri... *shit...*"

"Something wrong?" She looked at him with big doe eyes and swollen, sexy lips.

"No, nothing's wrong."

"Then I can do this?" she asked as she took him in again.

His hips came off the bed. "Yeah, more of that would be good."

She added some tongue this time and nearly finished him right off. "Brianna..."

"Yes, Noah?"

"Come here." He reached for her and arranged her so she straddled him, the heat of her core singeing him. God, he loved her.

"Is this what you wanted?" she asked, her innocent expression nearly making him laugh.

"Almost."

She flashed a coy smile that fired him up even more. "I might need detailed instructions."

"I thought you liked to be the boss of me."

"Only at the inn. Here, I want you to tell me what you want."

"How about I show you?"

"That works, too."

He lifted her and gasped as she slid down on his hard cock. "Now that is what I'm talking about."

"Mmm, you do know how to fill a girl to overflowing." She sat up straight and gazed down at him, her eyes on fire with desire and what looked an awful lot like happiness. He hoped he was making her happy. She deserved that more than just about anyone he'd ever met.

She tilted her hips and began to move, her breasts bouncing from the enthusiastic pace.

As he grasped her hips and held on for the ride, Noah's eyes wanted to roll back in his head.

"How am I doing?" she asked, sounding breathless.

"You're perfect."

"That doesn't leave any room for improvement."

"Absolutely no improvements needed." When he held out his arms to her, she leaned over to kiss him as he turned them so he was on top. "I love you, and I can't believe this has happened. I was so determined to avoid anything like this, until you came along and were constantly up in my grill, making me hard as a rock every time you pointed that finger at me."

"This finger?" she asked, poking his chest.

"That's the one." He grabbed it and pretended to bite it as he moved in her. "I wanted to grab that finger and pull you close enough to kiss the sass right off your sexy lips."

"Like this?" She drew him into a deep, tongue-twisting kiss.

"Just like that."

Sex had never been fun like it was with her. Everything was fun with her, even arguing. She was so incredibly responsive, and when Noah felt her inner muscles contract around his cock, that was all it took to fire his release right along with hers.

He landed on top of her, and when he tried to move so he wouldn't crush her, she tightened her arms around him so he couldn't get away.

"That was…" She sighed deeply.

"Not good?"

Snorting with laughter, she said, "Incredible. You're making me realize that my definition of good sex needed some serious calibration."

Noah pushed against her. "Happy to calibrate you any time."

She smiled up at him as she smoothed the hair back from his forehead. "And it was fun."

"Funny, I was thinking the same thing." He kissed her, lingering for a second before he reluctantly pulled back. "I want to take you to meet my aunt and uncle and see their barn."

"I'd love to meet them and see their barn."

GRAYSON WAITED OUTSIDE MELINDA'S HOME UNTIL FIVE MINUTES past nine. He figured with a small child in the house, they would certainly be up. He took one last moment to gather his thoughts and remind himself to stay cool, no matter what she said or did. It was up to him to help Noah gain access to his child. He needed to remain calm and get the job done.

He walked up to the front porch of a well-kept house, painted dark gray with maroon shutters and window boxes. As he reached out to ring the doorbell, he noticed outdoor toys stashed on the far right-hand side of the porch.

The maroon door swung open, and Noah's ex-friend Miguel's face immediately registered shock when he saw Grayson. Tall and muscular, Miguel had light brown skin, dark hair and eyes and stubble on his jaw. He quickly schooled his features to hide the surprise, but it was too late for that.

Miguel opened the storm door. "Help you?"

They'd met a few times in the years that Miguel had been friends with and worked for Noah. There was no way he could pretend not to recognize him. "Let's not play games, Miguel. You know exactly who I am and why I'm here."

Melinda came up behind Miguel. "Who is it?" When she looked around Miguel and saw Gray standing on the front porch, she gasped. "Gray."

"Melinda."

She glanced at Miguel. "Will you please give us a minute?"

He stared at Gray for a long moment without blinking. "Yeah, sure."

After he stepped back, Melinda came outside. As she pulled two sides of a long cardigan together, Gray noticed her hands were shaking. "What're you doing here?"

Melinda had light blonde hair and green eyes. Gray had always thought she was pretty, until he heard what she'd done to Noah. "My brother wants a divorce."

"You didn't need to come here for that."

"And he wants to see his son."

A whimper escaped from her before she seemed to recall that she shouldn't give anything away. "He's my son."

"And Noah's." When she didn't immediately deny it, Gray knew a moment of relief. "He wants a divorce and joint custody of his son."

She affected a mulish expression.

Before she had a chance to say anything, Gray said, "He hasn't ruled out full custody, and after hearing that you denied him his son for more than two years, the courts might give it to him."

Her eyes filled with tears. "Noah told me to go away and never come back. That's what I did."

"The second you learned you were pregnant with his child you were obligated to tell him."

She looked down at the porch. "I... I wasn't sure..."

"You didn't know whether the baby was his or Miguel's." Gray made no effort to hide his disgust. "But it couldn't have taken long after he was born to know for certain who his father is. At that moment, you owed my brother a phone call."

"He wouldn't have taken my call."

"You could've sent a certified letter, called my mother or me or done *something* to make this right."

She swiped at tears.

"Here's what's going to happen. You're going to give my brother an uncontested divorce. You're going to agree to joint custody, and within the week, you're going to make it possible for Noah to meet his son by bringing the child to Butler. You're going to allow Noah to see him any time he wants to and to be part of every aspect of his life, or we'll sue for full custody. Is there any part of that you don't understand?"

After a long pause, she said, "No."

Gray handed her an envelope. "You've been served. I suggest you move very quickly to fix this egregious omission. You've got one day to contact Noah and arrange for him to meet his son, or we'll see you in court." He started to walk away but turned back. "What's his name? My nephew?"

"Elliott."

"I look forward to getting to know him. We all do." Grayson turned, went down the stairs and was halfway down the walk when she called out to him. Turning back to her, he said, "Yes?"

"Tell him…" She shook with sobs. "Tell him I'm sorry."

Grayson wanted to tell her to fuck off with her apology, but he didn't do that. He bit his tongue and continued to his car. When he drove off a minute later, she was still standing on the front porch. "Well," he said, "that went well."

He was thankful she hadn't tried to deny that the boy was Noah's.

His brother had a son named Elliott.

Grayson was one hundred percent confident that she'd be calling Noah to set up that meeting. A half mile from Melinda's house, he pulled over to send a text to Brianna's phone.

I served her with divorce papers and put her on notice that we intend to file for joint custody. She has twenty-four hours to contact you to arrange a meeting with your son, whose name is Elliott. She understands that she has very few options here unless she wants us to sue for full custody. I believe you'll hear from her sooner rather than later. She said to tell you she is sorry. Congratulations, Dad.

CHAPTER TWENTY-SIX

"Lips that taste of tears, they say, are the best for kissing."
—Dorothy Parker

"Oh my gosh, it's *gorgeous*," Brianna said when she got her first look at the outside of his aunt and uncle's home. "It really is a barn!"

"It used to house cows. They said they could still catch a faint whiff of cow shit years after they moved in. It was a wreck when they bought it, and they did most of the work themselves."

"That's amazing."

"The joke in our family is if you're going to have ten children, you have to buy a barn."

"Ten children. I can't imagine that."

"I wonder how Gray is making out," Noah said.

"I've got my phone with me, and we'll ask your aunt and uncle for the Wi-Fi log-in."

Noah parked behind his uncle's Range Rover. "I suppose I'll find out soon enough."

"It's going to be fine. She doesn't have a leg to stand on in this situation, and Gray will certainly tell her that. He'll make sure she does the right thing."

"I hope you're right."

"I'm always right. I've proven that to you repeatedly."

Grinning, he said, "I walked straight into that, didn't I?"

She shrugged. "Truth hurts. Take me in and show me this beautiful home. I can't wait to meet your aunt and uncle, the parents of *ten* children."

They got out of the truck and met in front of it.

Noah extended a hand to her and led her into the house. "Hello? Are you guys decent?"

"Just barely," a man's voice called.

Noah chuckled and took her coat to hang it on a hook. "Check that out." He nodded to a row of ten hooks on the other side of the mudroom with names above them: Hunter, Hannah, Will, Ella, Charley, Wade, Colton, Lucas, Landon, Max. A second row was underneath the original: Caden, Callie, Chase, Savannah, Stella, Sarah, Carson.

"That's adorable," Brianna said.

"Carson already has a hook, and he was only born this week."

"His grandfather did that last night." The woman in the doorway had long gray hair, a youthful face and a warm smile. Brianna immediately noticed her resemblance to her sister, Hannah. "This is a nice surprise." She came to hug and kiss Noah. "Can't remember the last time you stopped by out of the blue."

"It's been too long. Aunt Molly, meet Brianna Esposito. Brianna, my aunt Molly Abbott."

"The mother of ten children." Brianna shook Molly's hand. "Nice to meet you. I bow down in awe to you—and your sister with the eight children."

Molly laughed. "A girl has eight or ten children, and it becomes the headline of her life."

"Not to mention two sets of twins for you guys," Brianna added as they followed Molly into a cozy kitchen. "That's a feat in and of itself."

"Are we talking about my wife's extraordinary baby-making skills?"

"We most certainly are not," Noah said.

"Damn, that's my favorite subject."

"Brianna, meet my uncle Lincoln. He's known for being the father of ten children, the CEO of the Green Mountain Country Store and the Beatles' number one fan."

"Oh, I love the Beatles," Brianna said, reaching out to shake hands with the handsome man with silver hair and sparkling blue eyes.

"Then we'll be best friends," Lincoln said. "Have a seat. Can we get you some coffee or hot chocolate? My Molly's hot chocolate is the best you'll ever have."

"I can't say no to that," Brianna said. "If it's not any trouble."

"No trouble at all," Molly said. "Some for you, too, Noah?"

"I'd love some. Thanks, Auntie. Could we trouble you for the Wi-Fi log-in? We're waiting for some news."

"Of course." Linc helped Brianna log into their Abbey Road network. "All set."

"Thanks," Noah said.

"The inn is looking great, you two," Linc said. "Coming right along."

"Yes, it's going well," Noah said. "We've got the plumbers coming in this week."

"That's wonderful. Mrs. Hendricks is eager to reopen."

"Hopefully by late spring, she'll be back in business."

Molly made the hot chocolate and brought two mugs topped with dollops of whipped cream to the table.

Brianna's mouth watered at the smell of chocolate. "That looks wonderful. Thank you."

Molly put a plate of cookies on the table and took a seat. "The secret is to heat the milk before you add the chocolate."

"Oh, I'll have to try that."

"Knock, knock," a male voice said from the mudroom. "Is everyone dressed?"

"For now," Molly said, smiling. "Come in, Dad."

"I've learned to be careful coming in here unannounced," Elmer said.

"That's right," Linc replied. "Your daughter and I are almost empty nesters. You never know what might be going on here."

"That subject is firmly off-limits," Elmer said as he took a seat at the table. "Nice to see you, Noah."

"You, too, Gramps. This is Brianna Esposito. Brianna, my grandfather, Elmer Stillman."

"Such a pleasure to meet you," Brianna said. "I've heard so much about you."

"All good, I hope?" Elmer asked with an adorable grin that made his eyes twinkle with delight.

"Of course," Brianna said, charmed by him.

"I just came from Hunter and Megan's," Elmer said. "That little one is a cutie."

"He sure is," Molly said. "Did they get any sleep last night?"

"Not much, but they don't seem to care. They're madly in love."

"Happens to all of us," Linc said with a smile.

A young, handsome man came into the room, carrying a blond little boy.

"Brianna, meet my cousin Max and his son, Caden."

"Nice to meet you."

"You, too," Max said.

"You want some cocoa, Dad and Max?"

"I'm good," Elmer said. "I had some earlier."

"I'll take some, Mom, if you don't mind," Max said.

"No problem."

As Molly got up to make more cocoa, Brianna noticed Noah staring at his cousin's son. "How old is he, Max?" Brianna asked.

"Almost fourteen months."

"He's adorable."

"Thanks, I think so, too."

When Brianna's phone buzzed, she picked it up and devoured Gray's message before handing the phone to Noah so he could see it.

Noah's eyes flew over the screen and then flooded with tears when he got to the part where he learned that his son's name was Elliott.

"Everything all right, son?" Elmer asked.

Noah made a visible effort to pull himself together. "It seems I have a son I've just found out about."

"Oh my goodness!" Molly said.

"When Melinda and I split, she was pregnant."

"And she never told you?" Linc asked, his expression hardening.

"No, she didn't. I asked Gray to find her because we never actually got divorced."

"I figured you would've done that right away," Molly said.

"I should have, but that would've meant having to deal with her. That was the last thing I wanted to do. I just pretended like I'd never met her and went on with my life. Gray hired an investigator to track her down, and he was the one who told us there was a child. When Gray and I saw the photos of him, we knew he was mine. He looks just like I did at his age. My mom has a picture…" His voice caught. "His name…"

"His name is Elliott," Brianna said.

"Elliott," Elmer said. "That's a good, strong name."

"When will you get to see him, Noah?" Molly asked.

"Soon. Gray told her she needs to make that happen, or we'll sue for full custody."

"You ought to think about that anyway," Linc said. "It's outrageous that she kept him from you for all this time."

"I agree, but Gray says it wouldn't be in his best interest to take him from the only home he knows. Even if he's living with my ex-friend and foreman, Miguel, the guy Melinda cheated on me with. The three of them are one big happy family."

His words dripped with bitterness, but who could blame him?

"Jeez," Max said, "that's completely effed up."

"Sure is. I need to call my mom and tell her the latest."

"Use the phone in the den," Molly said. "Make yourself at home."

"Thanks. I wanted to show Bri your super-cool house."

"And I'm dying to see it," Brianna added.

"After you talk to your mother, I'll take you on a tour," Molly said.

"Sounds good."

Brianna got up and went with him into the den, sitting next to him on the sofa.

After he dialed his mother's number, Brianna reached for his hand and cradled it between both of hers. She was determined to be there for him every step of the way in this situation, the same way he'd been for her.

∼

"They seem cozy," Elmer said, his eyes gleaming the way they did when one of his grandchildren found love.

"Don't get all crazy, Gramps," Max said. "You know how Noah can be. If we make too big of a deal about it, he's apt to decide not to bother."

"I don't think he's going to do that with this young lady," Linc said. "There's a real spark between them."

"You two are so ridiculous," Max said. "You have a few matchmaking successes, and now you're suddenly experts."

"We've had more than a *few*, my dear boy, and we had a hand in this one, too," Elmer said.

"Why am I not surprised?" Max said, rolling his eyes at his mother.

Molly took it all in, amused as always by her matchmaking

husband and father, who did, indeed, think they were the shit for all the successful matches they'd helped to make for their kids. They'd now turned their attention toward the Colemans.

"And from what I hear," Elmer said gleefully, "Cabot's shacked up with Izzy at her place, determined to nurse her through her recovery. I saw that coming a mile away."

"Sure, you did," Linc said disdainfully.

Not only were they matchmakers but also competitors, each trying to outdo the other in their quest for true love throughout the land.

"What I want to know," Max said, "is when you're going to use some of your matchmaking mojo on me."

"When you're ready," Elmer said.

"I'm ready," Max said emphatically.

"Not yet," Linc said.

"Why do you guys get to decide that?" Max asked.

"Because, my boy, we're the experts," Elmer said, "and you need to trust us on this."

"Do they honestly believe this BS they're spewing?" Max asked his mother.

"I think they do, sweetheart. You can't take issue with their track record."

"That's right," Linc said. "We know what we're doing, and don't you worry, my boy, we're going to take *good care* of you when the time is right."

"I'll believe it when I see it."

Noah and Brianna returned to the kitchen, and Molly immediately noticed the tears in her usually unemotional nephew's eyes. She was appalled to know what his wife had done to him, keeping his son a secret.

"You talked to your mother?" Molly asked.

"I did. She can't wait to meet her grandson, but like me, she's upset to know he's already more than two, and we've missed so much."

"Don't let it make you bitter, son," Elmer said. "It's a terrible thing she did, but what matters is now you know, and you can be part of your son's life going forward. The blessing is he'll never know you weren't there at the beginning."

"That's true, Gramps. Thanks for that."

"You wanted to show Brianna the house," Molly said.

"Yes," Noah said. "We're thinking about going into business together, restoring old barns like this one once was and making them into homes."

"That's an exciting idea," Linc said.

"I first started thinking about it when Gray moved into the church, and I thought that was the second-coolest house I'd ever seen, after this one, and how there might be a market for that sort of thing."

"Especially among the folks who come up for ski season," Elmer said. "I like it a lot. You'll do great at that."

"There's an old horse barn for sale up by Gavin's lumberyard," Max said, referring to his brother-in-law. "You should check that out. The place is crumbling, but the bones are there."

"We'll take a look. Thanks for the info."

"Let's take that tour," Molly said. "There's nothing I love more than showing off this house. Linc bought it sight unseen, not knowing that cows used to live here."

"No way," Brianna said, laughing. "What did you say when you heard he'd bought it?"

"I told him he was insane, but it turned out that he was on to something."

"He was definitely on to something." Brianna took in the massive family room that occupied half the first floor. "This is incredible."

"You should see this place at Christmas," Noah said. "Aunt Molly puts a massive tree at that end, and everything is decorated. It was always my favorite place to be at Christmas."

"I never knew that," Molly said, touched.

"We all loved being here."

"That's very nice to hear, my friend. We do love a good holiday around here."

She showed them the smaller sitting room where they spent most of their time.

"This is so cozy," Brianna said.

"We almost always have a fire going in here, even in the summer, and this is where you'll most often find us."

"I love this room," Noah said. "We've watched a lot of hockey games in here."

Molly took them upstairs and showed them the master bedroom that she and Linc had expanded to include an en suite bathroom after their children left. Max had moved back home after becoming a single father to Caden, and they were more than happy to have the two of them around. Their big barn had gotten quiet after the kids moved out.

"I love everything about this lovely home," Brianna said.

"The new master is awesome, Aunt Molly," Noah said. "I hadn't seen that."

"You were still in California when we did that."

"This was Wade's room." Molly showed Brianna a closet-size room that had little more than a twin-size bed in it. "He was our loner. I think if he hadn't had this room to escape to, his siblings might've driven him mad."

"That's great," Brianna said, chuckling.

They went back downstairs and rejoined Linc, Elmer, Max and Caden at the table. The little guy was now sitting on the lap of his delighted great-grandfather.

"This place is spectacular," Brianna said. "I'm incredibly impressed that you did most of the work yourselves."

"It was a labor of love," Linc said with a warm look for Molly.

"It was a good thing I loved him when he told me he'd bought this place," Molly said. "I had to break it to him that he'd bought a falling-down piece of crap."

"All I saw the first time we came here was potential," Linc said.

"Sure, you did," Molly said, laughing. "It was a mess, but we made it work."

"They were young and in love and determined," Elmer said. "And look at what they built together."

"A barn and ten children," Noah said.

"We didn't plan the ten children. That just kind of happened."

"And we have a deal about not discussing *how* that happened," Elmer said, glaring at her and Linc, who laughed the way they always did when he said that.

"We have no idea how it happened," Molly said. "Especially the two sets of twins."

Elmer covered his ears with Caden's hands. "Make it stop."

Brianna laughed hard, which made Molly happy. Her sister, Hannah, had told her about Brianna's ex-husband's murder as well as the hell he'd put the poor girl through before they split.

"We've got to go," Noah said. "I thought I might take Bri up to see Colton and Lucy and the sugaring facility. I also want to take her to meet Hannah and Dexter."

"Make sure you call before you go up to Colton's," Molly said. "According to Lucy, he likes to run around naked up there."

"Dear God," Noah said. "He really is feral."

"We did what we could with him," Linc said as Brianna laughed helplessly.

"May I use your phone again?" Noah asked.

"Our phone is your phone."

While Noah went to call his cousin, Molly placed her hand on Brianna's arm. "We're here for you and Noah if there's anything at all either of you needs."

"Thank you so much, Mrs. Abbott."

"It's Molly—and he's Linc, and he's Elmer."

"And I'm Max," her youngest son said with a cheeky grin.

"Your family is very kind and welcoming," Brianna said. "I've appreciated that more than you know in the last few days."

"We were sorry to hear about your ex-husband," Elmer said.

"Thank you, but I don't feel right about accepting condolences for him. We had a very acrimonious split more than a year ago, and while I wouldn't wish what happened to him on anyone, I'm relieved to no longer be married to him."

"It's a strange mix of emotions, I'm sure," Elmer said.

"It is," Brianna said with a sigh.

Noah returned to the kitchen. "Colton assures me he's fully clothed and would love to show us his mountain."

"You'll enjoy that," Molly said. "But I apologize in advance for my son."

Brianna laughed. "Thank you so much for showing me your gorgeous home and for the delicious hot chocolate."

"Come any time. We still do Sunday dinner, Noah, and you're always welcome."

"Thanks, Auntie." He hugged her, Linc and Elmer and gave Max and Caden pats on the head. "Good to see you guys."

"You, too," Linc said. "We're looking forward to meeting Elliott."

"I am, too. You have no idea how much."

"That boy has hit the father jackpot, son," Elmer said. "He'll find that out soon enough."

"Thank you, Gramps," Noah said gruffly.

Molly walked them to the mudroom and waved them off as they drove away.

"It seems our Noah is rather smitten," Elmer said when Molly returned to her seat at the table. "And with a lovely young woman."

"She is. I love that they're talking about going into business together."

"Weren't they fighting constantly a few weeks ago?" Max asked.

"That they were," Elmer said with a chuckle. "But your father and I conspired to see if there might be some sparks under the animosity, and lo and behold, look at them now."

"You're so full of yourself, Gramps," Max said with a chuckle.

"What can I say? I know love when I see it brewing."

"I can't with this," Max said. "Unless you've got something brewing for me, that is."

"Not yet, my boy, but your day will come, and when it does, I predict an epic love for the ages."

"As I said, I'll believe it when I see it," Max said.

CHAPTER TWENTY-SEVEN

"So it's true, when all is said and done,
grief is the price we pay for love."
—E.A. Bucchianeri

"*T*hat was fantastic," Brianna said. "What a gorgeous home. My brain is exploding with ideas and barn doors and wood-planked floors and cased openings." She gave a little shiver of excitement. "To be honest, that's the part of each project I enjoy the most—the design decisions. If I hadn't gone into architecture, I think I might've ended up in interior design."

"I'm glad it inspired you. Before we go up to the mountain, I want to stop at home and check my messages to see if she called me yet."

"Yes, let's do that."

Noah reached for her hand. "I can't believe I'm looking forward to a call from her."

"Only so you can see your son."

"Yeah."

"Your grandfather was right, you know."

"He usually is."

"Elliott will never remember the years you weren't there. You'll be his dad, and he'll love you."

"I hope so."

"He will, Noah. I promise."

"I know nothing about kids."

"You'll learn the same way every new parent does. We'll put together a room for him at your place and get him some toys, and you'll teach him to ski and take him sledding, and before long, he'll be following you around like a happy little puppy."

"That sounds nice."

"It'll be great."

"Thanks for the support today. I'd be going crazy without you here to keep me sane."

"Same goes, love."

"I'm sorry that my thing has taken over your thing."

She waved a hand to dismiss the statement. "Your thing is a big deal."

"Yours is, too."

"No, mine is a sad thing that happened to someone I used to know. It's got nothing to do with my life today, which is pretty damned good and getting better all the time."

"I'm glad you think so."

"I never thought I'd be so excited to check out a junky old horse barn."

"We'll do that on the way back from Colton's. I know exactly where it is."

Brianna clapped her hands together. "I can't wait."

At Noah's, they were surprised to find the house free of Colemans.

"Wonder where they all are?"

The red light on the answering machine flashed with a message. Noah pushed the button to play it.

"Um, Noah, it's Melinda. I, um, Gray was here, and well, I wanted to arrange a time for you to see Elliott. I, um, I'm sorry, Noah. I didn't know what to do after everything happened, and

I, ah, I'm sorry. Call me." She recited her number, which he wrote down.

Noah called her right back before he could come up with a thousand reasons to be nervous about talking to *her* for the first time since that dreadful day three years earlier.

Melinda answered on the third ring.

"It's Noah."

"Hi."

"When can I see him?"

"Would tomorrow be okay?"

"Yes. You'll bring him here?"

"I will."

"By yourself."

"I understand."

"What time?"

"Around four?"

"See you then."

He ended the call before he could lose his shit and start screaming at her. That wouldn't help anything.

"She's bringing him here tomorrow."

Brianna came to him and hugged him.

It took a second for him to release the rage and tension that made him want to recoil from her touch, until he remembered it was Brianna holding him. He loved her and was safe with her. Noah sagged against her, soaking up the love she gave him so willingly.

"It's going to be okay," she said softly. "I promise."

Because there was nothing else he could do, Noah grabbed hold of her assurances. "Thanks."

He held her for several more minutes and then pulled himself together to salvage their day. "I promised you a visit to Colton's mountain."

"We don't have to do that if you'd rather not."

"I want to. I need to keep busy so I don't spend the whole day stewing."

"Then let's go."

~

WHILE NOAH RAN UPSTAIRS TO PUT ON WARMER BOOTS, BRIANNA took a second to check her phone while connected to Wi-Fi. She'd received a text from her cousin, Dominique.

OMG, Bri. Heard about Rem. Are you ok? I don't even know what to ask. I'm here if you need me for anything. Love you.

I'm ok. I was shocked, of course, but ok. The cops questioned me, but I couldn't tell them much. It's all so tragically sad—every bit of it.

So sad. You have to figure you weren't the only one he pulled his gaslighting shit on.

Definitely not. Talked to his parents. I feel so bad for them.

Ugh, those poor people. They're so sweet, and he put them through hell. Do you want me to come up? I can if you need me.

Thank you for offering, but Noah is here, and he's been great. He's got some crazy stuff of his own going on (ex-wife with a 2 y/o son that's his, and she never TOLD HIM), so we're propping each other up.

OMG, seriously? Wow. So things are good with him?

Really good. Thinking about what's next after the inn and hoping it includes him.

OH, BRI! I'm so happy for you! I can't wait to meet him! I told you he was worth a second chance.

I can't wait either, and yes, you were right about that. I'll call you to catch up soon.

Take care and let me know if I can do anything.

Appreciate you checking on me. Xo

Noah came stomping down the stairs and walked into the kitchen as she finished the last text to Dom. "Everything okay?"

"Yes, that was my cousin. She heard about Rem and was checking on me."

"I guess the word is out."

"I suppose so."

"Do you want to see what the Boston media is saying about it?"

"*No.*" That was the last thing she wanted to do. "I think I'm better off not knowing."

"I tend to agree. You still want to go to Colton's?"

"Absolutely. Let's go."

Noah drove them up the mountain to his cousin's home at the top of a steep incline that required four-wheel drive to navigate.

"Do they ever get stuck up here?"

"Sometimes for days at a time."

"Gulp. Not sure I'd like that. What does his wife say about that? She's Emma's sister, right?"

"That's right, and Lucy is a good sport. She'd have to be to put up with Colton." He took another curve and headed up an even steeper incline that seemed to go straight up into the clouds.

Brianna held on a little tighter to the armrest. "Are you sure this is safe?"

Noah laughed. "Perfectly safe, or I never would've brought you here."

"How do we get back down?"

"Carefully."

"I can't with this place."

"I thought you were going to give us a whirl year-round."

"I was going to until you brought me to the top of the world."

"Good news. There's cell service up here."

"Of course there is."

The road finally leveled off into a yard with a driveway and several log-cabin-style buildings. Two yellow Labs came running over to greet them.

"The dogs are Sarah and Elmer, named for our grandparents."

"How does your grandfather feel about having a great-granddog named for him?"

"He was very honored."

A bearded man with long hair, wearing only a flannel shirt and jeans, came over to greet them.

"Is he barefoot?" Brianna asked.

"Looks that way."

"Are my eyes deceiving me, or has my cousin Noah Coleman come to visit?" Colton asked in a big booming voice as he hugged Noah and lifted him right off his feet.

"Put me down, you oaf."

Colton released him and pounded him on the back. "Good to see you, bud. I was so glad you called and asked to come up. I even put clothes on for the occasion."

"You forgot shoes," Noah said.

"Ah damn, I knew I forgot something. Who's this lovely young lady you've brought to meet me?"

"Brianna, meet my cousin Colton Abbott. Colton, Brianna Esposito, the architect on the inn project."

Colton gave him an arch look. "The architect, you say. Hmmm, it seems I'd heard about some—what's the word I'm looking for—*animosity* between the two of you."

"That was so last month." Noah put his arm around her. "We get along *much* better now."

Colton flashed a big, goofy grin. "Is that right? Well, good for you. Come in out of the cold and meet my Lucy." He whistled for the dogs and led them all into a cozy cabin, where the heat from the woodstove was a welcome relief after the icy air outside.

How did he walk around out there with no coat or shoes?

"Luce, we've got company. Noah has brought Brianna to meet us."

Brianna could immediately see that Lucy was hugely pregnant. "Don't get up." She crossed the big, open room to shake hands with Lucy, who had shoulder-length red hair and green eyes. Brianna noted an uncanny resemblance to her niece, Simone. "Nice to meet you."

"You, too. Welcome to our mountain."

"That ride up was quite something."

"You haven't lived until you've experienced the ride *down*," Lucy said with a grin.

"Ah, God, I'm already terrified."

"No need to be terrified," Colton said. "Noah knows his way around these parts."

"Brianna wanted to see the sugaring facility. Are you up for a tour?"

"I'd love to."

They spent the next hour in the building across the yard while Colton walked her through every step of the complex process of making maple syrup. Lucy begged off, saying she needed to keep her feet up so they wouldn't swell.

"I had no idea what was involved in making syrup," Brianna said. "This was truly fascinating, Colton. Thanks for sharing your incredible knowledge with me."

"It's always a pleasure to share our place with new people. Everyone says the same thing—that they had no clue what it took to turn sap into syrup."

"Are you and Lucy coming down to town before her due date?" Noah asked.

"That's the plan. She's due in two weeks, so we'll move in with Mom and Dad next weekend until Bruiser arrives."

"Bruiser," Noah said. "Tell me that's not really his name."

"That's what we're calling him, but my beloved tells me there'll be a different name on the birth certificate. I defer to her as the birther of the baby."

"Wise move," Noah said. "Speaking of babies…"

Brianna had wondered if he planned to share his news with Colton.

"It seems I had one about two and a half years ago."

"*What?*"

"Melinda was pregnant when we split and didn't think I needed to know that."

"Christ have mercy! How'd you find out?"

Noah shared the story with Colton. "She's bringing him here to meet me tomorrow."

"Holy shit, Noah. I'm so sorry that happened but glad you found out about him."

"Yeah, same."

"What the fuck is wrong with people?" Colton asked.

"That's an excellent question," Noah said.

Brianna curled her hand around his, wanting him to know she was there for him, no matter what. At some point, his problems and his pain had become hers, and there was nothing she wouldn't do to soothe him. The realization made her feel weightless, like Alice falling down the rabbit hole. She'd been down there once before, so gone with love over Rem, she hadn't seen the forest for the trees, even when they were smacking her in the face with the truth about him.

Noah wasn't Rem. She had to keep reminding herself of that. He knew what it was like to be hurt.

That made him about the best risk she could ever take.

If he disappointed her, she'd never get over that.

~

TWENTY-FOUR HOURS NEVER WENT BY SO SLOWLY. EVERY MINUTE felt like a year. Why hadn't he just gotten in his truck and driven to Burlington yesterday to see his son? Because Gray had determined how this would play out, and Noah needed to follow his brother/lawyer's lead. But he was losing his shit waiting for four o'clock.

Brianna had been close by all day, but she'd given him space to brood and pace and think.

"Do you want to eat something?" she asked around three.

"Don't think I could. My stomach is in knots."

"He's going to love you, Noah."

At her suggestion, they'd driven to Rutland that morning to

buy some toys to have at the house. They'd gotten a barn with little people and animals, a race car track and some trucks, hoping they were things the little guy would like. How did he know what his son liked or didn't like? He was flying blind where Elliott was concerned, and that made him so fucking angry.

But there was no place in this day for anger. This day was about meeting his son and beginning a lifelong relationship with the boy.

And it was about seeing Melinda for the first time since he caught her in bed with his friend. That was the part he was dreading.

While they were out yesterday afternoon, they'd gone by the abandoned horse barn. At first glance, he could see it would be ideal for the sort of projects they wanted to take on. They'd also enjoyed a fun visit with Hannah, her family and Dexter, the puppy moose.

He wanted to be thinking about their plans for the business and the fun day they'd had visiting family, but he couldn't focus on anything substantial until he'd met his son. He'd asked the others to clear out and his mother to hold off until next time so as not to overwhelm the little boy with Colemans at their first meeting.

Noah sat on the floor and fiddled with the barn animals, examining each of them and wondering which one his son would prefer. He was a cow guy himself. They fascinated him and always had. He wanted to know everything his son liked and disliked. He wanted to know what made him happy and what upset him. He wanted to know about his birth and what he'd looked like the second he was born.

He would never forgive her for denying him those memories. A soft knock on the door had him shooting up from the floor a short time later and race walking to open the back door.

There they were. Melinda holding a child.

Noah barely glanced at her as his gaze devoured the adorable little boy with pudgy cheeks and big gray eyes, the same color as Noah's. He stepped back to let them into the house.

"Th-this is Elliott," Melinda said.

Noah held out his hands to take the boy from her.

She handed him over to him, seeming reluctant, but that was too damned bad.

"Hi, Elliott." Noah took off the boy's knit hat so he could see his blond hair. It was like looking at himself at the same age, which was why Melinda couldn't deny who his father was. But Gray had insisted a paternity test still be done so there could be no doubt.

Elliott studied him with a serious expression on his cute face.

"Do you like trucks?" Noah took him into the living room to sit on the floor with the toys. "How about we take off your coat before you play?"

Elliott's chubby little hand went to the zipper on his coat, his brows furrowing with indignation when he couldn't operate the zipper himself.

"Let me help with that." As he unzipped and removed the coat, it was all he could do not to reach for the child and hug him tightly. He didn't want to scare him, though, so he refrained, but his heart was in his throat as he watched his little boy check out the toys he and Brianna had chosen for him. He wore a red and blue plaid flannel shirt, jeans and cute little work boots.

Elliott picked up the cow and held it up for Noah to see. "Cow."

"Yes, that's right. I love cows. Do you?"

Elliott nodded. "Moo."

Noah blinked back tears. "You're so smart."

"He knows all the animal names and sounds they make."

Noah ignored her. He didn't want to hear all the things his son had learned that he knew nothing about. He didn't want her in his house or raising his child. When the anger threatened to overtake him, he choked it back, determined to keep his focus on Elliott.

They played for an hour, with every one of the toys getting Elliott's attention. He loved the trucks Noah had chosen for him, and the race car track was a huge hit.

"Cookie?" Elliott asked Noah.

"Is he allergic to anything?" Noah asked without looking up at Melinda.

"Not that we know of."

Her use of the word *we* infuriated Noah. Fuck her, and fuck Miguel.

Brianna brought him a plate of cookies and the apple juice boxes they'd bought at the store earlier in the day.

Noah held out a hand to her, and she joined them on the floor, the three of them sipping from juice boxes and eating cookies.

"This is my friend Brianna," Noah said to Elliott. "Can you say hi?"

"Hi," Elliott said.

"Hi, Elliott," Brianna said. "We're so happy to meet you."

"Juice," Elliott said.

"You like juice?" Bri asked.

Elliott nodded.

While Noah watched them together, he pretended the three of them were a little family and that Melinda wasn't standing watch over them, her coat still on.

"He'll spend every other weekend here," Noah said without looking up at Melinda. "As well as a week at Christmas and three weeks in the summer. They don't have to be three weeks in a row, but I want three full weeks. When he gets older, we'll let him decide where he wants to spend most of his time."

She didn't say anything for a full minute, and then she said, "Okay."

"And he'll call me, and *only me*, Dad."

"He… he calls Miguel Miggy."

Noah was enormously relieved to hear that his son didn't call Miguel Daddy. That might've been too much for Noah. "He'll also have my name. That's nonnegotiable. If it's not on his birth certificate, you'll have it amended, and you'll provide me with a copy."

"Okay."

"I want pictures of him from every part of his life, from birth to now."

"I... I can get them for you."

"Thank you." Noah forced himself to look directly at Melinda. "I'll never understand why you did this to me, but I'll do my best to treat you with respect as his mother, which is way more than you've given me by keeping him from me for all this time."

"I'm sorry, Noah. I didn't know what to do after everything that happened. When I realized I was pregnant—"

"You should've told me! You *knew* I would've wanted him."

"I'm sorry. That's all I can say."

It would never be enough, but he had no choice but to accept her apology and move on—for Elliott's sake.

Noah reached for his son, who came willingly to him after playing with him and sharing cookies with him. "I'm your dad, pal. And do you know what that means? It means I'll love you and protect you and play with you and be there for you for the rest of my life. If you need *anything*, you come to me, and I'll make sure you get it."

Brianna sniffled next to him.

When the boy started to squirm, Noah released him. He kissed the top of the child's head. "I'll see you again soon, okay?"

"'Kay," Elliott said.

Noah got up off the floor and brought the child's hat and coat with him to the kitchen. He helped him into the coat and zipped it up before plopping the hat on his head. The last thing he wanted to do was let him go, but he knew he had to. For now, anyway.

"You can bring him here on Friday after work. I'll bring him back on Sunday night."

"I, um, okay. Noah, I just want to say—"

"Don't. There's *nothing* you can say that will fix this, so don't even try." He'd thought he might feel something for her, some of the old feelings, but there was nothing but anger and resentment for what she'd denied him—and Elliott. Eventually, he'd have to talk to her about things involving their son, but not now. Not yet.

"I'll see you on Friday, buddy. We'll play trucks some more, and I'll take you to see the big trucks at work."

"Trucks!" Elliott said.

"We'll see all the trucks." Noah smiled and waved to him as Melinda carried him out of the house. "Bye-bye."

Elliott waved back to him. "Bye."

He needed to get a car seat and a toddler bed, and what else did he need? How did he even know what he needed? What did he know about taking care of a toddler? His mind raced until he forced himself to take a deep, calming breath. His mother and aunt had raised eighteen children. They'd tell him what he needed, and he'd get it before Friday. He'd make sure Elliott had *everything* he needed going forward. He couldn't rewrite the past, but he'd do whatever he could to make up for lost time with his son.

"He's adorable," Brianna said after Melinda had driven off.

"I'm sorry I didn't introduce you to her—"

"Don't be sorry. I didn't want to meet her. It was all I could do not to punch her."

Noah laughed softly and wrapped his arms around her. "So that was my son."

"That was your son, and he's *beautiful*. He looks so much like you! I can't wait to get to know him."

"Me, too. I'm going to need help… So much help. I have to get a car seat and a bed for him and more toys and—"

Brianna pulled back to place her hand on his face. "Take a breath. We've got this. We'll get everything he needs and make sure he feels at home here."

"I want you to feel at home here, too."

"I already do."

"When your lease is up at your place, do you think you might want to move in here?"

"I believe I would."

"And the business... You might be into that, too?"

"Absolutely.

"Does that mean you're going to give notice to your job in Boston?"

"That means I already have. I called the office on Friday to let them know I wouldn't be coming back to Boston after I finish the project here."

"What did they say?"

"They weren't happy and tried to offer me a raise, but I told them 'no, thanks.'"

Noah's heart, already full to overflowing after the time with his son, felt like it might explode after hearing she was making definite plans to stay with him. "The horse barn... Do we think that might be our first project?"

"Other than meeting Elliott, it's all I've thought about since we saw it yesterday. I've even roughed up some sketches."

Noah released a deep breath. "We're going to do this, then."

"We're going to do it, but only if it's what you want, too."

He gazed down at her sweet, gorgeous face, memorizing every detail. "Before I met you, I would've sworn I was done with love and relationships and everything that goes with them."

"I was right there with you. All set, thank you very much."

Smiling, he kissed her. "But then there you were, shaking that finger at me and firing me up with your smart sexiness, and suddenly, there I was, right back in the place I swore I'd never go again. But it feels different this time. It feels good and safe and right."

"For me, too, Noah. I swear to you I'll never hurt you the way she did."

"And I'll never hurt you the way he did."

She curled her arms around his neck and kissed him.

"I love you."

"I love you, too."

He believed that when she said those words to him, she truly meant them. He had faith in her, and he trusted her to keep her word to him. "How about you show me those sketches?"

"I'd love to."

*T*en minutes after Linc slid into the booth across from Elmer at the diner, they were still waiting for Butch to bring them coffee. Linc was thinking about getting it himself.

"He said he doesn't need us to hire someone to cover for Megan," Elmer said, "but he seems overwhelmed. How can one person wait on the tables and cook the food, too?"

"I hate to say it, but I think you're going to have to start delivering coffee, old man," Linc said, grinning at his father-in-law.

"Who you calling old, boy?"

"Figure of speech. I want to be 'old' like you someday."

"You think we ought to pitch in?" Elmer asked.

"I think we'd better before there's a riot."

"How hard can it be? We watch Megan do it every day."

"Exactly."

"You get the coffee," Elmer said. "I'll take the orders."

"On it."

For the next hour, they ran their asses off, refilling coffee, taking orders, delivering food, messing up orders, redoing orders, making more coffee, clearing tables and wiping up after each customer.

When the breakfast rush was finally over, they dropped into their usual booth, completely exhausted.

"Holy. *Shit.*"

"What you said." Elmer guzzled the glass of ice water he'd poured for himself. "How does Megan do that every day by herself? And pregnant for the last nine months, no less!"

"I have a whole new respect for her," Linc said.

"Me, too."

Butch came out from the kitchen. "Thanks for the help, boys. You saved my ass."

"We need to get someone here to help while Megan's out."

"She won't be gone long, will she? How long does it take to get over having a baby, anyway?"

Linc snorted with laughter. "It's gonna be a while, my friend."

"Our company believes in full maternity leave," Elmer said. "As the official owner of the diner, I encouraged her to take all the time she needs. So, let's hire someone to help out in the meantime."

"I don't like change," Butch said, frowning.

"Well, I'm not going to pour coffee for you every day," Linc said.

"And I'm too damned old to work this hard," Elmer said.

"Oh, so *now* you're old," Linc said.

"Don't be cheeky, young man."

Linc lost it laughing. "I'm just pointing out that when it's convenient for you, you play the old-man card."

"If you live to be my age, you can play any card you want."

Butch refilled their mugs. "If you want more, get it yourself," he said as he walked away.

"He does know we're the bosses around here, doesn't he?" Elmer asked, grinning.

"He's well aware that we need him more than he needs us."

"Especially right now." Elmer settled back against the booth. "Well, that got the blood pumping. I'll sleep well tonight."

"Makes me realize how easy my real job is," Linc said.

"If it's too easy for you, I can find someone else to run my parents' business."

"I think that ship has sailed, my friend. You're stuck with me."

"All this excitement made me forget that I wanted to tell you I heard Noah and Brianna bought the Foster horse barn."

"Did they now?" Linc asked, beaming. "That's wonderful. They told us how they want to restore old barns and churches and other unique properties."

"It's a great idea. There are a lot of abandoned old places in need of a purpose. I love to see him coming out of his shell with her."

"I do, too. Brianna is good for him. Hannah told us that the police arrested a suspect in Brianna's ex-husband's murder, a business associate he allegedly scammed out of a ton of money."

"Jeez. That guy was a piece of work."

"Yes, he was, but there's good news, too. The ex-husband never changed the beneficiary of the life insurance policies they got when they were first married. His parents are insisting the money go to her, and it's a hefty chunk of change."

"Good for her," Linc said. "From everything I've heard about what he put her through, she certainly deserves it."

"Indeed. She's planning to invest some of it into the business she and Noah are starting together."

"I'm so happy for them," Linc said.

"Me, too. No one deserves to be happy more than that boy. And this weekend, I'll get to meet my new great-grandson, Elliott."

"Noah showed me some photos. He's the spitting image of his daddy at that age."

"He sure is. Adorable."

"Hannah is infuriated that we didn't know about him until now," Elmer said.

"Can't say I blame her. It's egregious."

"She wants Noah to file for full custody, but he's not doing that. It's not what's best for the boy."

"No, it isn't. It'll take a while for Hannah to get past that, but she will."

"She said she'll never forgive Melinda for any of it. You heard the full story about him catching her with his foreman?"

"Yeah, Molly told me the other day. It's horrible. No wonder he retreated from everything for a few years."

"Don't blame him at all. That's a bitter pill to swallow."

"Ah, well, he's on the right path now."

"Thanks to us," Linc said, raising his mug to toast his father-in-law.

"Oh, please," Elmer scoffed. "Sending Noah and Brianna to dinner was *my* idea. There was no *we* involved in that. You're getting your ass kicked in this competition. You're so far behind, you might never catch up."

"Whatever. Who do you think called Cabot to tell him Izzy was in the hospital?"

"Mia called him."

"Au contraire, mon frère. The first call came from *me*."

Elmer eyed his son-in-law with respect. "Is that right?"

"Yep, and I can have my friend Cabot testify to that."

"Very interesting. I've taught you well, my young protégé."

Lincoln rolled his eyes to high heaven. "Protégé, my ass. If things work out between Cabot and Izzy, that one is *all* mine."

"I'll concede that one to you, but only if they make a go of it. It's about time you won a round."

"Have you heard anything about how things are going at Izzy's?" Linc asked.

"Nothing more than Cabot is waiting on her hand and foot and plans to stay for as long as she needs him."

"He's a little bit older than our Izzy," Linc said. "How do we feel about that?"

"From everything I've seen of him, he seems like a wonderful guy."

"I think so, too. I'll be on the lookout for anything I can do to help things along so I can score this point you say I need."

Elmer sipped his ice water. "You need *a lot* of points to catch up to the master."

"Don't count your chickens just yet. I've still got six Colemans and one Abbott to work with."

Elmer leaned forward, grinning. "*Cluck, cluck.*"

~

THANK YOU FOR READING NOAH AND BRIANNA'S STORY! NOAH has been a bit of an enigma during the series, so it was fun figuring out what made him into a cranky loner and finding the right woman to bring him back to life. I hope you enjoyed getting to know the Colemans as much as I did.

Many thanks to all the people who help me behind the scenes, including Julie Cupp, Lisa Cafferty, Tia Kelly, Jean Mello, Andrea Lopes, Ashley Lopez and Kristina Brinton, for the gorgeous cover of *Come Together*. I appreciate the hard work of my editors, Linda Ingmanson and Joyce Lamb, and my beta readers, Anne Woodall and Kara Conrad. Also, a big thanks to the Vermont series beta readers: Marchia, Alice, Nancy, Betty, Katy, Jennifer, Deb, Doreen

A special thank you to Melissa Shufon for the insight she provided into the role of women in the construction business.

As you can probably imagine, Izzy and Cabot are up next in *Here, There and Everywhere*, and I'm looking forward to finding out more about them and whether they can make a go of it. I love that we have all these Coleman cousins to keep the series moving forward, and don't worry—I haven't forgotten about Max Abbott. He'll get his turn before too much longer.

Watch for *Here, There and Everywhere*, the next Butler, Vermont, book in 2022!

Thank you again for reading *Come Together* and for your excitement for more in this series.

xoxo

Marie

ALSO BY MARIE FORCE

Contemporary Romances Available from Marie Force

Book 5: Hoping for Love (*Evan & Grace*)

Book 6: Season for Love (*Owen & Laura*)

Book 7: Longing for Love (*Blaine & Tiffany*)

Book 8: Waiting for Love (*Adam & Abby*)

Book 9: Time for Love (*David & Daisy*)

Book 10: Meant for Love (*Jenny & Alex*)

Book 10.5: Chance for Love, *A Gansett Island Novella* (*Jared & Lizzie*)

Book 11: Gansett After Dark (*Owen & Laura*)

Book 12: Kisses After Dark (*Shane & Katie*)

Book 13: Love After Dark (*Paul & Hope*)

Book 14: Celebration After Dark (*Big Mac & Linda*)

Book 15: Desire After Dark (*Slim & Erin*)

Book 16: Light After Dark (*Mallory & Quinn*)

Book 17: Victoria & Shannon (Episode 1)

Book 18: Kevin & Chelsea (Episode 2)

A Gansett Island Christmas Novella

Book 19: Mine After Dark (*Riley & Nikki*)

Book 20: Yours After Dark (*Finn & Chloe*)

Book 21: Trouble After Dark (*Deacon & Julia*)

Book 22: Rescue After Dark (*Mason & Jordan*)

Book 23: Blackout After Dark

Book 24: Temptation After Dark (Gigi & Cooper)

The Wild Widows Series
Book 1: Someone Like You

The Treading Water Series
Book 1: Treading Water

Book 2: Marking Time

Book 3: Starting Over

Book 4: Coming Home

Book 5: Finding Forever

The Miami Nights Series

Book 1: How Much I Feel *(Carmen & Jason)*
Book 2: How Much I Care *(Maria & Austin)*
Book 3: How Much I Love *(Dee & Wyatt)*

Single Titles

Five Years Gone

One Year Home

Sex Machine

Sex God

Georgia on My Mind

True North

The Fall

The Wreck

Love at First Flight

Everyone Loves a Hero

Line of Scrimmage

The Quantum Series

Book 1: Virtuous *(Flynn & Natalie)*

Book 2: Valorous *(Flynn & Natalie)*

Book 3: Victorious *(Flynn & Natalie)*

Book 4: Rapturous *(Addie & Hayden)*

Book 5: Ravenous *(Jasper & Ellie)*

Book 6: Delirious *(Kristian & Aileen)*

Book 7: Outrageous *(Emmett & Leah)*

Book 8: Famous *(Marlowe & Sebastian)*

Romantic Suspense Novels Available from Marie Force

Historical Romance Available from Marie Force

ABOUT THE AUTHOR

Marie Force is the *New York Times* best-selling author of contemporary romance, romantic suspense and erotic romance. Her series include Fatal, First Family, Gansett Island, Butler Vermont, Quantum, Treading Water, Miami Nights and Wild Widows.

Her books have sold more than 10 million copies worldwide, have been translated into more than a dozen languages and have appeared on the *New York Times* bestseller more than 30 times. She is also a *USA Today* and *Wall Street Journal* bestseller, as well as a Speigel bestseller in Germany.

Her goals in life are simple—to finish raising two happy, healthy, productive young adults, to keep writing books for as long as she possibly can and to never be on a flight that makes the news.

Join Marie's mailing list on her website at *marieforce.com* for news about new books and upcoming appearances in your area. Follow her on Facebook at *www.Facebook.com/MarieForceAuthor* and on Instagram at *www.instagram.com/marieforceauthor/*. Contact Marie at *marie@marieforce.com*.

CPSIA information can be obtained
at www.ICGtesting.com
Printed in the USA
LVHW022030220721
693426LV00010B/668